Pray *for the* Light

Nightbringer

Nightbringer

James Byron
HUGGINS

WHITAKER
HOUSE

All Scripture quotations are taken from the King James Version (KJV) of the Holy Bible.

This novel is a work of fiction. References to real events, organizations, or places are used in a fictional context. Any resemblances to actual persons, living or dead, is entirely coincidental.

NIGHTBRINGER

ISBN: 0-88368-876-X
Printed in the United States of America
© 2004 by James Byron Huggins

Whitaker House
30 Hunt Valley Circle
New Kensington, PA 15068
www.whitakerhouse.com

Library of Congress Cataloging-in-Publication Data

Huggins, James Byron.
Nightbringer / James Byron Huggins.
p.   cm.
ISBN 0-88368-876-X (hardcover : alk. paper)
1. Alps, Italian (Italy)—Fiction. 2. Travelers—Fiction.
3. Abbeys—Fiction. I. Title.
PS3558.U346N54   2004
813'.54—dc22
2004018589

1 2 3 4 5 6 7 8 9 10 **ﻭﻭ** 10 09 08 07 06 05 04

To Sarah

You have been
and forever shall be

my princess.

PROLOGUE

He was not alone.

Wearing battle-scarred armor, his bloodred robe ragged from the storm of the last three days, he walked slowly through the bright, early morning light—the brightest morning he could remember.

He was aware that his hand no longer bled and burned as it had three days before. Nor was his sight clouded and white as it had been three days ago. Yes, his hand and his eyes had been healed in the same dark hour. Now he could see again... and fight again.

He saw the soldiers—so many men who lay as dead—sprawled across the glistening grass as if struck down by some soundless lightning. But he knew that they were not dead, just as he knew they would rise again when the great and mighty force that had also risen here was gone.

He passed the sleeping soldiers without further thought and reached the place where the sky had been so streaked and torn by lightning. And he gazed upon the gigantic grave-stone that lay white and alone in the close-gripping dust of the morning that would soon warm with the sun and rise and dance like ghosts.

He thought about the man who had been laid in the tomb and laughed.

Yes, it was a day for ghosts.

Holding the spear that had struck and finished the storm in his perfectly healed hand, he gazed upon the gaping black entrance of the cave with perfectly healed eyes. But he did not enter the grave.

He didn't have to.

———

A flintlock pistol trembled in the old man's hand as he staggered wildly through the Cimmerian corridor. He seemed to be searching for something, but there was nothing... nothing.

His face was streaked with blood from where claws had torn deep furrows across his skull. His eyes darted back and forth, wide and shocked and uncomprehending. His legs threatened to betray him before he could reach the door.

He cautiously entered the Great Hall of the castle.

Butchered bodies glistening black in the moonlight lay strewn about everywhere, some dismembered in a blood-bathed orgy beside others killed so efficiently that there was no blood at all. He tried to push down the fear that rose within him, but his shaking body belied his futile attempt. More quickly, he began to back toward the door and then turned to run, but with his first stride he froze.

A growl shuddering like tremors in the wake of an earthquake enveloped his blood-soaked boots and crawled up his knees to hold him in a vise of fear. The pistol wavered in his hand.

He turned.

Glowing red eyes gazed upon him from the night.

The pistol clattered from the man's hand as he fell to his knees, mouth opening in a silent scream. He raised trembling hands as if to beg for mercy but knew those eyes would never grant mercy.

Nightbringer

The thing half emerged from the darkness.

A scream rose in the man's throat.

Thunder struck the hall as the huge twin doors were thrown open. And even against his fear of the slouching horror that stood at the edge of the night, *that had brought the night*, the man whirled to behold—

Silhouetted by lightning that tore the sky apart in fantastic spiderwebs of fire, a stranger boldly entered the blood-drenched castle. He did not even hesitate as he stepped over a bloody body and said nothing as he coldly lifted a flintlock rifle at his waist and fired.

With a roar the abomination spun away from the cowering man.

The stranger heedlessly cast the smoking long rifle aside as he strode steadily through the swirling smoke and withdrew a flintlock pistol that he fired instantly. The creature howled and retreated again. And even before the sound of the gunshot returned from the bowels of the castle, the stranger had withdrawn yet another pistol to fire yet again with a dead-steady hand.

A guttural howl that seemed more human than demon erupted from the creature and it staggered back, *back* into the night.

Without a word—without even a glance at the old man sprawled across the bloody floor—the stranger stalked forward, withdrawing a long, broad dagger and rapier.

The old man saw the spectral silhouette of the stranger as he strode over his fallen form, glimpsed the flash of lightning as it slashed down the edge of the sword. Then the stranger disappeared into the vast darkness of the night, pursuing the creature, and was gone.

Artillery shells erupted as the man slid silently into a ravaged trench, crouching beside a soldier who hung headlong, his mouth open in what would have been horror if he had been alive.

As the man hit the ground, he raised his rifle, though he had not yet entered enemy lines. But what he hunted this night would not be found in enemy lines. No, tonight, it was here, feeding on flesh and fear.

Night had not yet fallen, and already it had emerged—*growing stronger with all this death*. The man knew that if he did not kill the creature soon then he would not kill it at all because the beast would fade into the darkness and escape again.

He moved quickly, teeth clenched in concentration, scanning everything, ready for anything. He heard a scream and moved, innately understanding the cause. Then he slowed because he knew the victim would be dead when he came upon the scene, and he did not wish to join him.

The creature was there when he arrived.

It whirled, its eyes blinking, then it vaulted incredibly high and far from the trench, coming to ground to run across the sulfur-clouded field. But the man was almost as quick as he raised his rifle and fired.

It howled and stumbled, clutching its thigh, and the man fired again and again, working the Enfield rifle as fast as the bolt would allow. His seventh and last shot went wide—he was certain because he did not hear another cry.

Crouching low, the man hastily shoved cartridges into the rifle while glancing at his surroundings, acutely alert to the danger that the creature might circle in its tracks and attack. Not that he expected to actually see it coming for him. In the smoke and fog, it was impossible to determine movement, but his senses were hyperacute—years of war had made them so.

Nightbringer

He rose and moved after it, sensing more than hearing a hideous cry at the far side of the battlefield. It had already reached enemy lines to kill again.

Instantly running, the man was enveloped by the fog and mist but easily tracked the creature by the bloodcurdling cries that cut through the gathering night. But when he dropped low into the German trench, he was not surprised that he encountered no attack. The creature had been here and was gone. The horrified, frozen stares of dead men—their throats and chests ripped open—were evidence enough.

Utterly still, the man listened. He had tracked it over a century, over a hundred thousand miles to this battlefield. Had determined *this one* would not escape him again. But he knew, as time passed, that the beast had, indeed, escaped him. Just as he knew that there was nothing to do but begin tracking it again.

Again and again we fight, but the fight must end.

Quickly he shed his British paratrooper uniform and donned the uniform of a dead Nazi colonel as a contingent of SS troops reached the site. They shouted questions in their language, and he sternly silenced them in their language.

Yes, he spoke their language.

He spoke a hundred languages.

CHAPTER ONE

An edge keen and white as a razor rose behind the whetstone as the man pushed it along the edge of the sword. His smoothness was the sign of a master, though there were few alive now who would know the sign of a master.

He did not care.

It was his purpose to ensure the age-old weapons within the Abbey of Saint Gregory's were preserved as if they would be used tomorrow in a war that men had not waged for hundreds of years. Before war became bloodless and the enemy faceless.

Saint Gregory's, the greatest abbey to rise upon the Alpine crest joining Italy and France, was in truth more museum than monastery. For throughout its Great Hall and innumerable chambers, corridors, and catacombs lay a great repository of weapons borne in all the wars ever fought for, or against, God. Nor was its purpose to glorify or condemn but rather to proclaim the truth that God would judge each man for the blood he had shed.

Having lived here for almost seventy-two years, Barnabas had meticulously polished and preserved the Roman armor— the swords and shields and spears—every day, though he could not explain why. But it was what he was compelled to do, and so he maintained the vulnerable armor until it burnished like deep gray waves of fire. So that a razor's edge honored all the swords and spears and daggers. And, last, he regularly replaced the royal red cloak on the marble Roman centurion that forever stood guard beside the altar of God.

Odd, yes, that a statue of a Roman centurion stood in the place usually occupied by angels and prophets. And it was in this cathedral alone that a centurion stood in that holy place. But there were also exquisite statues of Moses and Mary and Joseph. And along the wall were exotic runes and emblems of the Order of the Knights Templar—some curious form of calculus, it was held, that revealed the tombs of the prophets, the secret of perpetual motion, eternal energy, even life. Carved into the pillars and ceiling and panels, the enigmatic flowing symbols resembled waves crashing along the shore, each running over the next in air that slashed with foam.

Barnabas had watched a hundred scholars and priests, ministers, councils, and merely obsessed believers as they spent months, even years, trying to decipher the enigma contained within the runes. But they all eventually departed in frustration, and although Barnabas could not understand the runes, it was clear to him that the secret to the code was not contained within the code itself.

For he was also a mason, though not as most understood masonry. Indeed, he did not clumsily mortar stones together to construct a wall with less than perfect smoothness. In fact, such was his skill that he needed little mortar at all, and when he finished no one could determine where one stone ended and another began. For it was his particular gift to patiently shape the blocks until they fit so tightly that not even air could pass through.

Life had always been thus. Barnabas did not know why. He only knew that he had been raised within the abbey and that it had been a good life. But sometimes in the night he saw the face of the man who had left him here so long ago—saw in his mind alone, for his eyes were weak and opaque now—as the man emerged from the smoke and screams and war. He could hear the man's comforting words, and then the man lifted his small body from the frozen ground and carried him from the battlefield.

He remembered the man bearing him so strongly through a night torn by shrieks and screams, through fields of mist-shrouded dead, through the thudding of machine guns and eruptions and the wounded howls of still more men who did not yet know that they were dead. He remembered how the man had been so utterly unafraid, as Barnabas had been so utterly afraid. And then, hours later that same night, the man had climbed the slope to this forbidding place and boldly entered the abbey as if he owned all that it contained—as if he'd built it, and none resided here except by his will.

Yet as they rose on the slope, the man spoke soothingly to him about the gigantic stones of the abbey—their weight, shape, and purpose. He had talked until Barnabas had completely forgotten his fear, so fascinated had he become with the man's words. And Barnabas had studied each stone as the man passed them, describing a reason for each. In that moment Barnabas understood what he wished to do for the rest of his life. He would keep this place for the man. He would protect it for this man.

Then the man gently delivered Barnabas into the arms of the monks before assuming a different, dark, gigantic aura of authority—an authority so absolute and stern that none uttered a word as he instructed them to care for Barnabas as if for their own lives.

Even at such a young age Barnabas vividly understood that the monks answered to the man as if to a king. Then the man encouraged them to maintain their faith, their courage, and their strength—to remember their purpose, even when war threatened to crush the doors of this holy place. Because this place would never fall, he said. No, it would never fall because what it contained did not belong to man, nor would God allow man to possess it. Then the man turned without fear into the night...and was gone.

Days tirelessly faded into months, months into years, years into decades—abbots were appointed, grew old, and died, for no one who came to Saint Gregory's ever seemed to leave. And Barnabas continued to do what he had always done, working as he had always worked, and remembering the night of the storm—the night he would have known death but for the man who had so fearlessly delivered him from its clutches. Nor had a single monk ever voiced a question of it in all the years.

Some questions should not be asked.

Though he was old, even for a monk, he was strong and seemed not a monk at all in the cold manner in which he turned the petrified, shattered skull in his hands.

The fingers that slid over the bone were thick and callused, the hands wide and powerful. His huge squared head, where it emerged from his dust-shrouded habit, was completely covered with long gray-white hair streaked with spidery black. But his thick shoulders indicated no curse of age, nor did his senses seem diminished as he turned to the silent shape that now stood behind him.

The other monk spoke hesitantly to him. "Brother Melanchthon, the...uh...the father abbot wishes to know if you will participate in Compline Prayers today."

Melanchthon did not move within the amber sphere of his wall-mounted torch. "I will participate," he growled, like a bear roused from hibernation.

The other monk hesitated. "But...how?"

"As any participate—each according to his ability."

Slowly, Melanchthon turned his head. The other monk was smaller, but much taller, with a slender body. His hands were long and delicate. His fingers, as he folded them around his lamp, seemed to stretch almost to his wrists. In aspect he seemed breakable and precious, like porcelain. And though he did not tremble at the older monk's steady gaze, he seemed to fight the impulse to rush away.

Mercifully, Melanchthon smiled and nodded. "Yes, I shall attend evening prayers, Brother Jaqual. Tell Father Abbot that I beg his forgiveness for my absence this afternoon."

Jaqual nodded but did not raise his eyes as he turned away. The light from his lamp silhouetted his long brown habit until the darkness overcame the halo. Melanchthon watched him until he was gone, then turned his attention again to the crumbling wall that had once been stone. He once more studied the broken shard of skull. Then, frowning, he studied the wall as if it were an enemy.

Even an amateur's eye could see that the squared stones were once mortared together, though, just as equally obvious, it had been buried for centuries—perhaps for as long as Saint Gregory's had stood.

Melanchthon unceremoniously cast the skull aside and carefully struck a faint gap between the stones with a rock hammer. Though brittle, the stone returned a deep thud as if all the earth pressed behind it—lifeless stone refusing to let him enter.

Guarding its secret...

Shadows of rock and wind-blasted trees—their bark shorn away to leave them naked and white in the fading sunlight—began to pale as the sky darkened.

Wind exploded in gusts, lifting sheetlike ghosts of snow from the white-ribboned ground, swirling them down the mountain and toward the abbey that stood monolithic and alone against the blue outline of mountains merging with dark clouds.

The monk who stood upon the parapet, watching the slow gathering of the storm, seemed as placid and calm as the deepest of the ocean's unexplored depths. He turned with a faint smile as Jaqual approached with long, gangly strides that made him seem all ankles, knees, and hips.

Father Stephen laughed good-naturedly at the sight, waiting for the novice to speak first, though he already knew what his words would be. The younger monk folded his hands.

"Brother Melanchthon says he will attend Compline Prayers, Father Abbot. But, I...uh...gathered from his tone and actions that he...well...may not have been speaking truthfully."

With the words Jaqual bowed his head, as if he had failed. But Father Stephen laughed again as he gently laid a hand on the monk's thin shoulder. "Melanchthon must dig for his bones, eh?" he said with an indulgent smile. "I expected little more."

They walked toward the roof entrance of the abbey. "Come, my young Jaqual, let us worship God together. But first, I want you to use the telephone. We should make sure that Mr. Trevanian's tour group is already in the mountains. If not, then we must advise them to return to Lausanne."

"Because of the storm?"

"Yes, the storm. There was nothing on the last radio weather report, but I do not fancy the face of it."

Jaqual glanced back at the mountains. "But...uh...we have nothing to fear?"

Father Stephen laughed and grasped the monk's arm. It was thin and spindly as a broom. "No, Brother Jaqual. Saint Gregory's has withstood a million storms; it can withstand a million more. But if Mr. Trevanian's tour bus is caught on the pass, then we might be forced to assist in their rescue. And I do not relish the idea of trouncing into the gale bearing rope and ax."

As they reached the door, a gust of slicing cold wind cut across the roof in razors of ice. Father Stephen winced as he quickly pushed Jaqual into the stairway and slammed the door shut. The older monk angrily shot the bolt.

"Well," he muttered with irritation, "that's enough of that! Go now, son, and determine if the tour bus can beat the storm to our door. If not, they must turn back."

Father Stephen scowled as he descended.

"It seems we are separated from the world until the wrath of this beast has passed."

CHAPTER TWO

Grinding gears, Miguel eased off the clutch, and the tour bus climbed in a roar that was hoarse and large. The narrow road had no shoulder on one side and a shoulder two thousand feet straight down on the other, but he did not even glance at the precipice. Instead he glowered at the blinding snow that struck with such force.

Crowded but not over-packed, the bus bore Miguel, two elderly gentlemen, two women, two children, two other men, and a priest who, strangely, traveled alone. Although the priest had been predominately occupied with a satchel of official-looking documents, the rest of the tour group had seemed to enjoy pleasant conversation during the long, groaning journey up the Italian Alps toward the ancient Abbey of Saint Gregory's.

One of the elderly men—wearing an inexpensive three-piece suit rumpled from the long day—half turned in his seat toward the woman seated behind him.

In her late thirties—her age was not so easily determined because she was in superb physical condition—the woman wore her thick brown hair in a layered cut, bangs hand-brushed casually and attractively to either side.

Her eyes were bright green—almost jade—and seemed to pick up the smallest details of her surroundings. The bend of her head hinted that she heard every word spoken in her vicinity, as if she were effortlessly alert. As if she had unconsciously developed the habit of following every word and action of those around her.

Still, she smiled easily and frequently, but she could quickly turn a withering look upon the two rambunctious children who played beside her. More than once she had politely pardoned herself from a conversation to beam a warning that settled a dispute instantly and without words.

The children, a boy no more than nine years old and a girl no more than twelve, crowded her.

"Don't be afraid," Mr. Trevanian said with the gestures he habitually used as if not only did American tourists not understand Italian, but they didn't understand English, either.

The woman smiled at the tour guide.

"In my line of work, you learn to relax, Mr. Trevanian, or you don't live very long. I was just wondering why you seemed so preoccupied."

"Ms. Crockett, isn't it?"

"Just Gina."

"Thank you. And so what is your line of work?"

"Just a government job."

"Ah." He stared once more at the swirling snow.

"So, care to share why you're so preoccupied?"

He shrugged. "Saint Gregory's has not been open to the public since World War II. And, in truth, I have not seen it since I was a child—when my father took me on the very last tour."

The woman's eyes narrowed. "Why was Saint Gregory's ever closed to the public?"

"No one knows." He appeared to grow solemn. "It is actually the most fascinating basilica in all of Europe. It is certainly one of the greatest museums," he pondered. "Yes, from what

I remember—but I was very young—its treasury, which dates from the Roman Empire's golden age, is without peer. The relics seem to stretch on and on as you wander the halls—shields, candelabra, silver plates, chalices, ceremonial bowls. There are literally hundreds of spears, chariots, bridles, and even a bronze statue of Romatus, Julius Caesar's favorite stallion."

"Are you serious?" Gina laughed. "I thought Saint Gregory's sounded interesting when I read a little about it before we came, but I can't believe they haven't opened this place since World War II."

"Well...there was, perhaps, a legitimate reason." He gestured to canyons that delved into cloud. "It is very dangerous to be caught on the pass during a storm."

"Uh-huh," Gina said, staring carefully. There had been something in the tone. "Anything else?"

"Oh," Trevanian gestured, "there was some form of trouble before the war. But it seems Saint Gregory's has always been a site for the unexplained."

Gina was intrigued. "Really? What happened?"

For a moment Trevanian was motionless and silent. "Well, the story goes that one of the elderly monks—apparently the one responsible for ensuring the others maintained their separation from all things worldly—was killed. And rather horrifically, I believe."

Gina blinked. "Killed? As in 'murdered'?"

"Well, I didn't say 'murdered.'" Trevanian lifted a hand toward the Alps. "The mountains are filled with wolves, bears, wildcats, and the old man was found in the stable. He'd been torn to pieces, they say, as an African lion would do." He shrugged. "I don't know the truth of it. I only know that the abbey was closed afterward."

"But not 'closed.'"

"No, no...not 'closed.'" Though he had probably told this story a thousand times, the tour guide could not conceal his curiosity. "As I said, I don't know the truth of it. I only know that no one was ever charged with any crime." He laughed gruffly. "But that says nothing—the Church often handles matters in-house, so to speak. If another monk was involved, then they discreetly stabled him where he could do no more harm."

"Don't worry, Mr. Trevanian, I think we'll be fine." Gina glanced, bemused, at the cliff, then looked down at a map of the local region. "The map says we're less than a mile away. If we go off the edge, I don't think any of us will be around to sue. And I doubt that a mad monk that might have committed a crime in the 1940s is still hanging around."

Mr. Trevanian seemed not to notice the humor. He turned to look at Miguel, who had been speaking to someone on the CB radio and had just clicked off. The brief conversation had not disturbed the Spaniard's driving for even a second.

"What is it, Miguel?"

"The road down to Lausanne has been closed! I told them we were almost to the abbey! So, no problem!"

"No," Trevanian muttered, "no problem." A moment passed, and then he turned again to Gina. "We will be safe once we reach the abbey. It was built with stone walls over twenty feet thick. It's not amazing that it has endured for so long."

"Just how old is the abbey?"

"It was completed in 643 A.D." Trevanian stared at the snow swirling over the windshield as if the bus were submerged in a violent arctic current.

"The history proceeds like this. After Heraclius, the first and greatest of the Crusaders, defeated the Persians in 627 at Nineveh, he retook Jerusalem and, according to legend, reclaimed the Holy Cross and the greatest holy relics."

"The Holy Cross?"

"Yes, the cross of Christ. But in 636, when the Christian Arabs and the Monophysites betrayed Heraclius and killed his commanders in chief, Trithyrius and Vahan, all of Palestine lay open to invasion. Unable to hold Syria against the mounting armies, and perceiving that his army was doomed because so many of his soldiers had dishonored God in their wanton depravities, Heraclius personally gathered the relics and set sail from Antioch to Constantinople. Unfortunately, three of his five ships were lost in a storm during the voyage. Only two reached their destination."

"That's an incredible story."

"And true," Trevanian said. "Which is why Saint Gregory's is the most mysterious destination on the tour."

"And so Saint Gregory's has the alleged cross of Christ?"

"Unfortunately, no, the Holy Cross and many of the other relics were supposedly claimed by the storm."

"What relics does it contain?"

"Perhaps the head of John the Baptist. Indeed, there are uncountable legends and stories about hidden artifacts and treasures."

The nine-year-old boy beside Gina turned in his seat, staring at the Italian tour guide. "What about the Ark of the Covenant? Like in *Indiana Jones*?"

Gina tilted her head. "Josh..."

Josh's mouth tightened in a smile. "I mean...excuse me, sir. Do they have the Ark of the Covenant?"

"I'm afraid not, young man. It seems the Ark was too well hidden by the prophet Jeremiah—some say within a mountain in what is now Libya. And no one, as far as I know, has ever found it."

"Oh...bummer."

"But they have other relics that you may find fascinating," the tour guide said enthusiastically. "They have, perhaps, the staff of Moses! There are ancient swords and spears and armor worn by the Romans, the Persians, the Crusaders!"

Josh was not impressed. Yet the tour guide was not to be defeated.

"There is also the robe Peter surrendered in Rome before he was crucified! And they have the golden bowl that Pontius Pilate used to wash his hands before the Sanhedrin! And they have what many claim is a scrap of the original book of Romans, written by Paul. Uh...and they have vast catacombs!"

Josh sat bolt upright.

"With bones?" he asked, glancing at his mother. "Like we saw in the German catacombs?"

Trevanian waved off the Germans. "Who are these Germans? Saint Gregory's has...uh...millions of skull bones and leg bones and arm bones! All stacked in huge pyramids and piles and dunes! There are no catacombs in all of Europe to compete with the bones of Saint Gregory's!"

"Wow...cool."

Gina laughed. "Skull bones?"

"Oh, Josh," said the girl seated behind them.

Josh glared. "C'mon, Rachel! This is gonna be twice as cool as Frankfurt!"

Rachel leaped. "Look!"

Together they turned.

Rising from the crest of a wind-blasted hill, the Abbey of Saint Gregory's stood alone and gigantic and brooding on the crest of the mountain. A single square tower rose a hundred feet taller than the hundred-foot-high walls, and two parapets like huge black eyes glared down from above a length of white columns that supported the gigantic domed mouth of an entrance. The ominous impression was that of the mountain's gargantuan skull staring angry and displeased over a grave-yard of gray and scattered stones.

No one spoke or moved. Then Trevanian turned and gazed frankly at Gina. The tour guide attempted to appear relaxed, though his smile was clearly forced.

"Welcome to Saint Gregory's, madam."

CHAPTER THREE

S aint Gregory's seemed even more enormous inside its massive walls. The gigantic stones, each weighing tens of tons, had been fit together with such exacting craftsmanship that Gina couldn't imagine air passing between them even a thousand years from now. She wondered how men might have accomplished such a prodigious task using only primitive tools.

Skill, dedication, patience...

Curiously, she saw no signs of war—no pockmarks of cannon or mortars or even rifle fire that had scarred every historic structure she had seen across Europe.

Yes, this place had somehow avoided the armies that had fought World War II...or the armies had avoided it. But she laughed at the thought. Yes, it was scary, but it wasn't that scary. Saint Gregory's had probably escaped the war because it was so inaccessible and had no true military value—at least not enough value to risk a battalion on the road they had just exited. The closest place for an airstrip was in the valley eight thousand feet below, and, even today, there wasn't a nearby open site to land a helicopter. It was as though this place had been content to let time pass it by, as if it served its most profound purpose by remaining impractical.

Wandering about the outer courtyard alone, Gina seemed to study the abbey for more than its architecture. She noticed the doors and windows, as if searching for something specific. Meandering, she paced slowly down a wall, reaching up to touch the stained-glass windows set low to the ground. She touched the frame, pinching the wood as if to test its strength. She pressed softly against the glass.

Her athletic build was evident even in loose-fitting casual clothes, and she seemed every bit a woman in the prime of her life. Her tanned cheeks were high above full lips, and she showed no tension. It was only her eyes that revealed a detective's acute awareness to detail.

She turned, staring at the bus. Beside it stood the quietest member of the tour group—a man in his mid-forties. He had a strong build and spoke little. His hair was dark brown, and his eyes were blue like the sea off the coast of some Mediterranean island. He carried nothing but an aluminum case and a duffel bag.

She had attempted to speak with him several times during the past four days, and he had been unfailingly polite, but also mysteriously elusive. He did not seem to mind her questions, however, and so Gina had persisted. What she noticed most was that he always seemed to pause before answering—a trait of intelligence or deceitfulness.

His name was Michael Constantine.

She had barely walked out of the courtyard and back to the bus as the wide doors of the basilica behind her opened. The priest who greeted them was the personification of graciousness. He stretched out his arms as if to embrace the whole of them— men and women he had never met and knew nothing about.

"Welcome to Saint Gregory's," he said, chant-like. "I am Father Stephen, the father abbot. Please freely receive the blessings we bestow upon each of you, and please leave something of your happiness when you depart."

With formality, Trevanian bowed. "Father Stephen, I am Mr. Trevanian, the tour guide. We were forced to curtail the museums of Antigone to beat the storm to your door. I hope you expected us."

"Certainly we expected you!" Father Stephen laughed. "Each of your accommodations is prepared, and a meal awaits!" Then, sobering somewhat, he focused on Josh and Rachel. "And just which of these grown-ups do you own?"

Gina placed an arm around each of them. "They're with me, Father. I'm Gina Crockett. This is Rachel, and this is Josh."

"My pleasure, madam."

"Mine as well." Gina nodded and couldn't help but smile. "They won't be any trouble—I promise."

"Oh, worry for nothing, Ms. Crockett—"

"Gina, please."

"Of course—Gina. Worry for nothing, Gina. The abbey is quite childproof." He leaned into Josh's open stare. "There are no breakables within reach!"

Everyone laughed as Father Stephen looked over the rest of the party, and his eyes widened as he beheld a priest formally dressed in a soutane. Father Stephen focused instantly on the surplice—the tiny red threads of a cassock that marked a monsignor.

Openly shocked, the father abbot knelt and extended his hands.

"Arise, my friend," said the monsignor.

Father Stephen stood. "I did not know, Monsignor...?"

"Monsignor DeMarco, Father." The monsignor's tone was warm and comforting. "And it is I who should apologize. I am on a personal pilgrimage, so you could not have known of my coming."

"Yes, Monsignor—a pilgrimage, of course. Are there any special needs that we should—"

"No—nothing, Father. For this visit I am only another guest and wish to be treated as such."

Stephen bowed. "As you wish, Monsignor."

Slightly over six feet, in his late forties, the monsignor's elegant posture and manner indicated a natural possession of refined dignity and culture. His hands were broad and powerful, his face smooth-shaven, well tanned, and without scars. His forehead was broad and high, and he possessed eyes clear and intelligent and aquiline. There was a thin trace of Italian origin in his words.

Father Stephen turned and nodded to the rest of the tour group—an old man; a woman who seemed to be around Gina's age; a well-built, middle-aged man; and a large, bearded man who effortlessly held a huge duffel bag in a single hand. The man was utterly bald—his head apparently shaved—and he smiled with his every response or comment. His thick legs and arms were like marble pillars straining against his unassuming brown shirt and trousers. His sheepskin vest was his only fortification against the howling cold. He called himself Molke, saying one name is enough for any man.

He was good-natured and friendly, and had found himself crossing Gina's path more than once on her trip through Europe. During a journey they had taken together from Lucerna, he'd frequently reminded Gina of the men in the world's strongest man contests. He was by no means Olympian in build—his large gut, low center of gravity, and thick neck would have instantly disqualified him from any bodybuilding contests—but he had an obvious aura of gigantic strength. A gentle giant, Molke had playfully demonstrated prodigious feats of strength for the children, once lifting an Audi onto two wheels. At one of the castles they had visited at the same time, he hoisted a 1,000-pound cannon, inspiring the children to erupt with applause. Then he had laughed and replaced the weapon with as much ease as he lifted it. Gina felt comfortable in his presence and had come even to trust him, to a degree, to watch the children.

The abbot extended a hand to the huge double doors at least twenty feet high. They were built of thick wooden beams, possibly oak or hickory, looking much like square railroad ties. They were also paneled in iron plates recently painted glossy black.

"Please," the abbot smiled, "enter our home and consider it your home as well."

As the others began up the steps, Josh held his place. His utter stillness attracted Father Stephen's gentle attention. "Do you not wish to join us, Joshua? We've prepared an excellent meal for you, and you must be hungry from your trip."

Josh didn't move. "It looks scary."

Stephen laughed. "Oh, young man, rest assured. There is absolutely nothing to be afraid of in Saint Gregory's. Neither tempest nor storm can enter these walls."

After a long, uneasy stare, Josh tightly grasped Gina's hand and tentatively mounted the first step.

***

Melanchthon, bent upon a single knee, turned his head to gaze at the feet of the man who had arrived behind him. Nothing was said, for the other monk could not speak. Yet he was one of the few who dared approach Melanchthon so deep within the catacombs of Saint Gregory's, where hundreds of thousands of skeletons hung in mute anticipation of what they alone knew.

Melanchthon nodded slowly and rose.

"So, Brother Basil," he rumbled deeply, looking past the monk, "they have come."

Melanchthon sighed, then looked at Basil. "How is Brother Dominic doing today? Resting now, I assume, since you are here and not tending to his needs."

Basil smiled faintly and nodded, then stared pensively at Melanchthon.

"The guests, yes. They have come," Melanchthon said with another sigh. "Very well, advise Father Stephen that Melanchthon will be up as soon as he can wash and change."

With a single solid bow, Basil turned solemnly and walked in almost complete silence up the tunnel, surrounded by a halo of yellow light thrown from his lamp.

Unlike Jaqual, he did not seem to fear the darkness.

In the Great Hall—actually a stupendous cathedral-museum of relics that gleamed silver and gold in the light of a hundred oil-fed candelabra—they moved among remarkable displays of the weapons, uniforms, and armor of ancient Rome.

There were also holy relics, each presented in intricately carved display cases that, alone, were works of art. And Gina found it remarkable that this eighth wonder of the world had not been open to the public for almost sixty years. It was certainly a boon for the world.

Then she wondered vaguely about security and observed that the glass of the cases was over two inches thick and, for all practical purposes, unbreakable. Sure, it could be shattered, but it would take something like a bomb. Nor did she see cameras or guards or even monks who watched closely enough to be concealed guards.

She was staring upon the marble statue of a heavily armored Roman centurion when the oldest man of the tour group turned to her.

At least eighty, as his face reflected, the man's body was slightly bent and withered. As Gina shook his hand, she realized that it was soft and without calluses—the hand of a man who turned little more than pages. But his eyes were a scintillating blue and his hair a breathtaking white.

"Forgive me," he said with a humble, deferential bow, "I am afraid that I did not formally introduce myself on the bus trip. I am Professor Benjamin Halder, and this young lady behind me is my daughter, Rebecca."

Handshakes all around, and Gina recrossed her arms. "Yeah, I thought you were a professor, especially with the way you entertained the children on the bus ride. You kept them fascinated with all those stories about wars and soldiers and legends." She laughed. "I have to admit, you kept *me* fascinated! Are you a history professor?"

"Well," he said, "actually, I'm a sawbones, as they used to call us. But I no longer practice medicine. My greatest fascination in these past few years has been history—languages, mostly."

"That's wonderful!" Gina said instantly. "I hope you can teach Josh a thing or two while you're here!"

The professor laughed. "Latin?"

"English!"

He laughed as Rebecca placed a hand on his shoulder. Appearing to be no older than her mid-thirties—no older than Gina—she must have been conceived when the professor was at least fifty. Not so unusual among the English aristocracy, which the professor surely was.

"Father believes that people should continue to learn as long as they live." She smiled.

The professor tilted his head back and laughed. His affection for his daughter was natural and endearing. Gina was already enjoying their company and remembered how the professor had humbly shared his great learning as they'd driven over the mountains. He had been casual and polite—a man of genuine passion and great knowledge who simply enjoyed sharing it. He pointed to the walls. "Fascinating, is it not?"

Gina looked at the curious running-dog pattern of swirls and Latin letters with Roman numerals inserted at random intervals. She had intended to reply to the professor's assessment with polite disagreement, but then she looked closer. Her eyes narrowed. The pattern was not only fascinating, it was eerie. Clearly, it wasn't the eclectic or random artistry of a mason or sculpture. It was far too tightly...coded.

"What is it?" she asked.

"According to legend, it is a form of calculus."

"Calculus? Isn't that strange for a monastery?"

Professor Halder shrugged. "Perhaps, perhaps not. There are similar chapels throughout Christendom." He pointed to a section heavy with numerals. "According to legend—there is little fact to back it up—this is a secret message left by the ancient Order of the Knights Templar. Some say it reveals the vault of the greatest Christian relics."

"Relics," Gina repeated with a slow nod. "Yes, Mr. Trevanian told me all about them, but some of it seems too incredible." She became more considerate. "What do you think?"

Professor Halder laughed. "I suppose that some might be the genuine article, as they say. And some, for certain, are forgeries or fakes." Despite his scholarship, the professor was quite agreeable to reasonable skepticism. "You see, the medieval period is top-heavy with legend and lore—of witchcraft, sorcerers, holy warriors, and wars waged between angels and demons. And the Order of the Knights Templar is particularly shrouded in myth, since it maintained such fanatical secrecy. Even their initiation rites remain a secret."

"Just what, exactly, was the Order of the Knights Templar?"

Halder's eyes narrowed at the wall. "In layman's terms the Knights were a very select group of highly skilled soldiers who served only God. They did not answer to the authority of any country or even the Church. Yet they fought valiantly in a hundred wars, defending the weak, the oppressed, those tyrannized by cruel lords and kings. They were supposedly the bravest warriors, refusing surrender even when they were utterly doomed. They were not dependent on any kingdom for the means to fight their campaigns. In fact, their private treasury was enormous. Which is the reputed reason for their demise."

"Really?"

Gina's love for history quickly overtook her skepticism.

The professor shared his knowledge with the humblest tone. "Yes, according to the most reliable accounts, the pope at that time envied their wealth and influence, so he ordered they be executed for witchcraft and personally assumed control of their treasury."

"I've read about the Knights before, Professor. But I think there was more involved than just money. Tell me. How did the Knights become so rich?"

"Well, that occurred over a period of hundreds of years, of course. But they basically accumulated their immense wealth during the Crusades by collecting donations from grateful monarchs and taxes from those they conquered. In fact—and I hesitate to add this, since it seems most impractical—some say the Knights were never actually destroyed. Indeed, it is rumored in some secretive quarters that their heirs maintain a vigil over the relics to this very day."

"Why were the Knights so secretive?"

The professor paused, as if he'd never considered the question. Or because he had considered the question so completely that he was surprised someone even asked it. "Well, it was, of course, rumored that the Knights practiced ancient Hebrew rituals—intricate spells to forbid demons from interfering in our world. And, allegedly, they did not wish the world to possess such knowledge because it was so terribly dangerous."

He shrugged. "Who knows? But something that is not legend is their military prowess. The Knights were, without question, a great and influential force and are said to secretly influence the destiny of nations even today."

Gina was quiet, then, "You know, I don't doubt much anymore, but that sounds pretty fantastic." She carefully considered the wall. "Do you believe any of it?"

With a slight frown indicating humble uncertainty, the professor remarked, "Yes, I suppose I do believe that the Knights endured—simply because that is where logic leads."

"Logic? Why's that?"

"Well, it doesn't seem logical that an army as powerful as the Knights Templar could be destroyed so easily. In fact, if defeat in battle seemed inevitable, I would certainly not engage the enemy without first securing a number of my men within the nobility of a half-dozen countries. There would be no center of power—no target that could crush the empire. Then, even if they lost the war, they would continue in secret and, for certain, the accumulated wealth would have been hidden far too well for discovery. Of course, they would have sacrificed a measure just for credibility. But the lion's share would be dispersed to numerous strongholds—unknown even to one another—so that no single act of betrayal would be crippling."

Gina blinked. "You don't have to be a criminal to have a criminal mind," she said.

She searched and saw Josh sitting before a table, his chin supported on his hands. He was staring at a strange device with three rows of solid silver balls suspended on what looked like strands of fishing line connected to parallel sticks mounted on an iron bracket. She didn't know what it was.

"Excuse me, Professor." He nodded politely, and she strolled across the room as their Spanish driver, Miguel, paused beside Josh. Though still a dozen feet apart, Gina caught the words.

"No one knows what it is," Miguel commented dryly. "They think it was some kind of Roman game. But anyone who knew how to play it has been dead for a thousand years." He smiled. "Maybe you'll be the first to figure it out!"

Josh flicked the steel balls. They clacked for a moment before falling still, and Gina saw that the balls were suspended too closely to maintain momentum. "So, nobody knows what it is?" she asked mildly.

Miguel shook his head. "No, ma'am. It is a mystery, as many things within the abbey are a mystery."

"Yes, I've sensed that."

Monsignor DeMarco's dignified aura shadowed them as he approached. Gina turned and smiled politely as the middle-aged priest gazed over Josh. Then the monsignor reached out and lifted one of the sticks. He placed it in a notch, suspending the middle row of silver balls above the rest. He pointed to a row of strings.

"Push this one, young man."

Josh gazed up a moment, doubtful, then gently pushed the middle row. The movements were instantly free and rhythmic and seemed as though they could continue all day. Not perpetual motion, but the closest thing Gina had ever seen. "That's remarkable, Monsignor. Miguel said that no one has ever figured it out."

"I've seen one before, many years ago." The monsignor smiled. "It's a Roman chronometer, used for singing—so everyone could sing together." His countenance grew somber. "There must have been some happy times for that poor, spiritless empire."

"I thought Rome was the most powerful empire of the ancient world."

"Perhaps in scope," the monsignor commented, "but perhaps not...Rome spread even to northern England before its army became too thinly spread and was decimated by the Celts. But the empire was in decline, anyway, by that time.

"The power of the senate and the power of the militia had been displaced by the power of wealth and private armies. There was no one worth calling Caesar. Even centurions warred among themselves—those who worshiped the Christian God and those who remained loyal to the host of gods stolen from Greece."

Gina knew history well enough to follow.

"Actually," he added offhand, "Rome had no philosophy or mythology at all—not to speak of. They simply stole—shamelessly, I might add—from the Greeks; a rather remarkable action for such a proud nation. But as to your first comment, the most powerful nation of ancient times was not Rome at all.

"Indeed, the most powerful nation—the most powerful army, the most powerful people in intellectual depth and scope of influence—was unquestionably Israel when David ruled."

Gina's mouth had opened slightly as the monsignor finished. She realized she was gaping. "Israel?"

The monsignor laughed loudly, eyes gleaming. "Oh, dear! I suppose you, too, have been duped by those who say Israel was a leper colony led by vagabond prophets who hid in holes in the ground? A nation lorded over by an ignorant shepherd boy who never did anything worth remembering? A poor fool who managed to take the throne of Israel as both priest and king?"

Gina was already persuaded, but the monsignor continued with a smile. "Yes, poor Israel who defeated the Moabites, the Amalekites, the Egyptians, and every other nation that existed during its time."

He stood back, staring frankly. "Answer me something, Ms. Crockett. If David had wished to conquer the entire ancient world, who could have stopped him?"

Gina blinked. "Egypt?"

"Egypt sued David for peace when David was not even planning to invade," the monsignor pronounced, more serious. "Yes, a royal envoy delivered a thousand gold shields to David, begging him not to invade Egypt—a thousand gold shields to a man who cared more about playing with his children than storming their borders. And so, who else was there—mighty Askelon with its unconquerable walls three hundred feet in height? Yes, indeed, mighty Askelon, which archeologists have concluded was one of the most powerful city-nations of the ancient world?" He shook his head sadly. "Alas, Askelon, too, fell to David when he threatened to drive them into the sea if they ever raised the sword against a single Hebrew. And so no sword was raised—not while David lived. He allowed them to exist only as long as they remained within their boundaries and survived by their sea trade with Egypt."

With a quiet nod the monsignor turned to gaze across the vast display of relics. "And yet..."

"And yet?"

The monsignor's brow hardened as he gazed over the chamber. Or perhaps, Gina sensed, somehow, those within the chamber. The old priest's voice was abruptly strange.

"And yet there was, perhaps, one even greater than mighty David...."

Gina laughed. "I find that hard to believe, Monsignor. Who would that be?"

"Um..." he responded, "it is only legend, so I give it little merit." He blinked, then sighed. "Actually, I give it no merit whatsoever. I should not have mentioned it."

"Oh, come on. I have a curious nature. Who was it? And legend is always more interesting than fact."

"Well, this legend is certainly more interesting than any fact I can recall."

"And...sooo?"

The monsignor caved. "Well, my dear, there is a legend, as you probably know, that many people Jesus physically resurrected from death cannot die again by natural means. They must be killed by force—from bullets, swords, fire, or water." He waved vaguely. "Whatever. But according to legend they do not age, nor are they susceptible to sickness or disease."

"Ah, the legend of The Wandering Jew. Yeah, heard it."

"Of course you have, Ms. Crockett," he conceded. "And that is all it is—a story told by superstitious monks. And believe me, no one is more superstitious than a Gregorian monk."

"Call me Gina, please," she said.

With a deferential bow, the monsignor clasped his hands behind his back. "Of course—Gina. In any case—as I said—some legends are too incredible to accept, but some are truly worthy of consideration. Yet, I have always been fascinated by the way so many legends seem to come together in this abbey.

"Indeed, there are many things to amaze within Saint Gregory's. Perhaps you will allow me to explain some of its history another day."

Changed the subject smoothly enough...

Gina nodded.

"I'd consider it an honor, Monsignor DeMarco."

"Then it's a date."

They laughed as Father Stephen appeared in the main entrance of the Great Hall. Gina saw a banquet table behind him in what was apparently the dining hall. The father abbot raised his hands, as he had done when they arrived.

"Friends, dinner awaits."

Gina took a single step before she realized Josh was not moving and turned back. "Joshi? Time to eat, little man."

Josh still didn't move. His voice came from the very small center of him. "I don't like this place, Mom."

Brow hardening, Gina stared. Then she walked slowly forward and draped an arm over his shoulders.

"What's wrong, baby?"

"This place is...scary."

Gina smiled gently. "Honey, this is just an old, cool place with lots of skeletons and statues and stuff! Just like we saw in Germany! Remember that big church with all those bones that you thought was so cool?"

Josh's gaze roamed the walls.

"Places like this have monsters."

"Monsters!" Gina laughed, then seemed to realize it was a serious moment. She leaned forward, and Josh turned his face to her, eye to eye. "Baby, you're nine years old, now. You know there's no such things as monsters."

Josh didn't raise his face.

"Yeah...there's no such things as monsters."

CHAPTER FOUR

F ather Stephen turned to the hulking figure that stood unmoving in the doorway that led from a corridor buried deep beneath the abbey to the catacombs and ancient ruins.

"How long will you dare fate?" Melanchthon said like a judge pronouncing doom. "How long will you tempt the Lord with your acquiescence to the demands of Rome?"

"It is my *duty* to obey Rome!" Father Stephen's frown was resolute and conditioned. "You have no authority to question my actions as long as the archbishops ordain them."

"The archbishops are not here!" Melanchthon retorted. "If they spent even a single night in this tomb, do you think they would so rashly endorse these tours? Only a madman would sanction the presence of innocent people in this place of the damned."

Stephen sighed and lifted his hands to heaven. "And so, once again, we are damned?"

"Yes."

The father abbot faintly shook his head and glanced away before looking back. "Brother, your...your *warnings* have never been proven to be of any merit. I understand your cause of concern. There may be secrets buried here that no one should learn, but—"

"Or disturb."

"Yes, of course, or *disturb*. But we do not know that there are. In fact, despite your tireless searching, you have never discovered anything meriting even an open letter to Rome." His mouth tightened at Melanchthon's grave countenance. "Do you not think you should at least discover some type of evidence before you sentence us all to death?"

"What I have sensed is evidence enough."

"Yes, of course, again with this strange figure lurking throughout the walls of the abbey—the monstrous shape that has never been seen by any but yourself. A shape that leaves no trace, that eats nothing and drinks nothing. A shape that disappears like a ghost." He paused, staring. "My friend, I do not doubt that you have sensed something. But I have found no evidence to conclude that there is something strange here. And so I see no legitimate cause to disobey Rome. In fact, these tours are the best means of destroying these superstitious stories that have plagued us for years."

"If many men could see the harm in their actions, they would not die unfortunate deaths." Melanchthon's gaze was somber. "The halls of this place have seen much death."

"Death from what?"

Melanchthon frowned. "I do not know."

With a sigh, Father Stephen's face nodded. "Then I have no choice but to obey. And I abjure you to assist me—to accommodate our guests in a manner worthy of your great dignity, as I know you certainly will. For I know that, despite your vague misgivings, you mean no harm." He waited. "So...will you join me, Brother?"

Melanchthon's countenance was that of a displeased Moses. Finally he bowed his head. "I will join you," he said at last, "because neither of us will leave this place alive."

Nightbringer

Table conversation ranged widely from the fascinating to the unbelievable, and Gina suppressed a smile as she saw Josh following every sentence, especially those of Monsignor DeMarco, who had won Josh's complete allegiance when he helped him with the chronometer.

The monsignor and Professor Halder were obviously scholars of the first order. To amuse the children they had spoken in French, German, and Italian, and Josh and Rachel were, indeed, fascinated. Then Father DeMarco switched languages again.

"So your discipline is anthropology, Professor?"

"Yes, Monsignor."

The monsignor nodded, then glanced at Josh. "*Quod exspectavi aim sum adsecutus.*"

The professor laughed. "*In plerisque non civitatibus.*"

"Spanish!" Josh said. "I can speak Spanish!"

Rachel paused. "Josh, you can't."

"Yes I can!" Josh leaned lovingly into her and mooned. "Hablo Espanol me amor-a?"

Rachel rolled her eyes. "No, goofball, and neither do you."

The professor and monsignor laughed. Laughing also, Gina turned to Father Stephen, who occupied a chair at the head of the table. The father abbot had remained silent for most of the dinner, and even the small comments he offered had been concise. But Gina wanted to know more about the monastery. She told herself that it had nothing to do with the strange uneasiness that Josh had inspired in her.

"I think it's wonderful what you're doing with the abbey, Father," Gina said to soften the strange tension. "I mean, opening it so people can stay overnight and understand your cloistered way of life. It's a rich experience. Especially for the children."

"Yes," the senior priest replied with a smile. "Saint Gregory's is rich in history. In fact, I believe we have more documents and artifacts from the period of Christ than any other."

At that, the professor took a more serious tone. "I have also heard legends of a great religious relic buried deep within these walls, Father."

"A relic?" Gina asked coyly.

"*The* relic," said the professor.

Father Stephen paused for a sip of wine, then, "Legend is so much more exciting than reality, I'm afraid."

"And far more terrible," boomed a voice at once prophetic and angry—a voice that instantly commanded everyone's attention.

Gina turned to see an old but statuesque monk standing at the entrance. White-haired with impenetrable black eyes, he appeared centuries and centuries old, but it was impossible to determine his age. His fingers were slightly curled, as if from centuries of hammering. Then he entered the room with balanced, ponderous strides, as if undiminished by age.

"Allow me to introduce myself," he said gravely. "I am Brother Melanchthon, chief historian and theologian of Saint Gregory's. I shall explain anything you desire and give breath and spirit to empires long lost...reclaimed by dust."

Only Josh didn't seem intimidated. "Tell me about Rome!"

"At your service, boy." Melanchthon walked along a wall and lifted his hand. "The greatest majesty of ancient Rome is before you. Relics of wars against the Franks and Lombards—the Byzantines and Magyars and Patzinaks, who fought in small bands with bow, javelin, and scimitar. Here," he motioned, "are the Saracens, the most dangerous of all the enemies of Rome."

"Why?" Josh asked.

Melanchthon laughed. "Because, boy, the Saracens were experts at hit and run—at quick attacks where they would destroy a single platoon and then fade into the mountains." He nodded, confirming it all to himself. "Yes, the Saracens crippled mighty legions one piece at a time before the Roman generals Phillipus Arabs and Iunius Aureolis discovered their single weakness and learned to take advantage of it."

Josh was rapt. "What was it?"

"The weakness of the Saracens was that they *must retreat.* They did not command enough men for a forthright war, so they were continually forced to withdraw. What Aureolis discovered was that, instead of chasing them—a futile exercise— he could simply close all passes from the region where they'd attacked. Then his soldiers would simply advance and close the net, centimeter by centimeter, allowing not even a caterpillar to crawl through the line until the enemy was found and destroyed."

"Wow."

"Yes," Melanchthon said seriously. "Wow."

Professor Halder shook his head. "I had thought myself to be well-schooled in history, Brother Melanchthon. But you seem to have a firsthand knowledge of the ancient world."

"Thank you," Melanchthon replied steadily as he walked to the statue of the Roman centurion. "I have spent many years in the abbey learning what it contains."

The centurion's armor and red cape were in pristine condition. The ivory hilt of the short sword that hung at his waist was polished white. His breastplate had a lion emblazoned in gold within a silver circle. The steel gauntlets, certainly reproductions, were intricately woven from threads of leather sewn into a wool-lined leather sheath.

"Ah," Melanchthon whispered, staring at the uniform, "and as to fantastic legend—here is a man who became a legend even while he lived. And, as some say, never died."

Gina noticed the professor's minute nod. He was obviously familiar with this legend; she wasn't. "I suppose there's a reason for this...legend?"

"Yes," Melanchthon said quietly. "'Tis the armor of Gaius Cassius Longinus—the centurion who crucified the Son of God."

There was palpable shock in the room, and Melanchthon continued. "Yes, it was Cassius who nailed the Prince of All the Earth to the crucifix. Then, realizing what he had done, Cassius stared upon the cross and said, 'Surely this was the Son of God....'"

Melanchthon circled the table, drawing visions with his hands and far-staring eyes. "And then Annas, aged advisor of the Sanhedrin, and Caiaphas, the high priest, dispatched thirty temple guards to Golgotha—the Hill of the Skull— to break the bones of the one called Messiah. For Caiaphas remembered the prophecy of the psalmist: 'He keepeth all his bones: not one of them is broken.' And if the temple guards could only break a single bone, Jesus could not be the Messiah. But word of their intention spread to the very foot of the cross, and Cassius was prepared."

"Cassius!" Gina said before she could prevent herself. "The centurion who crucified him?"

"Yes," Melanchthon intoned, more serious. "Sword in hand, the centurion challenged the temple guards at the foot of the cross. They said they had come to break the legs of the one called Messiah, but Cassius would not let them pass. They said they were under strict orders from the Sanhedrin and would complete their mission by force, if necessary. Cassius still would not let them pass.

"Enraged, the temple guards threatened to kill the centurion. Then Cassius mounted his horse and charged upon Golgotha, stabbing at them with his spear, refusing to let them reach the body of Jesus. For he knew Jesus was the Son of God, and he would allow no one to break His bones. And when the pitch of battle demanded death, Cassius shouted that there was no reason to break the bones of the Messiah because He was already dead. And so he thrust his spear into the side of Jesus, and water and blood were released...."

No one in the room had moved in awhile.

"Caiaphas' ruse was revealed," Melanchthon added quietly, seemingly oblivious to the stillness. "For his guards had said that they only wanted to prove Jesus was dead. But the centurion had already proven that Jesus was dead, so there was no reason for them to break His legs. Unless what they truly wanted to do was desecrate the body of one who might well have been Messiah."

Melanchthon passed the chair of Father Stephen and approached Gina. His ominous tone continued, and Gina felt tiny hairs rise on the back of her neck.

"So...the centurion who killed Christ protected Christ, in the end. And it was rumored among those of the early Church that Cassius was then chosen by God to wander the earth until Jesus returned, protecting all the children of God."

Gina released a long withheld breath. "I don't understand. What's the legend? I mean, what does any of that have to do with this abbey?"

Melanchthon paused, hands heavy at his sides. "The legend, madam, is that hidden somewhere within these walls is the spear of Gaius Cassius Longinus—the very spear that pierced the side of the Son of God. And it is said that one day Cassius will return to claim his spear and fight within these walls the greatest battle he has fought in two thousand years. His greatest battle against his greatest foe—a battle that will decide the destiny of the entire earth."

"But what..." Josh asked tentatively, "...what if Cassius doesn't win?"

Melanchthon's face bent.

"Then, boy, God's warrior will die. And the earth shall suffer a dark night of horror so great that no flesh will survive, but for the return of the Son of Man, who is the Son of God."

CHAPTER FIVE

There had been no aperitifs, but a rich red wine was offered after dinner, and Gina was enjoying a glass. After enduring the grim Melanchthon's ominous dissertation on demons, monsters, the crucifixion, an immortal centurion, and the wrath of God, she could use a little relaxation.

She gazed at Rachel and Josh, who stood before a huge tapestry hung from a wall on the far side of the chamber. The obviously hand-sewn carpet was the image of some...gigantic beast battling against a dozen Roman soldiers.

Its head was sloped, like a gorilla's. Its eyes were bloodred and reflected a malignant, alien intelligence. Fangs like a lion's hung distended and bloody, and it possessed an overwhelmingly massive musculature and aura of power that eclipsed man.

Broken spears from the soldiers projected from its hulking arms and shoulders. Bearing the marks of uncountable sword wounds, it was covered in blood—and more than blood. For there seemed a bestial—and yet, far more than bestial—exultation.

Yes, Gina was certain, an exultation, as if it was enjoying the battle—as if it knew it would not be destroyed.

As she continued to study the tapestry, she saw the monk, Brother Melanchthon, walk up to stand beside Josh and Rachel. He, too, stared up at the tapestry.

Compelled by some reflexive parental instinct, Gina walked toward her children. She assured herself it was not fear and ignored the fact that she walked faster than usual.

⸺

Rachel raised her face to the monk.

"What's that?"

"One of the Nephilim," Melanchthon answered quickly with a single, defiant jut of his chin.

"The Nefleem?"

Melanchthon smiled. "Close. It is pronounced *neh...feh...LEEM*."

"Nephilim," Rachel repeated slowly and correctly. "Got it. So, what was it? A gorilla?"

"Oh no. It was a beast conceived by strange unions between the daughters of men and the sons of God."

"Like a demon?"

"Its father was a demon, but its mother was human. They are mentioned in the sixth chapter of Genesis and other passages of the Old Testament. They were, in fact, the primary reason God destroyed the earth by flood."

The big monk's gray beard lifted with his face as he spoke in a strong cadence. "For when God saw the whole heart of man was only a continual chasing after evil, He regretted He had made him. Yes...and the Nephilim were on the earth in those days, and afterward."

Rachel's eyes were wide. "These things were real? What...I mean, what were they like?"

"In the ancient Hebrew, *Nephilim* literally means 'giants.' It comes from a root word that connotes fallen ones. The Old

Testament says they were the strongest warriors, and the most merciless. They were virtually unkillable."

"Were there a lot of them?" Josh asked.

"Aye, boy. There were once entire nations of them, ruled by the Rephaim."

"Rephaim?"

"Like the one who was killed in battle by David, warrior-king of the Hebrews."

"Goliath! Wow!" Josh glanced from the tapestry to the old monk. "How big was Goliath?"

With a smile, Melanchthon lifted a large steel plate from a table. "This is the axle of a chariot wheel. It weighs twenty-five pounds." He held it toward Josh, his huge fingers white with the effort of maintaining his grip. "Take it."

As if this could be a trick, Josh gripped it cautiously, and Melanchthon released his grip.

"Rachel!" Josh yelled as he staggered at the weight, and Rachel leaped to him. Struggling and simultaneously shouting contradictory commands, they lowered and then dropped the axle to the floor, where it hit with a dull ring.

Josh was laughing. "Now that was heavy!"

"Yes," Melanchthon said, smiling, "and yet the point of Goliath's spear weighed even more than that—perhaps almost thirty pounds. His coat of chain mail weighed nearly two hundred pounds. He was thirteen feet tall and probably weighed nine hundred pounds," Melanchthon nodded. "Yes, the Nephilim were unnatural creatures of unnatural strength, and their thirst for blood was even greater than their physical power. It is also written that the Nephilim had no soul and that they would not rise at the resurrection."

"What were they doing here?" Rachel asked. "I mean, why were they fighting everybody?"

Gina arrived and Melanchthon nodded without missing a beat. "Satan knew that the child of a woman would deliver his destruction. So Satan attempted to corrupt the seed of woman—the hope of the earth. It was his plan to make his seed the ruling force on this planet—a plan God ended with the Flood."

"So they were all destroyed?"

"Yes." Melanchthon's reply to Rachel was faintly bitter. "God destroyed them all. But, once again, men opened the gateway to their world, and more Nephilim were born. And since God had vowed that He would never again destroy the earth, He would not destroy them a second time. For the one thing the Almighty will not do is break His word.

"In any case, it was said that a single Nephilim could destroy an entire legion—between three and six thousand men. And when the Nephilim gathered in number, they could annihilate any nation but Israel, for David and his mighty men ever stood against them and knew their weaknesses. Still, David's years were only the years of a man, and when he died, there was no one who could defend mankind from their wrath until..."

Despite herself, Gina was captured. "Until?"

Melanchthon made a low growl in his throat, something unconscious.

"Until a warrior—a great warrior—was born. A warrior who would hunt them across the length and breadth of the world, preying upon them as they preyed upon man. And thus began a mighty and terrible war that has spanned centuries.

"Long were the battles...and uncertain. And although the beasts are powerful, they can die—just as anything can die. And one by one, continent across continent, this single warrior began to reduce them. Nor did modern man know the secrets of how they were created, so their number could not be replenished. Then they began to conceal themselves in the shapes of men."

Rachel's eyes flared. "They can change shape? You mean they can morph to look like a real person?"

"Only to a degree," Melanchthon muttered with a hint of contempt. "But they can resemble men for a certain number of days—only Solomon the wise knew how many, and he did not reveal it—before they must revert to their original form to rest. And, of course, they must alter shape when they call upon their monstrous strength."

"Was Goliath the strongest?" Josh asked.

"No. Goliath, though enormous and gigantically strong, was the offspring of a Nephilim far greater. Its name is not even recorded in the texts of Solomon because, as Solomon said, it was far too dangerous to be spelled.

"But Solomon did record that the father of Goliath was the strongest, the most savage—the most cunning of all the Nephilim. For he was the purest—born of the first generation—and there was little of man in him to diminish his strength."

Rachel glanced at Josh. He didn't appear close to speaking. "I really hope you say he's dead," she said.

Melanchthon's mouth turned down at the edges, and he shrugged. "Who knows, child? They are unnatural creatures and do not have a natural lifespan. If he has not been killed, then he might yet walk the earth."

All of them stared upon the tapestry, and then Melanchthon turned and walked away. But Gina called after him, and the old monk turned, waiting patiently.

"You never said the name of the immortal warrior who hunted these things down and killed them."

"Is it not obvious?" Melanchthon glanced at the marble statue of the centurion. "It was Gaius Cassius Longinus, madam—the centurion who crucified the Son of God. And then vowed to protect the children of God until the end of time."

———

Father Stephen entered the Great Hall with the uncomfortable smile of a mechanic about to inform you that not only is your car dead but *good and dead*.

"I'm afraid I have bad news," he began. "The snowstorm has closed all roads over the pass. So, until they manage to clear them, you must remain at the abbey." He smiled more easily to the children. "But there's no need to worry. We are quite self-sufficient. We have our own generator, water, and ample food stores."

"You mean we're stuck here?" Josh asked.

Father Stephen seemed to genuinely warm to the subject. "In any case, young man, it will take you at least three days to see all aspects of the abbey and the labyrinth of catacombs. In fact, this storm may turn out to be a blessing. To be honest, I was hoping that you could extend your journey a few days so I could show you all our *secret passages*."

"Oh!" Josh reached his feet and grabbed Gina's hands. "Mom! Did you hear him? Secret passages!"

"Sounds pretty cool." Gina smiled.

Rachel muttered, "Dead guys lying around in secret passages is not cool."

"Can I see them now?" Josh asked.

Father Stephen laughed. "Oh, Joshua—may I call you Joshua? Thank you. It's a little late to see them today." He leaned closer. "But I promise it will be the first thing on your agenda tomorrow! Is that good enough?"

Josh was disappointed in a pragmatic way. "Yeah," he muttered. "Thank you."

Nightbringer

Extending his arms, Father Stephen added in a melodious chant. "Now, dear friends, we invite you to join us in Compline Prayers, scheduled to begin in one hour. And if you wish to participate, please consider yourselves invited."

<hr />

It hated the snow.

Snow that spread white even in the darkness that glared at him, blinded him. He wished there did not need to be snow, but there was snow—hated snow that was as white as the light that his father had hated and fled so long ago.

It reminded him of that light he would never see and did not wish to see. No, what he cared to see was darkness—darkness that spread across the world like a thundercloud lowering itself to the ground, enveloping all the world.

His step, though he attempted to move without sound, was thunderous despite the howling wind and the lightning-torn sky. Yet the most fantastic execution of the spell was its ability to command even lightning from the frozen heart of this storm.

But it had no more time to hate.

It slouched to the tour bus, already piled with drifts. And there, careful to make no sound but the inexorable crunch of powdery snow, it lifted the hood. It stared at the engine, considering whether it should make its presence known.

It was far easier to disable this engine with brute force and not the subtlety that it had been advised to use. But it did not care anymore for subtlety...or for hiding.

Yes, the time for hiding had passed. Now it was time to kill—to kill them all.

It reached its long arm past the engine, and his fingers curled against the gritty, oily base. He curled his fingers even more—until his claws cut deep into the steel.

It had always been so easy to tear through steel....

Fangs clenched in silence, he powerfully twisted his body toward the sky, wrenching the entire engine from steel bolts that twisted and tore like paper. Almost, he raised it completely into the air, compelled to lift it aloft in a single arm and hurl it toward the abbey—to announce his presence, to declare his might, to hurl them into fear so that they would flee into the bowels of the abbey. But then he paused, snarling, and released the gigantic block. It settled awkwardly.

No, he would not announce his presence—not yet. He would wait...he would catch the centurion unaware, and he would kill him. And then the nightmare would end and glory begin.

All that remained was to kill the warrior....

God's warrior...

And as he turned from the destruction of the bus's engine, he violently turned his mind from the fear that he could be afraid.

Standing alone in the Great Hall, chalice in hand, Michael carefully regarded a painting of the crucifixion. Even at a distance, Gina could read his face, and he seemed to neither approve nor condemn the artist's work. In fact, he appeared bored.

It was the wonder of how he could appear bored in a cathedral jam-packed with literally the entire history of the world that prompted Gina to approach him. When she stopped, Michael smiled pleasantly, and she, too, gazed upon the painting.

"You don't like it?" she asked.

"Oh no," he answered casually. "I think it's magnificent. I was just wondering..."

Gina waited. "Yes?"

"Nothing," he shrugged, but then, "I was just wondering why everyone paints Him the same way."

With a studious eye, Gina examined the painting once more.

Jesus was, indeed, portrayed more or less as she had always seen Him portrayed—slender, almost gaunt, long brown hair, dark eyes, a dead expression.

"I have a minor in humanities," she said. "So I've always had an affinity for art. I've probably been to the various Smithsonian art museums a hundred times. Studied in Paris... yeah, everyone pretty much paints Him in the same tone."

"Tone...good way to describe it."

Strange, she thought, that she had never considered how the historical Jesus of Nazareth might have actually looked. Because even if He had not been the Son of God, He was still a historical figure, and His life was extensively documented.

Gina found herself staring at Michael instead of the painting. "So what do you think He looked like?"

For a moment Michael was silent, but Gina had learned on the bus trip that pausing before answering was his habit.

"I don't know—He was a carpenter, and that was hard work. He walked over mountains, so he was a strong guy." He was silent for a second. "I've just always wondered why everyone portrays Him as some skinny guy who looks like He needs a handout."

Gina appreciated new thoughts, even one as strange as this.

"Good question. Come to think of it, I don't know, either. I guess because everyone else has portrayed Him like this, and the artist just followed the crowd."

"Followed the crowd," Michael repeated. "I wonder of all the mistakes men have made...following the crowd." He paused. "Crowds feed on the fear or the courage of others. They go with this group or that because they're terrified to think they might be alone in the universe.

"They join political groups—religious, cultural, sexual, whatever. They find their own identity in the identity of the group. They're not alone anymore. And if something threatens their group, they attack like rabid dogs." He paused. *"Weakness..."*

Michael regarded the painting in his longest silence yet. His words were faint and somehow distant. "I think the only thing true about this is that He was alone."

With those last quiet words, Michael turned and walked away. Nor did Gina watch him go. Then she realized she was staring dully at the base of the wall.

Blinking, she raised her gaze again to the painting but didn't see the soldiers or the weeping, moaning crowds. She only saw the truth of it—here was a man who knew the most terrifying, absolute loneliness. In the end He was abandoned by His family, His disciples—His nation. And yet He died with a peace and strength that scorned all those who mocked Him, nor did He condemn them.

Funny, Gina thought, how one man could possess strength as far beyond those surrounding Him as the stars beyond the earth. And suddenly she wished she knew more about Him.

Compline Prayers were upon them more quickly than Gina anticipated, and she sat with Josh and Rachel on a couch positioned to watch every facet of the ritual.

With a solemn pledge to remain quiet until the very end of the service, Josh sat with hands folded, mouth tight. But Rachel was truly enjoying the varied aspects of the abbey, for some reason undisturbed by Josh's onerous sense of doom. She was leaning forward, wide-eyed.

Gina was glad she'd read up on Gregorian chants before arriving. It gave her, if not a deeper appreciation, then a sort of self-satisfaction that she was staying sharp, always learning.

At the thought, she remembered the advice of the oldest man she had ever known. When asked how he made it, he told her it was by staying mentally and physically active. She'd expected the physical, but not the mental. Yet when she had thought about it afterward, she'd understood. Nothing ages someone faster than a hermit's life or a life without learning anything new.

So as the monks began the melodious chant, Gina tried to decide what type of process they were using. And almost instantly she knew it was the "gradual" because the song began with an operatic refrain, then a verse of psalm in psalm-tone style, and a repeated refrain.

As she listened, she studied the twenty-one monks, some of whom she had been introduced to during dinner. There was Jaqual, a thin, spindly monk with coal black hair, and next to him the mute Basil, a stunningly tall monk, equally massive in thickness, who could not join in the chant and held his cowl over his head for the entire service. There was a surprisingly small number, only five or six, of the very old, and then venerable Melanchthon, whom Gina still had not been able to judge.

The monk seemed older than the rest by far, but an unnaturally strong constitution allowed him to move like a man much younger. He also seemed to move with a solemn gravity, as if every move was his last and he wished it to have meaning.

The chant ended, and Father Stephen assigned individual monks to usher them to their rooms. But as Gina departed the Hall, she cast a glance at Michael.

He lifted his coat from a couch and casually cast it over his arm. But when he turned to study the monks, his face was serious. The thought that he was irritated by the chant flew across Gina's mind without notice—no, no, he was...searching.

He turned to gaze at the monk in the wheelchair—Brother Dominic—and Gina moved by instinct. She was grateful, in her first step, that her reflexes were honed to such an edge. Else she would have been noticeable when she walked back toward the table, as if she'd forgotten something.

But Michael didn't seem to notice, and she was close when he knelt before the crippled monk. Brother Basil, unable to speak but ever present to tend to Dominic and move him from place to place, bowed and stepped aside. Michael spoke softly, and Gina saw that Dominic's eyes did not move.

She caught Michael's tone but not his words, and it was a soothing tone. And, strangely, it did not sound like English. Then Michael reached out and placed a hand on the monk's shoulder and stood, nodding to Basil, who was already moving back behind Dominic to usher him out of the room.

Gina was already moving toward the stairway, having "retrieved" something from the table. She was almost startled as Monsignor DeMarco appeared in her path.

"Permit me to usher you and your children to your room," the monsignor offered with elegant, but casual, dignity.

Gina laughed. "There's some kind of danger?"

"Oh no"—he laughed—"certainly not. But I have journeyed to many faraway places, and I know the unease that sometimes accompanies the young in the presence of the old. So I wanted to assure myself that you and your children were relaxed and settled before the doors are locked."

Gina nodded quaintly. "Thank you, Monsignor. Somewhere in all that education you must have also learned nobility."

With a laugh the monsignor replied, "Nobility, madam, is something that cannot be learned."

Nightbringer

The one called Jaqual led Michael and Molke through the long second-floor corridor of the abbey. The corridor was lined with oil paintings and tapestries, but none bore the names or even initials of the artist. Molke stopped before one framed canvas that was almost six feet high and equally wide.

Molke paused, muttering a word of awe.

It was a broad panorama of a single knight riding a wounded white horse across a field spread with the butchered dead. Blood flowed in rivulets through fire-scorched stones as banners dipped drearily in the storm-clouded dusk, and the castle behind the lone rider glowed red with flame. It was the image of pure and bitter war, and yet it did not seem solely the effort of imagination.

"Incredible," Molke said quietly. "Does no one know who painted this? It is the work of a master."

Jaqual responded nervously. "No, sir. Even the old ones don't know who did it. I once asked, but no one in Rome seems to know where any of the paintings came from."

"Incredible," Molke repeated and looked at Michael. "Have you noticed these works?"

Michael shrugged. "It's similar to the style of European masters of five hundred years ago, but more carefully constructed." He pointed. "This ridge seems like part of the Carpathians—maybe Moldovia. And the armor indicates the twelfth century, when there was some vicious fighting between the Romanians and the Turks."

"A hard age," Molke said.

Slowly, Michael nodded. "Yes."

Jaqual turned and motioned to two doors. "These are your rooms, my friends. I think you'll find everything you need.

Also, each room has a telephone, just in case you desire to call one of the brothers, or anyone else."

"The lines are probably down with this storm. Do you have some other means of reaching the outside world?" Michael asked.

"Uh, yes, we have a radio. It's in Father Stephen's office. Do you wish to use it?"

"No," Michael said curtly. "Just curious."

Jaqual opened each of their doors, then moved aside and stood with his hands folded humbly in his sleeves. "Oh, and one more small thing, please."

They hesitated.

"Father Abbot told me to ask if you might remain in your rooms until morning. Some parts of the abbey are under reconstruction. They are not safe."

Molke nodded. "I will remain inside my room."

With a faint frown, Michael gazed at the spindly monk. "I'll be in my room until morning."

As they entered their rooms, the storm shook the abbey to its foundation.

———

The ubiquitous Melanchthon awaited Stephen when he closed the door to his private quarters. The father abbot did not even blink at the intrusion.

He carefully folded his mantle and laid it upon a wooden chair and spoke without looking. "I hope this isn't going to be the same conversation we had earlier."

"No." Melanchthon frowned. "It is to be much worse."

Father Stephen exhaled tiredly, then sat in a scarlet-cushioned mahogany chair and rested his hands on the arms. He bent his head, exhaled again. "Very well, Brother. Please begin."

"I sense something." Melanchthon's aspect and tone were obviously and sincerely concerned, but there was no judgment. "These people, and the brothers, as well, must leave quickly."

Although composed, Father Stephen's face betrayed that these vague forebodings of doom were beginning to grate pink against his skin. In a few minutes they would begin drawing blood.

"Brother," he said patiently, "why are you so compelled to warn me about this danger you perpetually sense? In all humility, your great mind is not beyond my comprehension. And I do not sense this...this thing you fear."

"If I am the only man who smells smoke, I will not hesitate to tell others the house is on fire." Melanchthon seemed equally as weary. "Would you prefer I keep these forebodings to myself when innocent lives are in danger?"

"The innocent lives of these tourists?"

"There are many here who are innocent and must leave. And some here who must never leave because of their guilt." Melanchthon came closer. "We both know the original purpose of this place. It was meant as a prison for priests whose sins against God and man were so great that the only safe harbor for them was within these mountains, all but inaccessible to the world.

"In times of old, this was known as L'Inferno, and it is still a prison—only in a different form. Now it is where the Church exiles those who speak too boldly against the Evil One." He smiled grimly. "How terrible it would be for priests to proclaim that they see the devil at work in the lives of men."

With a sigh, Stephen replied, "In this day and age, Brother, yes, it would be—not that you will agree. But, then, you have always been far more mystically inclined than I."

Melanchthon was the purest image of irony. His smile was sincere and utterly without humor. "That is true, but it does not change the truth. Nor can I remain silent any longer."

Leaning forward, Father Stephen spoke more pointedly. "Brother, do you remember the last time you came to me claiming to have seen this ghost, and I acquiesced to your demands to search the abbey? Yes, remember how we diligently searched the entire premises, only to find every door and window locked from the *inside*." He paused and clearly couched his words. "What you saw or think you saw was not here, Brother. And I am tempted to say that it never was."

Melanchthon was unexpressive.

"Please," Stephen appealed, "if you hate it here so much, Brother, then why don't you ask Monsignor DeMarco to re-station you? He has the authority to do so. And this is not the only abbey set aside for safekeeping."

"My place is here," Melanchthon muttered, and his mouth forged itself in the darkest frown. "My first...my last."

There was doom in the tone, and Stephen sighed. "All right, Brother. Tell me exactly what you think this danger is. And if you convince me—evidence or no evidence—I give you my word that I will achieve some means of evacuating the monastery."

"Why have you not offered such a thing before?"

"Because there has never been any evidence to substantiate your claims. And I cannot—for the sake of my sanity—chase ghosts every day of the year."

"Then I will not persuade you," Melanchthon said, bitter. "Because I can say nothing to you now that I have not said before."

Stephen pursed his lips. "Brother, if you want me to initiate actions to evacuate the abbey, then you must speak of more than mere feelings or vague premonitions." He grimaced.

"Melanchthon, you are mystical, but you are not out of touch with reality. You understand the seriousness of an evacuation, even if I use the excuse of this snowstorm. There are priceless treasures here. I can't leave them unwatched."

Melanchthon held the moment as a man holds a sword that he has fought with for an entire day—as if his hand is frozen to the hilt so that he cannot let it go.

"Very well," he began, "but it is difficult."

"But try, please."

The huge monk waited. Then, "I have had dreams of a creature that walks these halls. It is...old. For its years are not like the years of a man. It knows...evil. And it has done much evil. It is powerful. It does not fear us. And now it shall reveal itself, for whatever game it played has ended."

Stephen crested his fingers. "And when it reveals itself?"

"It will have to kill us all," Melanchthon said somberly. "It will protect its secret, and then it will slip away and hide again among men."

Stephen registered a hint of anger. "I know the legends, Melanchthon, because the Nephilim are legend!" He rose with a curse from his chair. "Brother, sometimes I believe your mystical inclinations are too vivid for your own good!"

"I wish it were so," Melanchthon answered. "But it is not so, and so I must do what I can to ensure that what has been... will never be again."

"The Nephilim are all dead, Brother."

"Are they?"

Father Stephen leaned upon his table. "Why in the name of God do you continue like this, Brother? No one has seen one of these creatures in three thousand years! The Church has even forgotten them. They are only overlooked passages in a book no one reads anymore."

After releasing a slow breath, Melanchthon raised his face. He blinked softly, as if watching the wind, detecting a scent, listening to a ghost. He gazed at a corner of the ceiling as a man who cautiously watches the approach of a lion.

"Something this way comes," he murmured, utterly motionless. "Something that has waited long for this hour." His beard tilted as he nodded. "Yes, it will not wait much longer."

For a moment, as if Melanchthon's utter certitude was contagious, Father Stephen bit his lip. "But...but if this creature is so perfectly hidden, why would it reveal itself at all?"

"Because someone has come that even it fears. So it will emerge from hiding...and soon."

Stephen was considerate or confused. "Brother, a mere feeling, without any logical reason, is not enough to justify calling up helicopters through the storm."

"It is no natural storm."

Stephen rolled his eyes. "There is no winning this discussion with you! You will believe as you will believe! But the simple fact is that I cannot evacuate the abbey on a feeling! The snowstorm has closed all roads, so we cannot use the buses. The nearest village is six miles away across mountains that have killed more men here than all the wars combined, so we cannot leave on foot."

He shook his head passionately, as if to convince the older monk of his logic. "Listen to me, Melanchthon. We are trapped here until the roads are cleared! And I can no more change that than I can make the sun retreat ten steps of this abbey."

"It is already too late to flee," Melanchthon said and bowed his head. "I only pray that the Lord will intervene. Because what is coming will kill...until there is nothing left to kill."

Nightbringer

Killing monsters left and right, Josh enhanced the drama of his handheld video game with growls, explosions, pleas for mercy, and then a dramatic long-drawn death cry that ended in a low mumble, swearing vengeance. It reminded Gina of something out of some kids' cartoon show.

She threw him a T-shirt. "Game's up! Time for a shower. Then brush your teeth and gargle."

Rachel, lying flat on the bed beside him, remarked dryly, "Unlike last night, dog-breath."

"I was busy last night, Rachel."

"Doing what?"

"Killing monsters."

"Game geek."

"No names," Gina said sweetly. "Josh, get on it. I'm tired. I want to go to bed."

With a meaningful drone Josh clicked the video game. "Man, I was just about to slaughter a plesiosaur." He set the handheld game on the night table and slouched toward the bathroom, closing the door. Rachel reached over and picked up the game.

In a few minutes Gina heard the shower. Laughing, she removed clothes from the suitcase and began laying them out for the next day. When she was finished, she reached in and removed a matte-black SIG Sauer P226 semiautomatic pistol.

She ejected the clip and locked the slide, ensuring the chamber was empty. She tapped the clip on the soft edge of the suitcase and slid it back into the handle. Then she placed it beneath her clothes and became aware that Rachel was watching.

"I thought you weren't FBI until we got to Rome."

With a smile Gina walked back to the bed and relaxed beside her daughter. "I'm not."

"Uh-huh. So why the gun?"

"Regulations, babe."

"You even have to carry a gun here?"

Gina nodded. "Want the short version?"

"No."

"'In any country where there's an FBI field office and an FBI special agent will be working with such office at the end of personal time, that agent must be fully prepared to assume duty at the end of said personal time.'"

"And after this we'll be in Rome—for four months!" Rachel stuck a finger into her throat and leaned forward. "Gack."

Moving beneath a halo of steam, Josh walked out of the bathroom, rubbing his head with a towel. He looked at Rachel, then at his video game. His eyes narrowed. "What did you do?"

"Nothing! I was just looking at your—"

Josh snatched up the yellow computer and quickly ran a diagnostic check, or something. He released a deep sigh. "You are so luuucky," he sang, "that my game wasn't eeeraaased."

"Okay, guys," Gina chimed, "it's time for sleep." She kissed them both and they lay side by side beneath the covers. "No more talking until I wake up in the morning. And do not drag me out of bed before I'm reeaaaady."

Josh had the last note.

"Oh, please, Mom, no siiinging...."

CHAPTER SIX

N *ight...*
Although the shadows that cloaked the Great Hall would have been depthless to human eyes, it moved through them without effort. Although the night outside—a night without a moon or even a star in the storm-clouded sky—was a solid cube of black to other creatures, it could see every wrinkle of stone, every stir of dust, as if darkness were only a lesser form of day.

But it had known true darkness before.

Yes, it had known true darkness in Egypt—so long ago, now—when darkness struck the land so completely that even he could not see through the blackness of it. And yet, still, the hated slaves had enjoyed the light that streaked down in interlocking crescents that flooded and followed every Hebrew home—a child playing in a muddy field, an old woman walking in the open street.

He had always hunted in the night—had feasted upon the slaves—but during those three nights he had not hunted. No, he had not dared violate the light for fear that—while life to the slaves—it would be his doom.

Long he had lived, and the empires that he had once ruled were still unknown to these...humans—as if human knowledge were enough, in itself, to measure. But he could, indeed, remember the kings who had come against him, the warriors he had torn into dead shreds of meat and bone. He remembered battles of sprawling hundreds of thousands—battles he had commanded and always won. Yes, that he had always won until the Hebrew dog rose and took the throne of Israel.

But he had escaped the wrath of mighty David—he that slew his tens of thousands on tens of thousands. Yes, he had escaped the fierce, bearded Hebrew and joined his own might with the expendable Persians, the effete Greeks, and, finally, Jerusalem itself.

He laughed.

Yes, always the Hebrews invited their own destruction. They were like fools returning to folly, dogs returning to vomit. For just as one generation was led by their king to honor their God, the next generation would dishonor Him. And then they would not trust their God to deliver them, but in their own right arm—devices of deception, engines of destruction. And the land would be taken from them once more.

But it was not truly their land. It had never been their land. No, for when the Hebrews arrived, Palestine was already inhabited by mighty nations that had stood for a thousand years. Nor were they quick to recognize the bold boast of a wandering tribe of Egyptian slaves. But war had decided the right to claim what could be claimed, and Israel had won in the end.

Yet he had almost undone it all when he led Tiberius' endless legions beneath the secret tunnels of the southern wall. For even Tiberius, upon seeing the great walls of Jerusalem, admitted that the City of the King would never fall unless it was betrayed from within. And so he had orchestrated the betrayal—nor had it been difficult, playing those who believed the Nazarene was the Messiah against those who so violently refused to believe—and such was the fall of it that not one stone stood upon another when the day was done.

He smiled, remembering how—

Sound...

He froze before the statue of the centurion. But the sound did not come again, and he bent his head. His breathing ceased, and his heart slowed, slowed more, until it barely beat beneath the huge twin shields of muscle mantling his massive chest. Hairs along his head and neck and forearms bristled.

Nothing...

What had made the sound had not moved again.

White lips separating to reveal fangs thickly set and saber-like, he turned in the direction of the noise. He gazed over the honeycomb of corridors that led upstairs to the rooms of the guests. Yes, the man was inside the corridors. But he was not moving, was not emerging from behind the walls.

He laughed silently. *So, you've come at last.*

I always knew you would....

With three monstrous strides—there was no cause for deceit if he was certain of the identity of his foe—he selected a passageway at random, expecting to hear the faintest step in another direction—was prepared to catch a whisper over his own soundless steps. He moved, increasing speed, hoping to catch the warrior unaware, for even the warrior could not hear as a wolf could hear—as *he* could hear.

He walked in and out and across and across again, and still he did not find his foe. Then he froze in place, head bent, listening. But there was nothing.

He snarled.

Fool...do you truly think you can escape me?

He moved faster through the corridors, poised to catch the faintest sound in the gray shadows—a glimpse of a silhouette.

Nor did he expect more than a glimpse, for the man was the purest warrior and possessed all the greatness of a hunter— patience, purpose, knowledge, skill, strength, and will. He would make few, if any, mistakes.

He listened as he moved, eyes roaming.

Nothing, nothing, nothing...

Nothing!

Fangs exposed, he bent and listened long, and longer, waiting with inhuman patience—with a millennium of patience. He waited until the Hall outside the corridors seemed to retreat before the first frantic light of dawn. Waited until the light was dangerously bright, though the humans who stirred long before sunrise were still far in coming. But to remain here any longer was a risk and, somehow, he knew....

The man was gone.

Discipline, patience...long had he exercised strict discipline and patience in the kill, and so he did not expect the tendrils of anger that bled slowly, inexorably, from the dark abyss of its center. But the anger did bleed until his taloned hands clenched and unclenched in murderous, frustrated rhythm.

Fang sharpened fang, and it struggled to contain the volcanic rage, to not lift its head for a single, challenging roar—a roar that would have been understood by only one other creature within these walls.

But it did not roar.

The time was not yet right, it had been told.

No, it did not roar. And its fangs clamped like a vise, shutting down the release of rage. Snarling, it glared once more into the empty corridors.

The man was *gone!*

NO!

It roared.

Nightbringer

Josh and Rachel sat upright at the same moment, staring at the stone wall before them—one second before Gina hit her feet and was moving, and one second later her hand closed familiarly around the grip of her pistol.

She instantly spun and raised a hand to the kids as they opened their mouths, but she was too late to prevent the triple series of screams, and then they were scrambling across the bed into her arms.

"What was *that!*"

Gina said nothing as voices and heavy footsteps in the corridor beyond approached, and then a fist was pounding on the door. A chorus of shouts and commands erupted outside, and Gina quickly pushed the kids behind her.

She snatched open the door and leaped back, the SIG Sauer P226 leveled directly into the door as it crashed open.

It took one heartbeat for those entering to see her crouching ten feet away in a shooting stance, and then Gina saw a host of bodies—the monsignor, Molke, Father Stephen—as they backed up in surprise before trying to enter the room, colliding and shoving one another to be first. At the last, it was Monsignor DeMarco—wearing an old-fashioned sleeping robe—who hurled the hulking German aside to beat him through the narrow entryway.

"It's all right!" Gina lowered the SIG. "What was that? Was that an animal?"

Holding his hand over his chest, dressed similarly to the monsignor, Father Stephen caught a breath. "We don't know! I was concerned for your safety!" He cautiously pointed at the SIG. "Is that a *gun?*"

"I'm an FBI agent."

Together they sighed.

Gina added, "On vacation."

"Yes, of course." Father Stephen turned to rushing feet. "Melanchthon! Barnabas! What are you doing here?"

"The guests!" pronounced Melanchthon. He lifted the torch high, gazing upon Gina. Then he looked past her and saw the children.

Gina was actually moved when the gloom-and-doom monk visibly released a sigh of relief.

"Barnabas!" Father Stephen clutched the old man's shoulder. "You've been at the abbey the longest! What was that sound?"

Barnabas squinted angrily. His frown deepened. Then he turned sharply, stepped into the hall, and lifted a Roman sword from the wall. His voice was indifferent. "I will go see what it was."

Gina stepped forward. "Whoa! Hang on a minute!" She held up a hand for patience. "I...really, really hate to say this. But if there's a wild animal loose in this place, I'm the only one qualified to find out what it is."

"Why do you say that?" asked Stephen.

"Because I'm trained in building searches and field survival techniques. Not just anyone—and I don't mean to imply anything at all—can do this safely. Plus, I have to ensure the welfare of my children. And last, I'm the only one with a gun."

"Well, give the gun to Barnabas!"

Gina stared. "I don't think so."

Michael waded into the room. He had obviously dressed hastily. He focused on Stephen. "You guys ever heard that before?"

No one replied.

With a quick nod, Michael stepped into the hall and lifted another Roman sword from the wall and looked at Barnabas. "Let's go, friend."

With the sudden shouts that seemed to come from one man—
"Of course!"—the monsignor and Melanchthon and Molke and
Father Stephen enthusiastically snatched Roman swords and
spears from the walls of the corridor. Then they encircled Gina,
who held the high-capacity semiautomatic at her hip.

Grinning widely, Josh and Rachel were *completely* ready for
this hunt!

Gina hesitated, as if debating whether to allow them to
accompany her, then seemed to realize their strength in numbers. For a moment she hefted the SIG, as if weighing whether
she could trust this group to completely ensure that the abbey
would remain safe or that they'd even come back.

She sighed, smiled tightly over her children.

"Okay, kids. Let's go."

The search through the abbey was electrifying for the host
of primitively armed men who had surrounded Gina. But with
the SIG tucked in her belt, she followed behind them now.

After the first ten or eleven hair-raising reactions to false
alarms, she'd decided it was much safer to move her kids—and
herself—out of reach of spear and sword.

They found nine doors that led to the outside slightly ajar
and unlocked "as usual" with tracks leading in or out. Bending
low, Gina could only determine that something had come—or
gone—this way. It seemed to move in and out, in and out, in
again, out again, *make up your mind....*

It was confused...or deliberately mulling the tracks. But no
animal would have the presence of mind to deliberately mull
its tracks.

To Father Stephen and the rest, a building search was a
truly thrilling experience. To Gina it was about as thrilling as
a bus driver going for a bus ride. She saw no signs of violence,

no sign of forced entry—not that force would have been necessary. The shock that had struck in the wake of the scream faded until she reasoned that it might even have been the wind from the storm raging outside. And by the time they arrived at the Great Hall, she was spending far more time appreciating the vast artifacts of the museum than searching shadows.

When Michael turned to gaze back, Gina had one hand hiked akimbo on her hip. She smiled.

"Tired yet, O great hunter of imaginary beasts?" she asked him.

Michael smirked. "You know, Gina, it might have been something."

"Michael, what are the odds of some rogue bear rampaging through an abbey? I mean—*really.*"

Michael glanced casually at the dispersing monks. "Million to one, I guess."

Gina walked forward. "You know, Michael, I actually like you. You're terribly, terribly strange, but you're gallant in an odd, medieval sort of way." Her tone was no longer teasing, and she was smiling. "Now what are the odds on that?"

He laughed. "A *billion* to one?"

The tension was gone, and Gina added, "Where are you from, anyway? You don't seem like the kind of guy who would join a tourist group."

"Actually," he answered pleasantly, "I'm headed for Rome."

"What about that! So are we."

Gina had expected some faint thought that they would be with each other for at least another three or four days to cross his face. But, if it did, she couldn't catch it. "So," she shrugged, "you going on business?"

Michael's gaze held some kind of sad resignation. "Yeah." He gazed over the Hall, glancing at all the monks who had joined in the search, then called Jaqual closer. The porcelain monk had not yet surrendered his shield. "Have you seen Dominic—or Basil?"

"No," he answered. "I...did not think of them. Dominic can't leave his room without assistance, and Basil is usually close by him in case Dominic needs help. Do you think I should check on them?"

A beat, and Michael shook his head. "No," he said curtly. "I was just wondering."

"Ah, of course, yes...uh, am I dismissed?"

"Yes, thank you."

"At your service." Jaqual bowed and was gone.

Gina shook her head. "What's this about Dominic? You think he might have been hurt or something?"

"I was just wondering where everybody was," Michael muttered and hefted the sword—not a conscious move.

Gina noticed that he must have handled a lot of weapons in his day.

His fingers were tight enough at the guard and the pommel, but his middle fingers held it lightly in the same manner an artist held a brush—poised for that single, deft, delicate move. Then he said, "Well, this was fun, but I think I'll get back to bed."

"Me too." Gina spotted her children. "Okay, guys! We're going to bed!"

"Mind if I walk you to your room?" Michael asked.

"Certainly not, and keep the sword with you. The kids love the adventure."

Michael laughed and they strolled slowly toward the staircase as Gina asked casually, "Ever used one of those things? You seem pretty handy with it."

"Nah. I'm not the warrior type."

Holding a long, blazing torch, Melanchthon walked fearlessly down the dusty, slanted tunnel where he had been working earlier in the day. Flames from the three-foot stick rose to the low ceiling and trailed behind him, where the inky black smoke hung like a malignant spirit long after the light, and the monk, sank down into the night.

Finally Melanchthon reached the wall where he been carefully chipping away layers of crushed concrete as old as Rome itself, for only Rome—of all the ancient nations—had possessed the secret of concrete.

Without any indication of weariness, Melanchthon set the torch in a crudely carved notch and sat upon a small stool. Within moments he was carefully chipping at the wall once more. And if someone had been standing directly beside him, they would not have heard his quiet words.

"It is time. I must find you...."

Monsignor DeMarco demonstrated a rich sense of humor about the affair, for the old priest had apparently endured quite a number of similar episodes amid ancient and shadowed basilicas. Gina laughed repeatedly as he regaled them with stories of terrified monks pushing him into a darkened corridor to confront the dreaded "It."

"Authority," the monsignor mused, "such a two-edged sword. In truth, I was as terrified as they were—not of a *thing*, mind you, but there might have been some animal, and yet I could hardly admit such." He laughed once more. "In any case, I rather enjoyed myself tonight. I am glad this layover has not been more of the mundane same."

At the corridor of Gina's room, the monsignor bowed, a deferential bend at the waist, his back ramrod straight like some character out of a historical romance. Gina returned a nod, and then the priest winked at the kids and walked steadily and slowly to his room.

Molke was not so cultured and patted her on the shoulder. Then he leaned down to Josh and Rachel. "Are you disappointed we didn't find a monster?"

Rachel: "Nope."

Josh: "Yep."

Molke laughed and turned to the hallway that led in the direction of Michael's room. Gina knew that it was one floor beneath them and contained smaller and older chambers.

In contrast to the monsignor, Michael had faded into the corridor with hardly a word. Only Molke seemed to notice and waved a hearty good-night to him.

The faint aura of secrecy that surrounded Michael had activated Gina's instincts. She knew the routine. Detecting lies was her special skill, and she reluctantly turned over what she knew.

He spoke little, remained in the background, never disagreed with anyone, or even agreed. But being unfriendly didn't make someone a liar. He didn't avoid eye contact—very important. His gestures were minimal, and she had not noticed any "micro-expressions"—an almost invisible tic of the face that revealed an emotion quickly concealed.

But he was definitely hiding something, though only an expert could have known because, as with any lie, his behavior and words too often didn't agree. He was friendly to her on an individual basis but faded into the background in a crowd. He verbalized no interest in anything at all, but Gina had watched his eyes. He narrowly caught every gesture, every movement.

There were other things, but that was enough for Gina. She began to wonder what he was doing. This wasn't a place for someone like him. Not alone, anyway. He had obviously seen a lot of the world. He didn't need to see more. So he had another reason for traveling in a group.

They arrived at their room, and Gina quickly tucked Josh and Rachel into bed. Then she settled into a chair to read some novel she'd picked up at the airport, but she couldn't stop thinking of Michael.

He's somebody....

She sighed and knew she wouldn't get anywhere with what little she knew. She could ponder all night, even make a few calls, but she was certain she wouldn't learn anything more, even if she stayed up the rest of the night.

No, she didn't have the strength for that. For even though the search had been stunningly uneventful, it had used up what little energy had remained after the long drive from Lausanne. And even though she had revealed no fear, she had felt sensations that she couldn't identify and told herself it wasn't fear.

Yes, the tracks had been disturbing, the endless dark alcoves and halls, the huge imposing doors with black iron bolts strong enough to withstand a charging rhinoceros. And, after awhile, the monks' collective fear had become somewhat contagious. She didn't ask herself whether there might be some unnamed cause for their fear—something about the shadowed abbey had made her resistant to knowing its secrets. In fact, all she wanted to do now was leave.

She soon heard the kids snoring and became aware she was staring at the cascading snow. She didn't need anyone to tell her they wouldn't be leaving here tomorrow or even the day after. No, this storm had hit hard and heavy and mean, and it didn't look like it was going anywhere anytime soon.

Nightbringer

She was aware that the hypnotic flow of flashing white snow seemed to foretell that something was coming—something stronger than the storm, colder than the storm....

Older than the storm...

"No, baby, there's no such thing as monsters."

Snow-eyes watched her from blackest night.

Something...

Monstrous...

CHAPTER SEVEN

The morning Dispensation Chant was even more beautiful than last evening's Compline Prayers, and Gina wondered vaguely if it wasn't because of the snow.

It had mounded so heavily upon the abbey during the night that only the highest sections of the stained-glass windows were unobstructed. Even the storm seemed more distant, as if the abbey had been buried beneath the mountain.

Gina mused over the most sumptuous breakfast she'd experienced in all of Europe, though the kids made short work of it—a shame. But Josh was eager to get moving, and Rachel—the twelve-year-old bookworm—wanted to see the archives.

The eternally grim Melanchthon volunteered to show her the abbey's repository of ancient books, located in the former dungeon. Rachel had blinked. "A dungeon?"

"Yes."

"You guys really have a dungeon?"

Grimly, "Yes."

Gina laughed and leaned back from the table. She was in no hurry to leave this exotic brand of coffee, suspecting she wouldn't find it again on this continent.

Rachel was beside her.

"Mom? Can I go? Melanchthon says they have books that go way back!"

"Go ahead." Gina focused on the big monk.

Though he did seem so utterly grim, Melanchthon could not conceal his warm and protective heart, seen easily in the painstaking, patient way he explained everything to the children. And Gina had long ago learned to trust her instincts. "You'll watch over her?"

"As God watches over His children."

Gina waved at Rachel. "See you later. Be good!"

They were gone in moments.

Gina saw the monsignor and Father Stephen engaged in deep discussion. The presence of a monsignor was obviously a great opportunity for the father abbot, and Gina figured red tape in the Church was probably as bad as in the FBI.

Maybe Father Stephen figured he could take his requests straight to the top. And from the expression on the monsignor's face, he was well received. She thought the rest of the group remained in bed, but when she asked after Michael, Jaqual said that he had already been up for awhile and gone outside.

Gina rose and donned her coat. Several monks stepped forward, attempting to warn her of the storm. "It's okay, guys. I just need some fresh air. I'll be back in a few minutes."

She could handle the monks pretty easily now. She just treated them like actual brothers. They were certain to protest, but they'd accommodate a request as long as it didn't interfere with their vows or her safety.

Two minutes later Gina found Michael standing on the outer wall. He smiled as she climbed the steps, and then she was beside him. She noticed the object of his attention. The road was so sheathed in ice that it was nothing more than a rising curve of the cliff. Squinting, Gina studied the rolling dark clouds—this storm wasn't going anywhere.

"What do you think?" she asked.

"I don't think we'll be leaving any time soon."

"Doesn't look like it."

Hands shoved deeply into her coat, Gina stared into a snow-covered valley that might have been a perfectly smooth ocean of ice. She understood how someone could go blind gazing at this white upon white. It was little better than staring into the sun.

Michael's voice had a faint edge of concern. "You said last night during the search that you're a special agent for the FBI. Do you have the authority to order an airlift out of here?"

"What?" Gina laughed.

She stared at him, but he didn't smile, didn't blink—*he's serious.*

"Yes, I can do that." But the necessity of having to answer the question made her more than suspicious. It made her faintly angry. "Why do you ask?"

"Accidents happen." He shrugged. "I was just wondering if you have authority over here."

"I've got a little authority, but I can't arrest anyone. That has to be made by Italian agents. But, as choppers go, I only have to make a call." She paused. "So are you gonna tell me or what?"

"Tell you?"

"You don't ask a question like that without a reason."

Michael hesitated to reply, and Gina tried to read all that could be read. *Highly intelligent but hiding...stoic...confident...no, not confident...predatory.*

Events began to coalesce in her mind: the oppressive atmosphere of this place; Josh's unexplainable, intuitive fear; whatever animal awoke them last night. And yet the unsolved murder of the monk that Mr. Trevanian had told her about on the bus was the most disturbing.

She was well trained to connect seemingly unrelated events to form a theory. But it did not require distinguished criminal training to connect what she had seen and heard.

The most disturbing premise suggested that the monks had a justifiable cause for fear—a premise reinforced by the fact that the abbey had only recently been reopened.

Perhaps this abbey had been troubled with acts of violence for years. Isolation, the haunting atmosphere, and demanding conditions could definitely exact a psychological toll on the inhabitants. And perhaps the Church had only recently identified and relocated those monks who represented a danger, both to other monks and tourists. That would certainly explain why the monastery had been only recently opened to the public. But it didn't explain the pervasive atmosphere of fear.

Gina was disturbed by how quietly she, herself, spoke. "What do you think about this place?"

"I don't think I'd pick it for a summer home."

"Uh-huh. And what do you think about that monk being murdered up here?"

Michael shrugged. "They're way up here—alone, isolated. There's no law, really. It's like being in the wild. A small thing turns into a big thing, and before you know it, somebody gets killed. I've seen it before."

"Really? Where?"

"Ah, I've been all over the world. Every place has some kind of backwoods story of a guy going nuts and hacking up his family and then killing himself. I'm not a psychologist, but it seems obvious that too much isolation is not a good thing."

The wind that hit the wall seemed to attack, and Gina hunched. Something about the place, the quiet, was far more disturbing than peaceful. She couldn't prevent her next words.

"I'm starting to get a bad feeling about this place."

"Me, too," he muttered.

"You, too?"

"Yeah."

"What do you think we should do?"

"If I were you, I'd tell Stephen that I want to leave." His demeanor became stern. "I don't think you'll cause an international incident if you get a chopper up here from Lausanne, Gina. It's less than an hour's flight. And I wouldn't take chances with my kids' lives."

"You think that's what I'm doing?"

"No, but look at the situation. An hour is a long time when you need help now." His aspect was one of a commanding officer's, and, strangely, it seemed natural. "I'm just saying that if one more thing happens, I'd make that call."

Gina stared over the mountains. "It's so beautiful. A monastery in the mountains. Seems like the last place in the world where someone should be afraid." She sighed. "If I make the call, are you coming with us?"

"Well, I certainly don't like the idea of being stranded up here with a mad monk running through the halls with an ax."

"I don't think things will get that bad. But I'll think about calling for a chopper." She shivered. "Okeydoke! I've had enough of this! Coming inside?"

"You bet."

They began down the steps when he said, "If your suspicions aren't enough, maybe you can talk to one of the monks."

"Like who?"

"Melanchthon seems pretty honest."

They crossed the courtyard shoulder to shoulder.

"True," she answered. "If he's got the guts to admit a two-thousand-year-old centurion is coming here to fight a monster, he's got the guts to admit anything."

Michael laughed. "Yeah, that's pretty weird."

———

Chin resting on hands, Rachel was watching Melanchthon dramatically act out some story when Gina walked into the library, which was, indeed, in a dungeon.

The old monk was walking up and down the gigantic chamber, imitating a dozen characters, but when he saw Gina, he stopped. He stood in silence. His arms fell to his sides.

Rachel turned and saw Gina. She immediately leaped up and grabbed Gina's hands. "Did you know that this place was once a headquarters of those guys?"

"What guys?" Gina smiled.

"The Knights! Those guys were cool! Do you want to know how they rescued the daughter of Behemius from the Sultan of Goth?"

"Maybe later, babe." Gina ran a hand over her head. "Right now I have to talk to Melanchthon about something. Why don't you run and see if Josh is in trouble yet?"

"But—"

"Best go find your brother, child." Melanchthon's voice no longer contained amusing drama. "Your mother and I have something to discuss."

Wise beyond her years, Rachel revealed no signs of alarm. She kissed Gina and was gone. Alone before the old monk, Gina knew there was no reason for ceremony or etiquette.

"What's going on, Melanchthon? If you care for me or my children, tell me."

Melanchthon smiled faintly—a sad smile.

"What's everyone's so afraid to talk about?" Gina pressed. "What's the doom that seems to hang over this place? I don't think it's some fantastic legend of an immortal coming here to fight his greatest battle against some mythical creature that never existed in the first place. But something is *for sure* going on." She paused. "Has someone been hurt lately?"

It seemed as if he would not answer. "Many have died here," he muttered. "And many more will die. This has always been...a place of death."

Gina walked forward. "Many have died here? You mean naturally? Or were they murdered?"

"Yes."

"Yes *what*?"

"They were killed."

"Recently?"

"No...not recently."

"How did they die?"

"Like the old monk was killed many years ago." The monk gazed about the room. "He is not the only one to be found torn to pieces, as if by a lion. But it is no lion, or dog, or wildcat."

"It's a Nephilim, right?" Gina asked tersely. She actually hoped he would say yes, because that would have encouraged her. She didn't believe in Nephilim and never would.

"You do not have to believe in truth," Melanchthon answered. "Truth is truth whether you believe in it or not."

The words angered Gina. She could deal with a threat she could understand. And she could understand almost any threat—human or otherwise. But a mythical beast was outside the parameters of what she could accept.

She shook her head. "Do you realize how foolish it is for you to believe in ghosts and goblins when you might actually have a legitimate threat? A threat that can be dealt with and stopped if you stop focusing your attention on these fantasies?"

He was silent and did not seem dismayed. He gazed upon her as if everything she said—and thought—was meaningless.

Gina understood. "Brother Melanchthon, I'm a federal agent. Do you know what that means? I have seen all kinds of evil in this world. And it is always caused by a human being.

"Listen, I know what it might seem like to you—up here, isolated in this strange place. It can do things to your mind. But if someone was killed here, then they were killed by someone or something else—like a bear." She considered everything she was learning. "When was the last person killed?"

"Nine months past. After Rome decided to reopen the abbey."

"How?"

"Like the others."

With an angry grimace, Gina bowed her head. "Why did the Church open the abbey if someone here is suspected of murder?"

"I do not know. The monsignor will know."

"He's here on pilgrimage."

Melanchthon grunted. "Is he?"

A terrified howl erupted somewhere deep within the abbey, haunting every room of the basilica at once, and Gina spun, reaching for the SIG, but it wasn't on her waist. She'd left it in the room, not thinking she would need it. She whirled toward the monk.

"Call for the police!"

Gina didn't look to see if Melanchthon was obeying or not as she turned and ran through the long corridor to the stairs. She was in good shape, and it felt as though she covered the distance in just a few leaps.

She cleared the first two steps to hit the third and within twenty seconds reached the door to her room. Throwing it open she snatched the SIG and an extra clip from her suitcase and was in the hall again, seeing two monks she didn't know standing on the landing.

"Where'd that come from?"

Whether it was her gun or her rage, they cried out and pointed, and Gina angled toward a staircase.

It seemed as though the cry came from beneath the monastery, and she doubted that even the monks knew half the passageways honeycombing this ancient place.

Breathing hard, trying to slow her racing heart, Gina noticed that her hands were slick with sweat. She released the grip only for a second to wipe her palm on her leg.

She knew fear was a *vivid* part of fighting—no one was unafraid in combat—but still, she had difficulty controlling her breathing, thereby reducing tunnel vision.

She reached the bottom of the stairs.

Nothing...

She poised, listening for the slightest sound.

No, nothing.

It was as if the howl had struck the entire abbey into silence. As the roar of a lion would silence every creature in the forest at once.

Terror told her to retreat. With a narrow glance she could see her chest lift with each rapid heartbeat. She was certain that her heart alone would betray her position.

Even worse, she was conducting a building search alone—completely against FBI regulations—but she had no choice. If this place was still inhabited by a killer, then she had to find him before he found her or her children.

She decided to make a slow reconnaissance down the tunnel to her right, sensing that it would lead back to the Hall and Josh and Rachel.

A distant chamber, where the tunnel bled into a dozen directions, was a pit of darkness. She'd almost reached it when she caught the scent of wicks—the odor of extinguished flame.

It was one of those moments when everything happens at once—understanding and reaction occurring simultaneously. It is a faculty of everyone—when instinct flares to danger and the body has already reacted before the mind comprehends why.

Gina stopped moving—completely.

She didn't lower the SIG, didn't breath. Then, very slowly, she bent her face twenty degrees, expanding her vision peripherally. She could see almost 360 degrees now, the only blind spot directly behind her.

She couldn't see more than ten feet, but that was as good as it could get. To hurt her it would have to touch her, and to touch her it would have to cross that ten feet. It was enough, in her position, to get off a half dozen rounds.

Cold—drenched in sweat.

She blew beads off her lips and focused her breathing.

She caught the very, very distant sound of water dripping, of wind moving to her left. She felt the cool air on her sweat-slick face, using the sweat to detect anything that might stir the air—an approach, a retreat. Her body was damp and cold, but she would not move, not until she was certain.

A large, rectangular table made of stone stood upon a small rising on the far side of the chamber with a dozen tall wooden chairs surrounding it. The large cobblestone floor had no other furniture, no emblems or displays on the walls. But two-foot-long iron spikes, similar to eighteenth-century fence posts, extended from the stone wall six feet above the floor, completely encircling the room.

In less than a second Gina memorized the position of everything—the table and spikes and tunnels. She didn't know the purpose of this place and didn't care. Right now it was an arena.

No movement, but she couldn't see the walls!

He could easily be standing there, just outside range, waiting. Gina lifted her gaze ten degrees, increasing her distance, listening...

When it happened.

One-tenth of a second before he struck, Gina had a flashing, incredible thought that he had waited patiently behind her until she shifted her gaze—a gaze he could not possibly have seen.

What felt like a wrecking ball hit her in the back, and Gina couldn't get off a shot. She knew she had screamed, and then she was in the air and on the floor, rolling. She hit the wall hard, and as she reached her knees, she saw the approach of...

Huge it was with mountainous hulking shoulders and a massive wedge-shaped head. Its chest was equally gigantic with inhumanly powerful shields of muscle sweeping out from the center. Its arms were thick with the strength of an anaconda.

And Gina vividly knew the fear that resides in the deepest, most secret place of the heart—the fear of *It*.

It was a fear Gina had not known since she was a child, since before she was old enough to understand what *should* be feared. It was the fear that even adults never kill, because it is bound to some part of them that yet lives, though it is subdued and trained by thousands of years of civilization.

But let that civilized adult stand alone in the darkest forest night, sensing its approach, and the fear will live again as vivid and breathless as it lived inside man five thousand years past. For some things are beyond science, beyond knowledge, beyond understanding.

She didn't see the blast that tore the semiautomatic from her hand to send it clattering into shadows any more than the hand that grasped her throat and lifted her from the ground.

Gina instantly kicked at the form and hit twice, but it was like kicking a brick wall. She tried to reach its throat—her only hope—but its throat was far beyond her reach. She began to panic as oxygen was shut off from her brain and struggled madly and then frantically.

Blindness, tears...

Floating...

"*God*," whispered Gina. "Help—"

It roared in anger, and then its hand was torn from her throat.

Gina's legs buckled as she hit the floor, but she instantly rose, despite the fact she hadn't yet drawn a breath.

It is a unique experience to stand when you are gravely wounded. Only the upper part of your torso seems to rise, all life centered in your chest with your head rising above it, seeing everything within arm's length with lucid clarity.

Her attacker was spinning through the middle of the chamber wrestling with...a man?

Michael!

Gina shouted—more from shock than fear—as Michael roared and slammed it thunderously into the wall and the creature came off the stone like a hurricane.

They went to the floor, revolving in murderous blows across the chamber. Then Michael threw out a leg to stop the spin and his right hand hit the beast in the throat with a crushing blow.

Gina followed every move like a cat.

Michael closed his right hand, and the beast *did* feel pain—for a flashing instant Gina glimpsed what seemed like fear—because it howled and with a vicious twist threw Michael to the side.

It rose snarling, grasping its throat with a clawed hand. Yet its right hand was open, fingers hooked like talons.

Michael also stood, snarling, crouched like a gladiator. His hands were open and flexed, ready to grapple. Gina could see his silhouette, framed by the faint light of the distant stairway.

Roaring, they charged each other.

Their collision was titanic, and Gina fell back against the wall, barely seeing arms intertwining and releasing, grappling. She saw the creature twisted, arm extended—it had thrown a terrific blow and missed. Then Michael charged forward again, completely lifting it from the floor, slamming it into the wall.

There was no finesse to this fight. It was pure power with the narrowest technique.

In awkward holds they swayed back and forth, each straining volcanically to overcome the titanic strength of the other. But it seemed that neither was truly superior, that they might fight for an eternity before either claimed a true victory.

Then Gina saw Michael's right hand flash up and close on one of the iron spikes protruding from the wall. Instantly Michael snapped it at the base and violently stabbed down. The sharp iron sank a foot into the beast's neck behind the collarbone.

Blood struck the ceiling.

Howling, the beast hit Michael with its uninjured right arm, and nothing could have resisted the wrecking-ball impact.

Michael sailed across the chamber as if shot from a cannon but somehow managed to touch one foot to the floor, turning himself in the air. He landed like a linebacker poised to rush his opponent.

Gina didn't watch the creature. She was too captured by Michael—his skill, strength, and agility. Michael had barely gained balance before he charged forward. Gina spun her head to see a sheet of black melting into a wall of black—it was escaping!

Michael was at the edge of the same darkened tunnel, pursuing it as if he would pursue it across centuries and continents and hell itself, when Gina regained her senses.

"Michael—NO!"

Even as he hit the edge of darkness, his left knee bent—a single step to absorb and halt the impetus of his hurtling rush with such strength that he did not need another. Gina knew she had seconds to decide a dozen things and didn't surrender to the rush—never, *never* surrender to the rush—and made only one decision.

Michael was a soldier—a highly conditioned and highly trained soldier—because only someone with extensive combat training could have done what he had done.

Frowning with an anger that pronounced judgment on all before him, Michael stared into the darkness a long moment. Watching alertly, Gina said nothing and suddenly wished she had retained the presence of mind to retrieve the SIG.

Slowly Michael retreated from the tunnel. Then he turned toward Gina, and his jaw tightened. He stared upon her as if she were a disobedient child—as if he ruled this world—a world Gina did not know and shouldn't know.

Without any words he walked toward a corridor that Gina hadn't noticed. "Wait a second!" she shouted. "Where are you going? Hey! Don't you think I deserve an answer!"

He was gone in the tunnel, and Gina spent six seconds to find the SIG and then rushed after him.

Gina found him kneeling over...something.

It took a second for her to recognize that it was a human being. Because whoever it had been was torn into huge, ragged, bloody chunks of meat, like a slaughtered bull.

The walls in this chamber were bright enough—horrible enough—to make the entire room appear black, though she knew it was blood painted across the walls, pooling upon the floor, thick and vicious, hurled in heavy handfuls across the ceiling.

Gina knew that it had been a man—a big man—but she could determine nothing else.

"Who is it?" she asked.

Michael's voice was somber.

"Molke."

Gently Michael laid a hand on the body, and Gina saw that Molke's head was still barely attached to his neck and shoulders, though the lower part of his body was eviscerated. She barely caught Michael's words.

"I'm sorry...."

Gina closed her eyes for a single brief moment so she could come to terms with this—*whatever* it was. She opened them when she heard movement.

Michael stood now over the body.

Eyes opening fully, Gina took the *whole of him* into focus. His physicality was accepted, but she had not yet come to terms with the brute act of strength that had snapped an iron spike like a candy cane.

She had once witnessed another agent, not a big man but one completely enraged over losing custody of his own children to his shrew of a wife, snap three iron spikes in a row off a fence. But afterward he couldn't remember doing it, and when asked to repeat the feat, he only cut his hand.

But for some reason she believed Michael knew exactly what he had done and could do it anytime he wished. Finally he turned to her. He glanced at the SIG and shook his head.

"That won't save you."

"Yeah," Gina replied, surprising herself with her own calm, "I figured that out. So what will?"

Michael walked toward a staircase.

"Time for you to leave."

———

A heated argument was already raging when Gina entered the Great Hall.

Josh and Rachel ran toward her screaming, and Gina knelt and held them until they finished asking questions, comforting them. Rebecca was close behind. She had been a surrogate mother during the rampage. With a quick glance Gina said to her, "Thank you."

Rebecca nodded, then sat down on a tan sofa next to her father.

Gently, Gina wiped tears from the faces of her children, hugged them close and tight. Then she rose slowly, holding their hands. She walked them back to the dais and sat them down beside Jaqual, always close. The monk seemed to have taken to them like a big brother. Gina lifted her face toward him.

"Watch them."

"Yes, ma'am."

"No!" shouted Josh.

Gina knelt again. Gently, she brushed his hair from his tear-slicked face. "Baby, I have to go talk to these men. I'll only

be ten feet away. Right there. You can see me every second."
She stared him in the eyes. "I'm not leaving you, Josh. Not
ever."

She let those words settle and glanced at Rachel to make
sure the older girl was adapting well enough to the stress. Then
she focused again on Josh. "You hear me, baby? I'm never leaving you."

Josh nodded slightly and let her hand go slowly.

With a grimace Gina turned and walked toward the group
of men.

Melanchthon was arguing forcefully with Father Stephen,
and then the monsignor joined. Miguel stood nearby the three
of them, then brushed past her, obviously frustrated.

"Not that it matters with all this snow, Ms. Crockett,"
Miguel said, "but something has destroyed the engine of our
bus."

Gina studied him. Miguel shrugged then jerked his head
toward Melanchthon, Father Stephen, and the monsignor, who
were now shouting at each other. Gina nodded at Miguel, and
he walked away. She turned to face the three men whose voices
grew still louder.

Gina didn't know who was arguing what and didn't care.
"Hey!" she shouted. "Did any of you call for help yet?"

With near-frantic emotion Father Stephen said, "The phone
lines must be down because of the storm!" But he did not seem
convinced of that, and he certainly wasn't convincing.

"Fine," Gina muttered. "I'll use your radio. We're flying
out of here—all of us!"

None of them moved or spoke—Gina knew. "What happened to the radio?"

Stephen seemed to gather himself. "It's broken. We don't
know who did it."

"It is *demolished*," Melanchthon clarified. "It cannot be fixed." He gazed at Gina. "We are alone."

But Gina had to be sure. It was a hard and fast rule. When your life is on the line, never trust that any gun is loaded or unloaded, never trust that you have the proper equipment, never trust that something works or doesn't. Check it yourself.

She cocked her head toward the distant office.

"Let's take a look."

Father Stephen glanced toward his office and hesitated.

Gina leaned toward him.

"Now."

———

Rebecca and the children, seated on the huge stone dais that supported the two gigantic pillars of the temple, were still visible when Gina reached the office and glanced back. She didn't have to enter the room to evaluate the condition of the radio.

The cover was still attached to wiring that descended almost to the floor. She saw broken fuses and torn circuit boards. Even the dials were crushed, as though they'd been hit with a hammer. Whoever had done this had obviously meant to make it permanent. She didn't doubt that it was unfixable—not with the equipment she saw.

"Do you have another one?" she asked Stephen.

"No."

Gina grimaced. "Don't you have spare parts? Surely you have spare parts. You said you guys were totally self-sufficient."

The priest moved across the corridor and opened the door to what Gina knew was a storage room. It was filled mostly with books and writing materials, catalogues, treatises, and church-related material. But one shelf contained a box—a very old box. And when Stephen brought it down from the shelf Gina saw instantly that it contained a host of spare radio parts.

She shifted them around, though she knew nothing about radios. She was aware of the monsignor as he stepped forward. "Here," he said quietly. "I know something of this."

He, too, moved the parts, but with a definite aura of purpose. He nodded once, twice. "Yes," he said. "I believe I can build something that will work well enough."

"Do you know the emergency frequencies?" Gina asked.

"I know all of them quite well, yes. And if the other radio can be made to function at all, I am confident that I can—at the very least—transmit a message to Lausanne." He lifted the box and spoke tersely to the abbot. "Collect everything in the office that is even remotely related to the radio—torn wiring, broken fuses, anything. We will assemble a device in the Hall."

Gina reentered the Great Hall with more hope than she expected as she took the hands of Josh and Rachel, again thanking Rebecca with a nod. But Gina had a haunting sensation that this was far from over. Despite a single bright moment, there was too much happening—too many unknowns—dangerous and unpredictable. If even one of them influenced the situation, all chance of survival could be erased in a single moment. And she sensed something else. She sensed that, win or lose, this would take something out of her. It had already taken something out of her—her very grasp on reality. And when the rest of this left, it would leave with her guts in its teeth.

She collapsed on a cushioned scarlet divan, and her kids plopped down next to her. She rubbed her head and tried to deny what her intuition told her, but it would not be silenced, and her fatigue flared into anger. She glanced at those nearby, saw Rebecca with Professor Halder on the tan sofa. Mr. Trevanian stood at the nearest entryway, talking to Miguel.

Gina closed her eyes and hung her head.

Then, a sharp ring, steel striking steel.

Gina opened her eyes but didn't lift her head.

Furniture moving.

Gina blinked—there were no screams, no sound of combat. They were safe for now. She intended to spend enough time in her own mind to find an emotional plain—a flat space where she could stand and deal rationally with the situation once more. But finally she couldn't resist raising her gaze toward the movements and saw that almost everyone in the room was gazing as well.

At the other end of the Great Hall, Michael stood before a long table, Barnabas moving silently at his side. Upon the table was an open aluminum case. Barnabas must have retrieved it from Michael's room.

Calm and steady, Michael lifted a Colt .45. He slid a clip into the grip, racked the slide, flicked on the safety, and shoved the weapon into a harness already bearing what Gina recognized were additional clips, antipersonnel grenades, flares, and another Colt.

She rose to her feet, saw Rebecca already moving toward the divan to calm Josh and Rachel.

With a slight bow Barnabas handed Michael an MP-5—a fully automatic short rifle.

Gina knew the weapon—she'd trained with it. Just as she knew it was only used by the elite strike teams. And the way Michael worked the weapons—his hands moving easily, reflexively, like someone turning the pages of a book—confirmed that his training was beyond her.

She stopped four feet from the table.

Michael cast her a single glance.

"You'll stay here," he said.

He wasn't asking for her cooperation, wasn't asking for her opinion. Wasn't *asking* anything at all.

Gina studied the arsenal of what she knew were very expensive armaments. "Going after it alone?"

He nodded.

What was happening didn't fall within the strange and unusual. It was fully in the realm of the inconceivable. But concern for her children inspired Gina to maintain balance.

"Let me get this straight," she began cautiously. "You're going after it alone while I'm supposed to stay here and hold the fort?"

"Got a better idea?"

"Yes, the monsignor thinks he can fix the radio. With this much firepower, why don't we just hang tight? This room is built like a bunker. Then, if it comes in here, we'll just open up on it. I don't care what it is. It can't survive this much ordnance."

Michael briefly lifted his face to the windows. "Look out there, Gina. We're snowed in. We have no radio, no phone—no way to call for help. Maybe they can fix the radio, maybe they can't. But the longer this goes on, the bigger the chance we'll make a mistake. That thing can make mistakes all day. We can't make one."

"Who are you with?" Gina didn't blink at his gaze. "At least you can be courteous enough to tell me that much."

He shrugged. "I'm with the same people you are. At least the paychecks come from the same account."

"Then you're CIA, because I know you're not FBI."

"Close enough," he said. "Just a soldier like you, Gina."

Gina nodded. She could accept that. But if he was lying, there was no way to know. She wanted to ask him something that might trip him up but didn't know enough about covert operations. The only thing she could think of was, "Here for a reason?"

He laughed harshly. "What do *you* say?"

"What I say is that you're bad news, pal. You are someone who is not supposed to exist."

For a moment, he frowned.

Gina shelved questions about his strength. There was no time. And if he was really CIA—the only logical assumption—he wouldn't explain it anyway. She skipped thoughts of experimentation. She'd heard enough rumors to believe anything was possible. And, actually, he was right. *Someone* had to go after that thing because there were too many variables to depend on a rescue.

He secured the vest, obviously bullet-resistant, though much thinner—hence, far more expensive—than the ones issued to special agents. Then he lifted a leg and began strapping a hideaway .45 to his ankle. He was seconds from departing.

"Since you seem to know so much, tell me what that thing is," Gina demanded.

"I have no idea." He shook his head. "It's something big and tough, and it ain't friendly. But if it lives, it can die."

He lifted the MP-5 and slung it over a single shoulder.

"You're lying, Michael."

"About what?"

"You know exactly what it is."

Michael gazed—almost painfully—on her.

"What it is isn't important, Gina. What's important is that we kill it before it kills us." He nodded at the case. "Take anything you want. If I'm not back in six hours, and if they can't get the radio working, then...I'd take my chances in the snow."

"It's six miles to the nearest village."

Her last comment didn't anger him, as she expected. So Gina felt confident that she could question his authority, should the need arise. But at this moment she felt he was right.

"Taking a chance in the snow is better than staying here," he said.

Gina saw his gaze center on Josh and Rachel for a split second.

"Listen...to stay here is death. You can't stay awake forever, and no one else is trained to deal with this."

"Then why don't you lead us out of here?"

"Because it'll chase if we run, Gina. *Any* animal will chase if you run. They smell blood. And I don't want that thing chasing us through a snowfall unless there are no other options."

He settled, separating his words as if Gina were a child. "Listen, in the woods you can't pick a place to make a stand. You have to adapt—you have to be quick. And you absolutely have to know what you're doing. These people aren't trained. Making a run is a last-chance move. Besides that, they'll be half-dead from cold before the fight even begins, and, believe me, cold will make a coward out of anyone. It will be impossible to control them and fight that thing at the same time."

He sighed deeply. "If I don't come back, then you'll know I'm dead, and you'll know it survived all this ordnance. If that's the case, then there's nothing else that will help you. You won't have any choice but to run."

"How do you know so much?" Gina whispered.

"I told you."

"You said you were a soldier—pretty vague."

Michael hesitated and, unexpectedly, seemed deathly weary. For a split second Gina was frightened. Then he straightened and briefly shook his head.

"A soldier's a soldier."

For a moment it seemed as though he would say something else. Then he simply lifted the MP-5 and walked across the Hall toward the very tunnel they had exited. But a group—the others had obviously heard every word—awaited him.

Gina saw Melanchthon bearing a lance. And there stood the ancient Barnabas, armed with a sword and dagger. Also, Father Stephen, armed with a lance. Even Jaqual was there, bearing a lance almost as long as his gangly form. Other monks she had not met stood nearby, all armed with antiquated weaponry. Together they were resolute. They would not allow Michael to confront the beast alone.

Gina stepped forward, sensing something...surreal.

The entire scene had an eerie, medieval feel to it—almost as if she were gazing upon this from the past. Yes, as if this very scene were being replayed from centuries and centuries ago, and the same walls cast the same deathly pallor upon the same defiant priests armed with fire and sword...as they were following a great and mysterious warrior into battle against the beast.

Michael reached up to lift a torch from the wall. The others, wordless, duplicated the action.

And followed him into darkness.

It was almost evening, and Gina had long passed dread and even panic so that she seemed to rest in a dead nothingness. And she knew too well that the first news she heard or saw of the group that followed Michael deep into the tunnels would determine whether she exploded with pent-up emotions, smashing everything she saw, or simply lean over and cry from relief.

For the entire day she had loaded and reloaded weapons. She had talked soothingly to the children, encouraging and supporting, but without making the mistake of minimizing the danger. She knew their instincts confirmed they were in danger, and they could read her every word, gaze, and action. They were far too smart to be deceived.

Yes, the best course was honesty—as honest as she could be anyway—and it had worked out better than she expected. They didn't cry or panic. They didn't huddle close to her with every step. In fact, Gina concluded, they were taking it a lot better than she was. They continued to eat and drink and talk with Rebecca and sometimes Miguel and Mr. Trevanian. Professor Halder even lent a hand by telling tall tales from long ago— stories without any mythically terrifying beasts, Gina noted.

Once again, she found herself standing over the monsignor, who continued to work minutely upon the remnants of wire and circuit board at one of the smaller tables in the Hall. Shutting down concern, she recalled an earlier statement, when he remarked that it would be much easier to repair if it had not been damaged so "precisely."

"Precisely" is not exactly how Gina thought a madman would disable a radio, but then there was only a single step between genius and madness. Still, she wondered why the rest of it had been so heavily damaged. It was as if it had been two creatures— or a single creature of two minds. Or, as she began to suspect, the greater damage had been done simply to hide the precise-ness of it. But she couldn't conceive of any reason for that.

The monsignor's face was strained with fatigue. Rather easily, he read her thoughts. "Worrying will not change what God has decided," he said quietly. "Try to get some rest."

"Huh," Gina grunted. "What a joke."

"It is better than wearing yourself out with worry. I believe I can construct a functional radio, but not before tomorrow."

Michael's words returned to Gina. "An hour can be a long time when you need help *now....*"

She glanced at her watch—ten minutes later than last time. She wandered back toward the long table to load more ammunition—

A cry...

Gina stopped and bent her head a quarter turn.

Yes...distant cries, but she couldn't determine the nature—terror or joy. She made a quick motion to the kids to stay on the dais as she ran to the exit of a corridor that echoed most heavily.

Darkening the distant bend, six men rushed forward. Two were carrying another between them, and Gina needed no more. Yes, they had found it. Or it had found them.

She searched desperately but didn't see Michael. Then Melanchthon's huge body came into the lamplight, and Father Stephen. They were carrying Jaqual between them.

He was alive but bleeding badly.

Gina saw that the monk had been hit in the chest—a massive wound, but mostly muscle. He was moaning.

Good—if he was moaning, he was in pain. If he was in pain, he was closer to living than dying. Everything beyond that was technique, and Gina quickly stripped the slashed robe from the monk's chest, applying pressure with bandages. She heard Melanchthon gasp and turned her face as the big monk collapsed to his knees.

His sweating face was pale. His hands shook violently. His first word was an eruption of anger, hate—shock.

"BEAST!"

The others collapsed at the word as if struck, sprawling across the floor, not even trying to reach a chair. Weapons clanged sharply against stone, and Gina saw that they were all injured.

Melanchthon lifted his torso, arms stretched wide, and inhaled deeply. His grimace was a portrait of a prophet whose prophecy assured his own destruction. But the prophet was not yet destroyed. The prophet would yet have words with the Almighty!

"Will You only *watch* as we are destroyed? *Then destroy us! Destroy us quickly and be merciful!*"

Gina recoiled at the pain of betrayal—of the most cherished, most terrible betrayal—that emerged from the priest. His eyes were maddened and searching. Then he lifted a spear and began to rise.

"I would not be so merciless!" he whispered through clenched teeth. "If *You* will not fight, then *I* will fight! If *You* will not destroy it, then *I* will destroy it!"

He stumbled toward the corridor.

Gina hit and tackled him behind the knees, and Melanchthon fell forward. She didn't have time to worry about which of them would be killed by the spear, and then it clattered harmlessly across the distant floor.

Like a she-wolf, she pounced on top of him. "*Nobody's* going *anywhere* until I get some answers!" Gina waited for a challenge, but the old priest was far too exhausted.

He had spoken in rage and pain and horror, but he could speak no more, nor could he rise. She waited until Melanchthon drew heavier, slower breaths. She spoke slowly and distinctly.

"Where...is...Michael?"

Melanchthon lifted a hand, as if to point. "They were on the ledge," he gasped. "They were on the ledge...fighting.

Michael had been wounded. He told us to run, and then he did something...I don't know."

"What! What did Michael do?"

"I don't know." Melanchthon shook his head. "He fired one of the weapons into the cliff. Then the mountain fell on us...on them. I saw no more."

"Is Michael alive?" Gina shook him. "Melanchthon! Priest! You're not passing out on me! *Is Michael alive?*"

Melanchthon was gone.

He would awake when shock faded, but he could say nothing more now. Gina groaned as she stood, holding the SIG tight. She stared over the rest of them. They were covered in dust and were in various states of consciousness.

Monsignor DeMarco retained his senses, having watched the whole affair from his chair at the small table. And as Gina glanced at him, the oldest priest slowly stood. He stared over all of them and shook his head, and Gina thought she detected... guilt in his eyes. But she didn't understand, nor did she understand the quiet words he spoke in such a terrible tone.

"Habebor...exstinctor terra...."

With a trembling hand the monsignor wiped his brow and turned away. And for the first time, his shoulders fell. His bearing was only the bearing of an old man, not a man of faith.

No, Gina did not understand his words, but she understood his tone of horrible, deep regret—the tone of someone who could not be forgiven, or could not forgive himself.

It was the tone of Judas, who killed himself when he realized what he had done.

⸺

The Hall glowed brightly with every lamp-wick stretched to full extension.

After he recovered, Father Stephen had commanded that even more lamps be brought into the cathedral-size room, as if light alone would protect them from this thing that preferred the darkness. But Gina knew that was fanciful. This creature didn't fear the light. It feared nothing.

Remarkably, Melanchthon had recovered twice as fast as those half his age. After rising, he drank from a bottle of wine sheathed in straw. After wiping his mouth with his sleeve, his black eyes focused bitterly on Gina.

"Yes," he muttered at last, "it was Michael...who held it so that we might escape." He nodded long and sighed.

"We tracked it for a long time—deeper and deeper into the mountain—deeper than I had ever gone. It was...not the place for man, but Michael hunted it as if he had hunted a thousand...as if he had *never* known fear. Often enough he bid us halt and then proceeded ahead for a space. Then he would return again and say the road was clear."

He slaked his thirst with another sip of wine.

"Such thirst..." He wiped his beard on his sleeve. "We followed it to where strange things glowed—things I have never seen. To where the walls seemed crushed by the tons of earth upon them. I thought we would descend into hell itself. It was hot—fiercely, terribly hot. But Michael gave no sign of weariness. Then he stopped, and I thought he meant to rest. But he did not move, did not speak."

Slowly, Melanchthon lifted a hand. "He stood without a breath, staring into a dark pit before him. It seemed to descend straight down into the earth, like the path of some huge worm that fed on the deepest parts of the world.

"Long he waited—until I almost spoke. Then he took a single step—a single step—away from the pit...and it happened."

His hand fell and Melanchthon's head rolled back before he shook it angrily. "It erupted from the pit, and though Michael braced to meet it, it blasted him back. Then I lost sight of Michael. He disappeared into the blackness. We rushed forward as one man, shouting, prepared to die. But when it turned upon us, it strewed us like dogs!"

He groaned. "Against that hellish strength we were like *nothing*—less than nothing! It crushed and struck us down and lifted men above its head, tearing them in half and flinging them aside, showering us with blood! It *slaughtered* priests you did not have the honor of knowing! Jacobi! Durnam! Reuben!

"Insane with fear, I lifted my spear and stabbed deep into its back! And it turned into me with...with eyes that opened into *hell*!" He collapsed forward, releasing a deep gasp. "I fell back...I didn't have the strength to stand. We were doomed—all of us. But then Michael reached his feet once more!"

Inspired, Melanchthon lifted his head, his hand clenched tight in a bloodless fist. "He *caught it* by the mane as a man would catch a lion! It twisted to escape, but Michael held it fast! Its fury was wild! It roared and struck and struck again and again! But horrible as it was—as *strong*—Michael was not less!"

Suddenly, the monk's voice softened, as if he were remembering something glorious, not horrible. "Never have men been so blessed by God to witness such a battle. It was like a battle between gods—of man as God *meant him to be* against the beast. I can speak of it now, though at the time I could not move. I could not speak."

His voice became softer.

"Long was the battle, and savage. Then Michael reached a weapon—some weapon he had not lost—and I was blinded by the light...the noise.

"I heard stalagmites shattering. I saw titanic shadows struggling against the other cascading along the walls. I heard roars, but I did not know if it was Michael or the beast...or both."

It took the weary monk a moment to catch his breath, for the telling took as much as the living.

"Then there was a crashing sound, and then silence. And I have never watched the darkness as closely as I watched it then. I could see a thousand shades of blue, black, silver, and white. I could see circles and pits. As if the very darkness itself were alive.

"I shouted as Michael emerged out of the night. Then I saw he was hurt...badly hurt, and bleeding. He shouted at me to get up, but I had no time before he *lifted* me from the floor."

Gently, Melanchthon grasped his upper right arm. "We fled—*flew* until we reached the ledge. And there we heard the roar of...the greatest beast. It was coming; we were doomed. But Michael only pushed us across the ledge. He lifted poor Jaqual and flung him into my arms. 'Take care of the boy!' he shouted.

"I turned back when we reached the crest of the stairs and saw Michael standing at the narrowest section of ledge. The beast crouched before him."

Gasping again, Melanchthon rubbed a bruise on his temple. "The rest...is unclear."

Gina leaned forward. "Melanchthon! Michael might still be alive! Try to remember!"

"I will try." He focused, then blew out a long breath. "Yes, it seemed to come forward, and Michael stepped toward it. He was not retreating. He was going to hold it there. Then he fired some kind of weapon—I know not of these things— into the cliff, and we were thrown back together. We could not enter the cavern because huge stones choked the entrance, so we made our way here." He paused and gazed steadily upon Jaqual. "Will the boy live?"

"Yes, he's...coming through well," Gina said tiredly and, with an effort, stood. Her weariness, she realized despondently, was deep—*meaningful*. And it scared her. Because it meant she was beginning to care for something more than surviving—for something far more.

Without fear, she stared into the darkest corridor.

"This thing won't beat us."

———

The monsignor was patiently bandaging injuries, administering comfort, both physical and spiritual, to the wounded. He gave no sign of shock when Gina appeared beside him.

She gave no indication of leaving.

When the monsignor lifted his eyes, he saw her expression and lowered his face again. He nodded. Then he rose to his full height like a man accepting a death sentence with dignity.

"I am sorry," he began simply, "for all of this." He lifted a hand to silence Gina's question.

"No," he continued, and it sounded like a verdict rendered from a far higher power, "I can say nothing. The secret things belong to God, and should, and I will not further risk my soul in stupid human attempts to force the hand of the Almighty. I have seen enough. It is my sin—all of it. For had I not bowed to authority—earthly authority that dies when men die—none of you would be in peril. But it is too late. We are here. And now the only good thing I can do is give my life to save you and your children."

Gina was on the edge of a dozen questions before she spoke in a dead calm voice. "So what is that thing?"

His face tightened in control—the last of it. "It is a creature born out of time, Ms. Crockett. A creature that is neither man, nor god, but wishes to be both."

"One of the Nephilim," Gina said bitterly. She was acutely aware of the SIG in her right hand. "You opened this place and you knew all along that it was here."

"No, I did not know. And, more important, I did not believe that any mythical creatures—half-man, half-demon— once walked this planet." His smile was tragic. "I was a skeptic, Ms. Crockett."

Gina's disgust was visible as she turned away.

"Weren't we all."

Unlike the rest, Gina was unable to sleep and fell into a deep discussion with Melanchthon, who'd recovered from his ordeal. But the heavy brow of the large priest was clouded now.

Gina sensed he'd cast off all vows and secrets. As she rested beside him, Melanchthon spoke in a hoarse, ravaged voice.

"It is Cassius," he said simply.

Gina said nothing for a time. But she knew she could not deny her thoughts forever. "Why would God destine a man to live forever, Priest? I have...a hard time with that."

Melanchthon laughed, a genuine laugh. "Men can watch the ocean collide against the shore forever and never admit the ocean is there. Yet they change their mind quickly enough if they are caught in the tide." He laughed again. "Better to live saying you were wrong than die saying you were right."

He focused on the flames, and they seemed to remind him of something. "War...what it must have been like, for him—two thousand years of war, of fighting. Every man he killed, despite the cause, wondering if he were right. Battles...endless. What kind of pain would such a man know?"

Silent, Gina stared into the flames.

"Even Cassius, probably, does not know why he is here. He knows what he understands as his purpose. But, though Cassius has lived so long, God is beyond wisdom of years." Melanchthon smiled at Gina. "Cassius, my dear, is as unknowing of God's ultimate plan as you or I. But he fights with courage—with all his strength, hoping, just as we hope, that we are right."

Then, with a groan, Melanchthon bent his head and laid it upon an outstretched arm. Gina watched him until his breaths were deep, rhythmic—until she was certain he was asleep.

She did not try to stop herself from reaching out, smoothing the hair upon his head. Her mouth tightened, and she fought the tears. Tilting her head back, she took angry breaths, struggling.

In a moment, it passed.

She rose, feeling strangely alone, and walked silently to where Josh and Rachel slept, close beside Rebecca, who had now fully assumed the role of surrogate mom, for which Gina was thankful.

Gina folded a shirt behind her head and lay down, wanting to think it through. Before she knew it, she was fast asleep.

It was *still* not morning when Gina awoke. She reached her feet in a blast of anger and bitterly searched the chamber. It was as though the sun had risen inside the temple. Lights were burning across the entire expanse.

A glance assured her that the kids were safe, and that was enough. If this beast hadn't attacked before now, then it probably died with Michael in the cave-in, which meant she needed to lead these people out of here at first light.

But she had to be sure.

Nightbringer

With almost everyone sleeping, she donned another MP-5, her SIG, and a belt of clips. She inserted tiny flares into her pocket. They would light the way if she became lost. When she reached the monks, they were already softly protesting.

"Don't worry," she said calmly. "I know what I'm doing." Her training told her that it'd be best to give them something to do. "I want the two of you to make sure we've got enough food and water to cover six miles in that storm. Can you do that?"

They nodded nervously.

"Fine." Gina slung the strap of the machine gun higher on her shoulder. "Then pack some food, stay alert, and I'll be back in a few minutes."

She was gone before they could object, though she knew they would make direct lines for the senior priests.

Whatever.

She'd just about had it with them all.

———

This was refreshing!

Gina slid along a wall, the SIG tight in both hands. She felt alive for the first time in days. Her vision was reading light that she knew she couldn't read unless she was in a combat mode. It was all white at the edges, and she had to blink often or lower her gaze.

She regulated her breath—sometimes holding it to reduce oxygen—ensuring that she didn't lose clarity on the periphery.

The flow...*the flow, stay in the flow*....

She knew it, even liked it. It was home—a place where she felt confident and skilled.

A sound.

Gina knew it—solid, sure.

It hadn't been some harmless brush inherent to these walls. It was something that had been *made.*

Utterly still, she waited a full sixty seconds, an agonizing long time. Sweat dripped heavily from her lips and forehead, stinging her eyes. She blew drops of perspiration from her lips, ignoring the overwhelming scent of fresh blood and her own fear. Then, finally, she rose from a crouch and lifted the SIG.

If it was coming, it would come. But it wasn't going to reach her without getting hit. And suddenly she wished she'd remained in the Hall, though she knew tragically that she might at least wound it and give the others a chance to run.

Her jaw tightened in control. She was trained to deal with situations like this. Was trained to shut down emotions and follow procedure, however emotional she might be. But it took every fiber of control to not begin running, screaming and enraged, back toward the abbey to warn the others.

Her eyes were like white lasers centering on and catching everything. But in the space of a minute, the stress had red-lined. She closed her eyes for a tenth of a second.

Don't panic. Come on, think, think. Keep your head.

It was all too much. She hadn't been prepared for this, but *nothing* could have prepared her for this! She spent only one second thinking of what had happened and turned into Michael. No, not Michael—

Cassius!

What happened next was too fast to follow, but Gina had the impression of a lion leaping upon her from ambush. And although, strangely, Cassius seemed to be moving in slow motion, Gina felt his hand on her gun hand and knew something had happened. Next she was staggering back, and Cassius was holding her gun, and her forearm came up automatically to protect her face.

Gina shouted as she gained her feet, her mind only now catching up to what had happened just as someone flings their hand away from a hot stove *twice.*

In the sound of rumbling thunder, Cassius took a single step toward her, and then Gina lifted a hand to her chest in shock. His torso was crusted in blood—his injuries deep and severe. His eyes were dead—weary with death. He took a single step, and Gina knew it might be his last.

She lunged forward as he fell, and they sprawled back, shattering or scattering whatever the monks kept in this corridor. Wrestling hard against his weight, Gina pushed him to the side and was screaming for the others. She knew her voice probably woke some of them to pure horror, but she didn't care. Cassius groaned and began to rise.

"No!" Gina leaped over him. "Cassius!" She didn't even think about using another name. "Cassius! It's me! *Gina!* Lie still, okay!

Cassius' eyes flared, even from the edge of death, glaring at Gina to *know* if she knew. He coughed violently, then grasped her by the collar, pulling her close. His teeth came together in pain.

"The children?...You?...All right?'"

Gina was stunned.

"Yes! We're all okay!"

The sound of rushing footsteps halted, and Melanchthon, along with the monsignor and Rebecca and Josh and Rachel, surged through the doorway. The professor, Miguel, and Mr. Trevanian followed.

Cassius cast his gaze upon the kids and made a brave attempt to laugh. "Are you two still here?"

Gina knew it was the children and suddenly wished they hadn't been here, because Cassius abruptly threw off her hand and rolled on his side. Then—and Gina groaned, only imagining what pain he endured—Cassius stood. He took only a moment, bent, breathing, before he straightened. When he turned toward them, he was steady, and his eyes were gentle.

Gina was speechless.

He nodded to the kids. "You two better get your things packed. You and your mom and everyone else are leaving."

Father Stephen quickly ushered the shouting children out of the room, and Rebecca followed. Standing silently, Gina and Melanchthon stared upon the centurion.

Swaying, Cassius bent his bloody face and nodded with the darkest frown. "I am...sorry," he whispered.

Instinctively reaching out, Gina stepped forward, but Melanchthon instantly grabbed her shoulder. No, no...what stood before them was also beyond them.

Cassius raised his face.

Ice-blue currents of love and strength that Gina could not fathom stared upon her. And, incredible as it seemed, Cassius was recovering far more quickly than any human being could recover from such injuries. His voice was dry.

"You say it...yourselves." He grimaced with compassion. "You are chosen.... And I will see...that you live. It is not your fault...that you are caught here."

He took a moment, breathing. Then he tilted his head back, inhaling, and whatever strength came to him seemed not to come from this world. He lowered his head again and was steadier. He nodded and whispered, "Please, the rest... need not know...."

Melanchthon responded instantly! "No, brother! They shall *not* know!"

Gina joined, but gentler. "No, Cassius...don't worry."

Cassius' head bent farther, and by her intuition alone, Gina knew that her words had painfully touched his soul.

Without looking upon her—as if he couldn't—he spoke in a low growl. "Not in a thousand years...have men known me. But I am *glad*...that *you* know me!... Yes! He is merciful! And I promise that both you...and your children...will live."

Gina lifted her hand to her mouth.

"Brother!" Melanchthon whispered. "Tell me what you require! I shall do it!"

Cassius nodded wearily and raised his face.

Gina and Melanchthon leaped forward as one, catching him, supporting him. She felt Cassius' left arm enclose her shoulders, holding her gently. But she saw Cassius' right arm embrace Melanchthon like a steel vise, holding him firmly.

Cassius smiled and nodded to the priest.

"*We shall overcome, brother!*" he whispered.

Melanchthon's smile was beatific.

"Aye! We shall!"

CHAPTER EIGHT

Gina waited, watching the high red swirls of the windows as the dimmed sun rose. She watched so long and so steadily that she began to read the wind as it passed—edges of blizzard that slashed like snow-edged knives past slivers of crimson. Watched until she knew the cold of it—a cold deep and merciless that came from the depth of something she was only now beginning to understand.

Cassius stood on the far side of the room, slowly preparing more weapons. She had bandaged his wounds, and he had promised to rest for a time, but he never truly rested.

He could not allow himself to rest, for the burden of what he placed upon himself was stronger than his weakness. But Melanchthon had seen to it that he ate and drank. And Barnabas, too, somehow sensed the secret, for he was ever at Cassius' side, obedient and vigilant, ensuring that the centurion had all that he needed or desired.

Gina had settled into it as she had watched the storm brew across the windows, but it hadn't been a completely content acceptance. Rather, it was like the acceptance of ominous, threatening weather—something that could not be changed and so should be endured with as much peace as possible.

Melanchthon was at Gina's side, and she raised her eyes. She felt herself smile but knew it appeared as wan as her spirit.

"We must discuss something," he murmured and gestured to where Cassius stood.

With a nod Gina rose and dusted off her blue jeans, though it made little difference. Her entire body was wet with sweat and dust so that her clothes clung like a loathsome skin. But she accepted it. She was learning to accept a lot of things.

When she and Melanchthon reached the table, Cassius raised his face and smiled. He searched her, and Gina knew her fear could be seen like still water beneath ice. If you knew it was there, all you had to do was gaze deeper, and you would find it.

"So," she said with a tight smile, "what's the plan?" She didn't want any cosmic discussions and didn't really think he'd initiate one.

"Simple enough," Cassius began. "First we see if the radio can be repaired. If not, then I'll lead all of you out of here. It's six miles to the village, but the paths down the south side of the mountain won't be as treacherous. We'll bundle the kids up as much as possible and, without any incidents, we should make the village by noon."

"What about what you said earlier?"

For a moment, Cassius stared upon the weapons. "It's still a risk," he said finally. "But now I think it's best to take our chances in the storm."

"You didn't kill it, did you?" Gina said it with no judgment. She only wanted to confirm what she had suspected but he had not plainly stated.

"No," he admitted. "I don't believe it was killed when the ledge collapsed. I don't know for certain, though. I was a little busy at the time."

"Think it might still chase us?"

He scowled. "Not as certain as I was before."

Gina waited. "Why's that?"

"I don't know." Cassius' response was moodier. "It's just a feeling. But I don't think it really wants to fight me—not really. But then that doesn't really add up."

Gina understood, finding some comfort with familiar ground. It was detective work—a mixture of common sense, careful analysis, and deduction. Casually, as if checking on the kids, Gina glanced over her shoulder. None of the others were close.

"On the first night, it called you out." Gina blinked at her own mention of the first night, not so very long ago. "And this storm—I understand, now—it's not natural. It wants to keep you here. But it still isn't initiating another fight.... So, no, it doesn't add up."

Cassius pondered, then grimaced. "If it wants a fight, then why doesn't it make a real fight?" He paused. "It knows where we're at, but it's still trying to play some idiotic game of cat and mouse. In one way, it seems in total control—unafraid. In another, it seems scared to finish this. Almost as if it has two minds." No one found fault with the logic. He shook his head. "I don't know...."

"Dominic...Basil," Gina whispered. "You asked where they were when we first heard the beast howl. You believe it's one of them?"

He sighed. "It seems probable, but there's no way to know for sure." He glanced over the room. "I only know it's not anyone who's been in this room since yesterday."

Melanchthon was gazing somberly across the room. "The only ones who have not been here are brothers Basil and Dominic. Perhaps—"

He looked at Cassius. "Perhaps it is both of them."

"Yes," Cassius agreed, "two of them. I've considered that. It's the only thing that makes sense. I don't know which one is older and smarter, but he's the one that...conjured...this storm. The other is probably the one playing cat and mouse. He'll be younger, weaker—a *lot* weaker. He'll be less knowledgeable about sorcery—things that only the oldest Nephilim remember—and less confident."

They did not seem to sense that Gina was shocked by the words they spoke so quietly and calmly. Her breath was short and hard, and she glanced from one to the other. Melanchthon understood, then, and placed a hand on her shoulder.

"Do not fear," he said quickly. "I am sorry. I did not think."

"You didn't think to tell me there's *two of them*?" she hissed, anger sharpening each word. "Did you think something like that would just occur to me? I'm the one with children here! I'm just a little bit preoccupied!"

"Of course." Melanchthon bowed his head. "I am sorry. I did not think of it myself until this moment."

Cassius gazed upon her with compassion. He waited patiently until she had recovered. His voice was gentle. "You okay?"

"Sure," Gina replied, bitter. "I'm okay. But that changes our plan a little, doesn't it?" She glanced over the weapons. "If there's two of them, you still want to chance the storm?"

He was uncertain. Gina saw it in the bend of his head and understood something of him. Yes, he was the ultimate warrior. But he was only human. He had no magical power to alter anything at all. He was as limited—as trapped—as they were. He merely had the faculty of experience and near superhuman strength and endurance. He had no black bag from which he could conjure a reality that did not exist.

Finally he shook his head. "I...don't see any other choice. One of them, two of them, the longer we stay in this place, the worse our chances are of surviving."

"What would you do if you were alone?" Gina asked.

"I'd stay."

"Why?"

"It's what I do."

He met Gina's gaze as if he would like to tell her more, as if he needed to tell her more. But she could see that, for some reason, he couldn't.

"Kill them, you mean," she said.

"Yes."

She wanted to ask him why—to hear him say it. She needed to hear him say it. She wasn't certain, but at his gaze, it meant something to her now. But it wasn't the time. She decided to go with, "Do we have enough ordnance to put both of them down for good?"

"Yes," Cassius replied with comforting certainty. "Just think of it like an ape—a gorilla. Hit it from a distance and keep hitting it—it's not bulletproof. But, like anything else, it won't die instantaneously unless you hit it the heart."

"What about the head?" Gina was thinking tactically now and found encouragement in it.

"No," Cassius answered firmly. "Don't try for the head."

"Too much chance of deflection?"

"Yes."

"What about bone structure—vision, hearing, endurance? Do they have a weakness?"

"No weaknesses. They don't have a blind spot, and their bone strength is like iron. They have the heightened senses of a cat. Strong as a gorilla, but a lot faster."

"How fast?"

Cassius calculated. "It varies.... And listen to me on this. They are not the perfect predators."

Melanchthon rumbled, "What is?"

"Man." Gina and Cassius said it together and at the same moment.

Cassius' eyes flared with surprise, and then he laughed as Gina laughed—a genuine laugh.

He continued. "Just remember that any round that hits a bone will probably be deflected. But bones don't surround their guts. If you can put a clip into their guts, they'll probably go down, but they might not, too. Like anything—like any animal—it depends on the animal."

He was talking more freely now that there were no more secrets. Or, Gina wondered, were there?

"Nephilim can reproduce, like anything, but when they mix with the human race, each generation becomes less pure than the one before. Which is why some are less knowledgeable, weaker, whatever. But even one of the Nephilim that's only three or four generations removed from pure blood is nothing you want to meet. There's a good reason why the human race has never been able to completely cast off horror stories of men or women who could transform themselves into monsters. Those legends are based more on fact than people know."

"This one," Melanchthon asked, "he is pure?"

"No," Cassius answered solidly. "This one is at least twenty generations removed from pure, which is why I could fight him. His strength is nothing compared to one that's truly half human and half...fallen god. One that's pure is hard to kill."

Gina was alarmed to see a veil of fear cloud his face. "But you've killed pure ones before, right?" Gina didn't like her question, didn't like, even more, waiting for his answer.

"Yes...a long time ago. And it was a long, bloody fight. And I wasn't alone. I was with twenty other men who were great warriors in their own right."

"Templars," Melanchthon stated.

"If it helps, I don't think that any first generation Nephilim still live."

Gina was suddenly aware that no one spoke of the legend—of the centurion returning to his very abbey to fight his greatest battle...against his greatest foe.

"But we've only seen one of them," she mentioned cautiously. "What about the other one? I mean, if there *is* another one."

"We'll have to deal with that when the time comes. Right now, we put our hopes on the radio. If the monsignor fails, we walk out in the morning. In the meantime, I think we can make a quick trip to your room so you can collect what the kids will need for the walk—their heavy clothing, coats, boots, whatever."

Gina looked over the room. Everyone appeared surprisingly calm. Either frantic emotion had been exhausted or a quiet confidence was building or both. "We'll be taking a big chance, though, leaving this room."

"I won't allow you to go alone," he said. "But I can go, and you can stay here."

Gina didn't like that idea, either. Yes, he was fully armed again. But if there were actually two Nephilim, then he wouldn't be coming back unless she was there to back him up. And she knew with certainty that she couldn't protect this group through six miles of mountains. Plus, she didn't trust Barnabas' eyes in the storm.

But Cassius would know every ledge, every cave. So if they were to have any chance at all, Cassius had to lead them.

She couldn't risk letting him get killed on a simple trip to her room.

"Either way is a risk," she said finally. "But the kids will need their clothes, their boots and coats. Okay, we'll make it quick. A quick run up, I grab their stuff, a quick run back. Think we can keep it under two minutes total?"

Cassius looked at Melanchthon. "You have any reservations about using a gun?"

"No."

Cassius gave him the MP-5. "That's the safety. Flick it off and hold down hard 'cause the barrel will rise. It's set on fully auto. Remember, we'll only be gone two minutes. And if we hear gunfire we'll be back here in thirty seconds."

"Understood," Melanchthon said and grasped the weapon. His broad hands folded over it, and it seemed much smaller than when Cassius had held it.

Gina turned toward the dais. "I'll tell Rebecca and the kids, and then we'll get it done."

"Okay."

Cassius lifted a long Japanese-style sword—a katana, Gina remembered—from the case. Even with a casual glance Gina saw that it was a sword of stunning quality.

The highly polished steel blade, perfect in design, was slightly curved with a thick, angled point that seemed unbreakable. Gina sensed that it reflected something of Cassius—something created by a holocaust that would have destroyed anything less than the purest strength. Something forged and reforged in holocaust after holocaust so that no weakness remained, for no weakness could have survived the white, glowing edge where a man and blade were remade into something far more than they had been before.

She exhaled. "Think it's gonna come to that?"

"No, but I've never regretted carrying more weapons than I thought I would need, 'cause I always end up needing them."

"Huh." Gina laughed and wished that had been funny. "No kidding."

It was difficult for Gina to assure the kids that she'd be back in two minutes. But Rebecca helped, and Jaqual had become a big brother who never left their side. Gina was also grateful that Father Stephen and Professor Halder so closely attended their needs, ensuring that the monks did not hold conversations within earshot.

She wasn't certain whether Rebecca or the kids were more comforted by the other's presence, but the arrangement had worked perfectly so far.

Pausing, Gina stood over the monsignor, who had worked through the morning relatively undisturbed by the monks— thanks also to Father Stephen's vigilance. A lot crossed Gina's mind, questions she was determined to ask the priest when the time came.

She studied the radio. It was crisscrossed with wires and was using only a circuit board. A number of vintage fuses were hooked together with a maze of copper line and aluminum foil. It didn't look very promising.

"How's it going?"

With a sigh the monsignor leaned back from the ragged remnants of the radio. "Well enough. I believe I can design what we called a 'whip antenna' in World War II. It is, actually, a little more powerful than a conventional radio and has better range. But we are limited to using Morse code."

"That shouldn't be a problem. There's a dozen rescue teams that monitor this area for transmissions in Morse code. It's the international language for emergencies."

"True," the monsignor answered, and he apparently did not sense or did not care for Gina's acute attention. But when she did not say anything more, and did not move, he raised his face.

"I believe that I shall have it operational this evening. Then we will be one hour from leaving, and it will be as if this never happened."

Gina actually laughed. Now *that* was funny.

She saw Cassius waiting for her beside the stairs. He was heavily laden with weapons, but she knew the extra weight wouldn't slow him down. In fact, she wasn't worried about *him* covering the distance at all.

With a last smile and a kiss and a wave at the kids, Gina walked to the stairs and took a belt he presented. It was loaded with three clips for the MP-5—almost a hundred extra rounds, three antipersonnel grenades, and four flares. It was heavy when she strapped it around her waist, but for the extra fire-power, she was willing to bear the weight. She'd carry the MP-5 in her hands for a quick first shot, but she'd let the shoulder strap bear the load.

"Ready?" he asked gently.

"You bet."

He glanced at the kids.

"They're okay," she added, a sure nod. "They're scared. But they haven't seen it yet, remember? They could be more frightened. "

"True." He nodded. "And they don't need to be."

They walked slowly up the staircase, not expending any more energy than necessary. But at the crest they stood before the longest corridor in the abbey. Far at the other end was another stairway, then another corridor, and then Gina's room.

Gina ran over the plan in her mind, taking deeper breaths—down this hall, up a flight, down another hall to the corridor with their rooms and back. At least a quarter mile, all together.

She felt light-headed from the breaths and knew she was oxygenated. She nodded tightly to Cassius. "I'm ready when you are."

With a curt nod he led, beginning at a lope that Gina felt immediately she could maintain there and back. It was fast, but not so fast that she'd burn out, yet neither would she be able to hold it for more than the short distance.

Her mind was acutely alert to any sounds from the Hall, but she heard nothing as they reached the second stairway, and Cassius took the steps four at a time to emerge twenty feet ahead of her on the crest. She knew he'd done it because the crest was a blind spot. There was no way to know what was there until you reached it.

Thirty seconds, maybe.

He motioned quickly, and Gina cleared the last step, and then he was ahead of her again, a single leaping stride putting him in the lead. The second corridor was longer and contained more doors, so Cassius would slow, just a hair, ready to react to anything.

Then they were in the corridor they sought, and Gina was in the door of her room instantly. She was glad they had barely unpacked because she knew where everything was. She grabbed the kids' heaviest coats, stuffed socks in the pockets, grabbed two sweaters and their boots.

"Got it!"

They were down the hall together when Gina realized something was wrong. She wasn't certain what it was until she realized it was smoke. But Cassius had already sensed it because at the stairway he leaped the final fifteen feet to hit the floor.

Gina had only begun the descent when she heard flames roaring.

Cassius cursed.

The last corridor was fully aflame, and Gina knew it as she hit the floor and threw the clothes and boots to the side, instantly raising the MP-5 for an attack. But there was no attack, and then she heard the howls—human howls of horror.

"The children!" she cried as Cassius spun.

Gina began to take a chance and ran toward the flames. If she was fast enough she might be able to—

With a cable-strong arm Cassius caught her across the chest, spinning with her to prevent injury.

Gina hit the floor livid. "Those are my children!"

Cassius kicked a door that exploded off the hinges as though it'd been hit by a truck. He snatched the MP-5 from her hands and raised it at the window. He fired for two seconds, shattering the stained glass. Smoke was already choking Gina as he smashed the remnants of glass from the rectangular opening. Instantly a blast of black air and flashing snow poured through, shocking Gina with cold.

"Isn't there another staircase?" she shouted.

"No!" He threw a leg over the sill. "They'll be burning that too! Our only chance is to get outside and follow the wall around to the front!" He stretched out an arm to her. "Hurry up! It's a drop but I can let you down!"

Gina slung the MP-5 and squirmed through the window beside him, and Cassius lowered her into the night. She raised an arm over her face, shielding her eyes from flecks of ice that hit like sandpaper, and she saw a slope of snow.

The ten-foot drift reduced the force of her impact, and two seconds later she heard Cassius hit the ground beside her.

He had leaped from the window, completely past the gigantic drift to land hard on his feet. She didn't expect him to be injured—he wasn't.

Trusting nothing in this storm, which reduced visibility to less than four feet, Gina grabbed Cassius' dark blue shirt, and he kept tight against the drift as they moved. It was slow work, and tedious, because they post-holed with each step, legs sinking to their thighs.

Then Cassius began to powerfully move against the heavy crust, bulling his way through the drifts, and Gina understood. He was making it easier for her to keep up. He was doing all the work. All she had to do was stagger in his tracks.

Still, it seemed like forever, though Gina knew it had been less than three minutes since they hit the ground, until they reached the front steps of the abbey. Cassius dragged her past the ice-sheathed stones with uncanny balance and pushed open the gigantic twin doors, and then Gina rushed into the Hall, raising the MP-5.

At least half of the monks who had been in the Hall lay across the lapis lazuli floor, torn and bloody and dead.

Gina scanned the dais—Josh and Rachel, as well as Rebecca, weren't there. She swept the MP-5 across the hall, but she didn't see the creature.

Instantly Gina knew who else wasn't there—the professor, Mr. Trevanian, Miguel, Melanchthon, Barnabas, the monsignor, Father Stephen, Jaqual, the two other monks—*Samuel and...Zachary*—yes.

"Rebecca!" she screamed but didn't expect a response.

Smoke from the burning section of the abbey had not invaded the Hall. But she could smell the scent of burning timber. She whirled as Cassius bent over the radio.

"What about the radio!"

Cassius took another moment. "The monsignor took the circuit board with him!" He nodded. "Good.... If we still have that, we still have a chance."

"We need to find them, Cassius." Gina's voice was calm in the calm of someone who sees a snake too close already and knows he can't move without risk. He stood and nodded hard.

"We will."

As they exited a mildewed staircase, Gina moved close beside Cassius. Without breaking her vigilance at connecting corridors, doorways, or the irregular, elevated ceiling where the beast could pounce on them from the darkness, she spoke. "Rebecca wouldn't run farther than she had to. She'd find some place safe and hide."

Cassius didn't answer.

"Cassius?"

Slowly, he turned his head toward a corridor. A good professional would have followed the gaze, but Gina was better than that. She looked in the opposite direction so they couldn't be blindsided. Still, she caught his minute hand movement and stepped silently into an alcove. Then Gina heard frantic voices at the far end of the corridor, and she moved past him fast. It was Samuel and Zachary.

Doubtless, Gina saw them before they saw her, for at her first stride they turned as one and began to run.

"Wait!" she shouted. "It's us!"

They seemed to hover between escaping and approaching, and then Samuel took a single hesitant step. "Ms. Crockett?" His voice was thin with fear. "Ms. Crockett?"

"Come up here!"

She met them halfway and gripped Samuel's shoulders so tightly he fell to his knees. "Where are the children!"

"I don't know!"

He was shaking violently—in shock—and Gina understood. She ignored guilt and made a conscious effort to loosen her hold. She calmed her tone. "Samuel, I'm sorry. Listen to me very carefully. I want you to think. Where...are...the *children*?"

He lifted trembling hands.

"I don't know, Ms. Crockett! I don't know!"

"What happened in the Hall?" Cassius asked sternly.

Samuel gasped, "W-We were waiting for your return! And then...then it came out of the north corridor. It just stood there! Staring at us! I...I didn't know what to do! Then it just walked into the room, killing everyone it could kill! Forgive me! I didn't know what to do! I grabbed Jaqual, and we ran! It was a demon!"

Frowning, Cassius held the monk's gaze. "Was it wounded?"

Samuel gaped. "Wounded?"

"Was it *injured*?"

"No, it was not injured! But it looked like it wore the robe of Dominic!"

"Dominic!" Gina hissed. "I'll kill him for this! Samuel! What happened next!"

He pointed as if the corridor were beside them. "Rebecca ran into the corridor beside the kitchen! She had the children!" He nodded and recovered—somewhat. "They were not hurt!"

Gina closed her eyes tightly to shut off tears because they wouldn't understand that it was just stress. They would misunderstand it as a sign of fear, and they didn't need any more inspiration for fear.

Straightening, Cassius lifted his torch at a hallway. "Down this hall was a sanctuary. Is it still there?"

It took Samuel a moment to understand either the question or the strangeness of it. "I believe so, yes," he answered, then added curiously, "It is very...ancient. No one is allowed there. We have never been allowed there."

When Cassius turned toward Gina, the glistening ice of his eyes was almost startling. She had never seen him like this, not even after his struggle with the Nephilim. Then, he had certainly been enraged. But what emanated from him was greater than rage—colder, more calculating, and more merciless. He was in a pure killing mode.

Even the hardest soldiers caught in life-and-death situations had a glimmer of fear in their eyes. But Cassius' eyes were pure to the center of whatever ice reflected the light.

At his mention of the sanctuary, his entire aspect altered, or, rather, it was as if a cloak had been lifted and his true essence was revealed. His brow was inspiring, his bearing noble and bold and lordly. The glint within his gaze was unconquerable.

"We'll have to double back," he stated, as if there would be no debate. "There's no good way to get there from here without going past the sanctuary."

Gina met his gaze. "What's at the sanctuary?"

"It's not safe."

It was all he said and—Gina knew—all he *would* say. But she would come back to it, guaranteed. "Fine," she said and looked at the two monks. "You guys coming?"

As if she needed to ask.

Professor Halder, Melanchthon beside him, entered Dominic's room to find it empty as the rest.

Breathless from the chaotic run from the Hall, finally finding themselves together as surrounding corridors boomed with the roar of the beast and howls of those it continued to kill, they gathered their wits and gained enough distance to recover and plan.

Melanchthon immediately spoke of Dominic and Basil, and Professor Halder had agreed that they should search both their rooms for any clue of a purpose or plan.

Halder stood guard with the MP-5, which Melanchthon had shown him how to use, as the monk roughly rifled the shelves, lifted the mattress, and opened books, only to hurl them aside.

By accident, it seemed, the monk brushed against a loose stone in the wall beside the shelves, and it fell with a dull thud to the floor. Both of them stared. A hole, previously hidden by the stone, contained a bundle wrapped in canvas, tied with a string. Melanchthon glanced cautiously at the professor.

Halder nodded.

As if he were laying his hand on a living serpent, Melanchthon slowly touched the canvas. Then he gently pulled it from the niche so that he was not forced to reach inside the blackness. He paused, then untied the string and opened it.

With the darkest aspect, Melanchthon stared. But the professor had no patience for enigmatic postures. He spoke angrily. "Speak, man! What is it?"

Melanchthon seemed shaken.

"So it comes to this...."

Entering the room, the professor stared down at a very old, discolored spearpoint. Three nails tied with threads of gold, silver, and copper held them all together as one weapon. The professor did not immediately reply, then a word came in a whisper.

"Cassius'?"

"Only Cassius will know," Melanchthon replied somberly. "I suspected it was buried within these walls, but...we were not meant to know of it. Or touch it."

What was left unspoken spoke more loudly by the manner Melanchthon tightly wrapped the spearpoint and closed his fist so tightly around it. The professor placed a hand on the monk's shoulder.

"There is no need..."

Melanchthon expressed no surprise. "I did not forsake my vow. It was the Lord who told you." He moved toward the door. "So be it! We must find him! Quickly!"

He snatched a torch from the wall and led them down a corridor, not looking to see if he was being followed.

"The children didn't run for the catacombs!" the professor shouted as they rushed forward. "They probably hid in the first room that offered protection. And Cassius will be searching for them. But so will this creature!"

"Why would this creature search for the children?" Melanchthon responded, already breathless.

"Because it will want *bait*!" The professor's certainty was contagious. "It knows Cassius will come for the children, no matter the risk! It will use the weakest to destroy the strongest!"

"Of course!" The monk's next words were a vicious growl. "Evil has its own wisdom!"

"Legend *lives* in this cursed place!"

Melanchthon's frown was bitter.

"And kills."

Without warning Cassius froze in the center of a crossroads of corridors. Head bent, he stood and listened intently. The torch pitched his shadow into the wall to his right.

Nightbringer

Watching from twenty feet away, Gina crouched with the MP-5 close. It was a formidable weapon—capable of hurling two thousand rounds a minute if the barrel didn't melt. But the best way to use it was in short bursts—squeeze and release, squeeze and release—and not to let the barrel overheat.

Subtly, she allowed herself to wonder.

Cassius—and she no longer harbored any intellectual doubt that could withstand the overwhelming force of her instincts—was, in one way, not unlike other soldiers. She'd seen it in his eyes when they had spoken and laughed.

He needed companionship. He had lived two thousand years hunting and killing creatures that were never meant to walk the earth—creatures that first made man retreat from the darkness. He was the ultimate warrior. A man so skilled, so strong, so fearless that he could have decided the fate of continents—even the world. Yet he lived in secret and fought his battles in secret—battles fought to redeem the world, and yet the world knew nothing.

She understood.

If they knew of him, they would hunt him down and destroy him. Because they would fear him.

Yes, he was utterly alone—alone in a way Gina could scarcely imagine. Because he had known centuries upon centuries of loneliness—of hiding among men, of fighting valiantly to save the human race, yet feared and even hated by the very ones he saved. She could not think of a greater curse for crucifying the Son of God, but Cassius did not seem to reckon it a curse. Either that, or, even now, he could still not count himself redeemed, and so he was resolved to fight forever to win his salvation through his own power.

She wondered what he pondered deep in the night when he could not sleep and all he had were his memories—ghosts, regrets, visions of battles fought centuries ago—before him. Watching hundreds of thousands fighting against him, thousands more fighting for him, following him as kingdom upon kingdom was saved or conquered.

Still, Cassius had not moved, and Gina moved up quietly beside him. Her voice was barely audible. "What is it?"

"It's playing for position."

Her eyes flared and she took a heavier breath.

"How close is it?"

Cassius pointed his sword to the stone ceiling. "It's moving parallel with us, stopping when we stop."

Without removing his eyes from the ceiling, Cassius lifted three extra clips from his belt and gave them to her. Gina slid two into her back pocket and one into her belt. Now she had over six hundred rounds. Her thinking was purely tactical now. "It's going to try for an ambush. Or it wouldn't be staying out of sight."

"I know."

"Or maybe it's injured."

"Maybe...but this one is using sorcery to shape-shift. It's difficult—very difficult—and maybe even beyond the power of the young one. But the old one...it could do it."

He began walking slowly forward, watching the ceiling as if he could see through the stones. He held the .45 in his right hand, the katana in a sheath at his waist.

"What's the point?" Gina whispered.

"The point is that if it is using sorcery to shape-shift, then it has the power to reduce injuries. When it shifts shape, it can alter its surface. It can eliminate shallow wounds."

Gina was so into it now that she understood the rest. "But not deep wounds," she added.

"No. If an injury is mortal, shape-shifting won't save it. It doesn't have the power of life and death. It can rearrange just its appearance. But even that takes very old sorcery—diabolical power this world doesn't even know existed."

"Like the storm," Gina muttered.

"Yes."

"How long can it keep it up?"

Her questions didn't even touch his concentration. "It took very little power to manipulate wind this high, which is all it did to cause the storm. If we were in a desert, it couldn't have done it at all."

"Why not?"

"Because sorcery isn't what you think." Cassius stopped in place, his brow hardened in concentration. "It's stopped. It's waiting."

Gina wanted to know if the storm could be reduced somehow. Anything was better than what was raging outside right now. "What do you mean about sorcery?"

"Sorcery can't create anything at all, Gina. Sorcery can only use what's already here. A spell can borrow something, open a gateway, or even influence someone to a degree. But it can't force anyone to do anything against his or her will—even the gifts of God are subject to the control of the individual.

"As far as this storm goes, this spell is only shifting winds that are already here, but even that takes wind from somewhere else. So nature will fight it, and nature will win. Nature always wins. It's just a matter of time."

Gina didn't care to add that they were almost out of time. It was ridiculous to tell him the obvious.

For a split second Cassius, or what was *him*, seemed to ascend from his body, from the corridor and the abbey, then just as quickly he reappeared behind his ice-blue, deadly eyes.

"It's gone," he whispered.

Gina caught a faint alarm in his voice. "Gone?"

"Yes."

He ran toward a staircase.

Gina matched him step for step. "How do you know?"

"I know!"

He took the stairs three at a time, and they burst together onto the fourth floor. But even before her second step, Gina knew the long corridor was empty.

"What happened!"

Cassius' face was a mold of fury. He stared in each direction.

"It heard something."

"Like what?"

"Like the others."

———

It was the strange sense of a presence that provoked Professor Halder to turn and look behind the small band led by Melanchthon's torch. He stared into the darkness as if someone had called his name. He lifted the torch higher.

"Rebecca?"

Melanchthon had turned. It took him a moment to understand, and then he leaped forward. "No!"

A thunderous roar like the blast of a hurricane erupted mere feet outside the light, and then they glimpsed a monstrous arm sweep in and sweep out with the last monk. Then they were running wildly and waving torches, and Melanchthon threw his shoulder against a door.

They did not wait for stragglers as Jaqual cascaded through the portal and Melanchthon and the professor slammed it shut. The monk shot the bolt as a fist struck the timber like a sledgehammer.

The bellow on the far side thundered with a bestial note of frustration, and it pounded the door again and again—a strong, rhythmic pounding that knew neither fatigue nor pain—relentless impacts that promised the ancient timbers would not hold for long.

"Marcus!" Jaqual cried and clutched frantically at the door. "He's outside!"

Together they pulled the hysterical monk from the bolt, hurling him into the chamber. Melanchthon bent over him, grasping his shoulder. "He's dead, boy! He's dead!"

"But—"

"No!" Melanchthon hauled him to his feet "Come! There is a passage to the Hall!"

Past weeping stones they moved to a very narrow stairwell that led upward. The sounds of cracking timbers grew louder step by step until suddenly it stopped.

Everyone spun and stared, waiting tensely. But no abomination came hurtling up the stairway. No door crashed across stones, echoing in the shadows. No, nothing—nothing but silence.

"What's this?" the professor hissed.

He began to move, but Melanchthon turned and pushed him against the wall with his greater bulk. "To go there is death, man! We will find your daughter and the children! But not along the way we came!"

The professor took a quick breath and made a decision just as quickly. "Lead!"

Together they moved up the stairway, the loudest sound the flame of their torches, and within seconds emerged in the maze of tunnels located south of the Great Hall.

Melanchthon paused, as he had also heard someone whisper his name. He stared long into the darkness. His teeth clenched angrily as he strode immediately into the darkness.

"I will not be deceived!" he bellowed, holding his spear before him. "It is using tricks! Sounds! It is not close, else it would have attacked!"

"Then what?" the professor shouted.

"It's trying to drive us from these passages!"

The professor rushed forward. "Rebecca and the children!"

In seconds they were running hard down another corridor, throwing open doors, calling to Josh and Rachel and Rebecca. Even Jaqual forgot his fear as he searched, boldly throwing open door after door, moving with astonishing agility into a corridore.

"Follow me!" Melanchthon began to descend a stairwell. "And brace yourselves like men! We will run no more!"

Josh whirled and screamed at the cascading crash that rolled through the corridor outside the door. It was the sound of a door torn completely off its hinges and hurled aside.

Again the sound repeated...and again.

"It's coming," Josh whispered as Rachel grabbed his hand and pulled him toward the far side of the room. Rebecca was attempting to unlock a door that led from the room into another. She pulled and strained at the bolt.

"Hurry!" Rachel shouted, casting a quick glance at the door. "Hurry, it's coming!"

Rebecca picked up a broken beam and struck the bolt, but it didn't move at all. She staggered back, shocked, and spun as the door on the far side of the corridor was struck with a single titanic blow. Her words died in a choked gasp.

Rachel's eyes fled the walls. "We're *trapped?*"

Rebecca reached out and pulled them close. "No!" she whispered. "We're safe! We're safe as long as we don't make a sound, okay? So be very, very quiet—both of you."

"But —"

"Shhh." Rebecca turned Josh's face into her chest. "Shhh... It'll be all right."

Josh rolled his eyes toward the door. There had been no sound since the timbers on the opposite side of the corridor shattered. "No," he said softly, "it knows we're here."

The door seemed to grow closer.

Rachel whispered, "No, Josh, it can't."

"It does."

"Josh..."

"It's coming, Rachel."

Then the atmosphere beyond the door seemed to darken somehow, as if what stood before it brought its own darkness— a darkness more substantial, heavier, and more dense than any natural darkness.

Josh whispered, "It's..."

Rebecca grabbed their heads and covered them, and Josh's last word was lost in the sound of a prehistoric beast colliding fully against the door. A force that struck without fear and without mercy—a force that would not be denied.

"Here!"

Gina spun in full stride, reacting as if she had shoved her hand into a flame—a reaction far faster and superior to conscious thought.

"Josh!"

She turned toward Cassius but there was no need. He was already descending into the stairwell four steps at a time, dropping fast and strong and balanced.

The thunderous attack upon the door did not falter a single beat, and iron hinges spiked so deeply into stone began to retreat. Then an impact on the door behind them caused them to leap away, shrieking in escalating horror.

Rebecca whirled from one to the other.

"What's happening!" Rachel screamed.

"There's two of them!" Rebecca shouted.

In the next second they were running wildly through the room, shouting incoherently, though Josh's screams proved the loudest and most frantic as he screamed for his mother.

The huge door leading into the corridor shattered midpanel, sending jagged splinters through the room like knives. The smaller door also began to splinter—slowly, inexorably.

A railroad tie in the portal shattered along its entire length, and they froze together, staring. No one moved as a blackness beyond anything they had ever known bled into the gap, and a single red eye of malignant, evil intelligence stared over them.

Fangs split in a smile.

Rachel screamed again—a scream that lasted and would last forever. Then the smaller door shattered, and they grabbed one another, all of them howling in terror, unable to run or even think as a shape appeared in the opening.

Barnabas!

Ax in hand, the old caretaker nodded once.

Behind him, one monk clutched a large bottle of liquid. Then Barnabas saw the thing that stood beyond what remained of the door on the far side of the room, and he shouted angrily in German. He cast the ax aside and fairly flung Josh into the arms of waiting monks.

"Run!" he shouted. "Now!"

Enraged at his presence, the creature bellowed—a hideous, shrilling reptilian roar—and struck the portal with such force that concrete rocketed across the room.

Nightbringer

Without another word Barnabas snatched the bottle from the monk and shattered it across the floor—and hurled his torch.

The soundless explosion rocked the walls and floor and the abbey itself. Rachel was vaguely aware of fire snaking through the shattered remnant of the doorway in what, at the moment, seemed to her so much like black fangs of a dragon.

Gasping at the superheated air, Barnabas dragged them to their feet, and they fled up the corridor. He slammed the first door they passed and bolted it, and then they were through another, and another, which he bolted one after another.

Rachel spun as somewhere far behind them, somewhere deep within the abbey, a door shattered with the rending sound of paper. She was still staring when Rebecca grabbed her hand, and she heard Josh screaming at her to hurry.

They raced, putting one door after another behind them, but the rending sounds began to stack one after another, as if the creature were splintering the doors as fast as they bolted them.

"Where are we going!" Rebecca shouted.

"Only Cassius can destroy it!"

Rebecca whirled. *"Who?"*

"There!" Barnabas shouted and pushed them quickly through a doorway where a long staircase wound up a square tower. The stairway was securely anchored to the walls, leaving a clear and unobstructed view to the top landing, six floors above.

"Hurry!" the old mason cried as a door too close fell to the fury of the beast. They rushed past Barnabas, and at the last, Rachel clearly caught the expression of true fear on his wrinkled face that only a child somehow seemed able to see.

153

Cassius selected corridors without hesitation as they rushed faster and faster through the abbey. Gina had no thought but one—she would kill *anything* to save her children.

Without even checking the doorknob, Cassius crashed through a door, sending planks flying, and didn't lose a stride as he came up against the rail of a colossal staircase that stretched into the depths of a huge square tower.

Gina looked down and saw Rachel and Rebecca and monks rushing frantically upward, trying to escape something—the beast. Then she screamed as she saw Josh sprawled across the lowest landing. He was trying to rise, but he was exhausted. He fell again, trying to reach the step. Barnabas reached down to lift Josh from the landing when—

Gina screamed again as the door behind Josh exploded into jagged planks and Barnabas was sent sprawling awkwardly across the landing and the creature entered the stairwell.

As the beast beheld Josh it howled in triumph.

"Run!" Barnabas screamed to Josh and turned into the beast, swinging the ax hard.

The creature hurled a contemptuous backhand that blasted Barnabas across the stairwell, where he hit the wall and slid to the floor.

The hideous Nephilim stood above Josh, laughing.

Rachel reached out, even as Gina reached out, though neither could reach him.

"Josh!"

Sword in hand, Cassius vaulted over the railing.

Gina screamed, *"Cassius!"*

Cassius dropped through empty space, falling faster and faster past flight after flight as the beast sixty feet below them moved solidly over Josh. It drew back a clawed hand and wasted a single moment to raise its bestial face in triumphant glee.

———

"RAPHAEL!"

The beast whirled with a curse as Cassius crashed thunderously into the base of the shaft, shattering planks that ricocheted across the entry like jagged knives. He rose up instantly, sword in one hand, the Colt .45 in the other. Instantly Cassius fired a full clip—seven big rounds—and the beast staggered, howling at the eruptions of blood and flesh from its chest. It took a single swipe before Cassius leaped across the landing, taking it completely from the stairwell and away from Josh, who pressed himself against the closest wall.

Descending fast, Gina passed Josh with only a glance to enter the corridor to see them wrestling fiendishly across the stones, revolving in a whirlwind of blows and blood and scarlet tatters.

She didn't have a shot but held aim with the MP-5 in case they separated for even a second. But they weren't separating. They were locked eye to eye, and Cassius wasn't letting it escape as he struggled to strike a single clean blow with the sword, but they were too close for the sword.

Incredibly, even beneath the snarls and roars and curses, Gina heard words hiss between them—words of a language she did not know and had never heard. Then Cassius whirled and hurled it headlong into railroad ties that splintered like twigs.

As the beast stood again, encircled by torches, Gina saw it clearly—no shadows, nothing hidden. Its face was her first sight. It was almost flat, like a man, but with large eyes that reflected red. It had wide flaring nostrils and fangs similar to an ape's. Its forehead was strangely void of the short coarse hair that covered the rest of its body, casting a humanoid aspect of dark intelligence.

Head and shoulders taller than Cassius, it was mammoth in every proportion, from the thick, sloped shoulders to massive curved pectorals that connected into wide, sweeping shoulders worthy of a wild bull. Its hands, much larger than a man's, were far thicker with long fingers that ended in black claws half again as long.

It crouched before Cassius, who still stood in Gina's line of fire, and laughed. Its voice was a ragged growl, like a human voice raked across coals to emerge scorched, blackened, torn.

"Even here...you would come for me."

"To the ends of the earth, Raphael."

Cassius' hand tightened on the sword. In the same action Raphael leaped as the sword flashed out, cutting stone from the wall in a slice of sparks. But the leap had carried Raphael beyond the bare remnant of a wall composed of more ties.

Momentarily separated from the centurion, the beast moved down the beams, poised. "You're as quick as I remember, Cassius! But not quick enough!"

Raphael's laugh was striking—each bark separated distinctly from the rest—a laugh that had built for centuries finding slow release. He smiled, "This was a trap, Cassius, if you have not realized! And you are outmatched!"

"I know of Basil," Cassius retorted spitefully. "Your game was poorly played—Dominic!"

"You know all, do you?" Raphael clearly found victory even in defeat. He cast a laughing gaze at Gina. "It does not matter! The mortals cannot help you. You are alone...against the two of us."

Raphael had almost reached the end of the beam.

Cassius awaited him.

"So be it," he answered. "The God whom you sought to destroy will decide it."

"That *I* destroyed?" Raphael roared in laughter, his fangs unhinged widely. "Have you forgotten who nailed Him to the tree, Cassius! Was it I? No! It was a *fool* of a centurion who traded salvation for the stuff of swine!"

A blur of black, and the entire section of ties was torn from the wall as Raphael struck them.

Gina saw the huge forearms upraised and knew the beast had struck with its full strength and weight. She glimpsed Cassius raising one arm against a ton of timber that crushed him to the floor as Raphael leaped forward, doubling the weight.

Then the entire corridor shook with the impact of a cannon that hit the heavy stone wall ten feet to Gina's left and she whirled, shocked. In one second she realized what was happening.

There was no door at the site of impact, and then the stone wall was hit again. Rock fell from the ceiling—the floor trembling in the wake of it with a short pause—and the next impact sent a stone weighing half a ton rocketing across the corridor like chalk.

It was *the second Nephilim*, but it didn't have a door, so it was blasting a hole through solid stone.

Training made her decision, and Gina turned and opened fire on Raphael, who crouched over Cassius. She concentrated on his stomach but couldn't prevent the barrel from rising and knew rounds struck both walls far to the side, deflected by bones.

Still, Raphael was howling, and it was all Gina could do to discern him as he twisted and retreated in the swirling smoke billowing from the torches. Then suddenly the Nephilim made an effort to move on her before Cassius roared and shifted the entire wall of ties. Gina glimpsed Cassius surging to tear a path through the ties. She fired again.

The long blast hit Raphael solidly in the chest and Gina glimpsed a huge arm, much larger, much more powerful than Raphael's battering stones from the wall to her left. As Raphael fell back, hitting the wall, Gina spun and fired thirty rounds at the second beast.

She didn't have a line to the target, so she rained lead upon the broken wall hoping to frighten it. As Raphael regained his balance, Gina whirled to hit him again. She shouted and raised the MP-5 toward the ceiling to reload as Cassius suddenly erupted from the floor, hurling off ties, standing squarely before Raphael.

Gina changed clips and spun toward the broken wall and heard Cassius shout something in Latin as a whirling, titanic battle raged less than ten feet from her back. She didn't have time to be astonished that she was not concerned—she knew Cassius would never let the beast reach her—as she fired another clip at the jagged section of wall, preventing the second Nephilim from engaging.

A sharp, wounded howl like a dog compelled Gina to turn, and she vaguely saw Raphael rush horrifically toward Cassius, who angled smoothly to the side. The katana flashed from right to left, slashing horizontally across the Nephilim's stomach.

Raphael grunted and bent double at the cut, grabbing his stomach with a forearm, and didn't turn back as he hit another door that—amazingly—slammed into the far side of the hall in a solid piece. Then the Nephilim turned and fled, vanishing into the darkness.

Cassius saw the broken section of stone, and for the first time, Gina saw fear follow shock. With his free left hand he ripped out the Colt .45 and held aim on the section and Gina followed.

Cassius didn't wait to see if there would be another attack. He moved directly into the hole, staring without any semblance of fear. If the other creature had remained, they would have been eye to eye, but nothing happened. Slowly, sweating and covered in blood—Gina couldn't discern whether it was his or Raphael's—Cassius stepped back and didn't even bother to look at the door where Raphael had fled.

But Gina couldn't handle such control. She ran to the door, dropping the second clip and inserting the third while opening the bolt again as she boldly stepped through. The corridor was long, dimly illuminated, and empty.

She stepped back into the demolished section of hallway.

Cassius shook his head and leaned, or fell, against the wall. Gina saw claw marks torn deeply across the left side of his face, and blood flowed heavily from his forearm. But without any indication of pain, Cassius wiped his left hand on his leg and removed his shirt so that he wore only a T-shirt, blue jeans, and black boots.

Gina knew he would be making a field dressing and turned back to see Josh, visually checking him for injuries because she knew, shocked as he was, it would be hours before he felt anything.

But he was fine, except for minor bruises and scrapes. Then she noticed Josh watching Cassius closely as the centurion finished the crude bandage on his forearm. As Cassius roughly wiped blood from his face, Josh walked slowly forward.

Gina didn't attempt to stop him. Whatever was happening was beyond her. And, sensing the approach, Cassius waited until Josh stopped a single small step away.

The boy whispered, "Those were real monsters, weren't they."

It wasn't a question, and Cassius gazed gently, compassionately, into Josh's eyes. He nodded softly.

"Yeah...they're real."

Unable to move now, Josh could only hug himself, and Cassius' face twisted in pain. Without hesitation he stepped forward and lifted the boy in a cable-strong arm.

Then Cassius stood solid and balanced in the center of the corridor as if he feared nothing in this world, as if nothing in this world could hurt either him or Josh. And Josh hugged him more tightly and rolled his face into his chest. "Are you gonna kill them?"

Watching, Gina saw Cassius tightly close his eyes. He lifted his face to the ceiling in what seemed like a prayer.

Cassius' effort to reach Josh before Raphael had been mythic. But, clearly, the Nephilim was stronger and faster. And now—his tightly closed eyes revealed it, though Gina was the only one to see—Cassius was no longer certain as he had been.

He bent his face closer to Josh.

"Yeah, buddy. I'm gonna kill them."

CHAPTER NINE

N one of them had failed to follow the tremendous battle being waged in the corridor two floors below their position, and Professor Halder and Melanchthon quickly gathered Rebecca, Rachel, and the scattered monks, descending.

Only when they were about to enter the area where the smoke was strongest—where the air itself seemed warmer, as if heated by the conflict—did Melanchthon pause and grab the professor's arm.

"Prepare yourself," he rumbled.

The professor needed no more. He was first through the opening, though the others were not far behind.

The wide corridor resembled a scene out of World War II after interminable bombs had been dropped on the same city night after night. It was difficult to conceive that anyone could have survived whatever destruction had raged there. Shattered stones the size of desks lay in the walkway. Stout wooden timbers were cracked as if they'd faced the relentless force of a hurricane. Everything was broken stone, shattered wood, chalklike dust with hundreds of shining gold cartridges littering it all like treasure surrounding a shipwreck.

Cassius and Gina—Josh was resting on a broken stone beside Cassius—displayed little or no emotion as they rushed forward.

Gina didn't trust herself to make more than simple greet-ings. The painful noise of the MP-5 had both deafened and angered her. Her emotions were boiling from the sheer racket and would continue—until her head stopped ringing and she regained at least a portion of hearing. It had even affected her balance so that she only trusted herself to sit and watch.

She was thankful that Cassius revealed none of the after-battle anger or impatience that she was experiencing. She wasn't surprised. He could probably fight all day and all night and still be as calm and composed as when he began. It was the first thought of genuine anger that she'd had toward him, and she knew it was just aftereffects of the fight.

As she watched the professor, Rebecca, Melanchthon, and Jaqual with the children, so joyous to be together again, she resented that they thought fighting exacted no toll, no price. She hoped they didn't expect her to share their relief too soon.

Cassius had been injured, but not as grievously as Gina had anticipated. In fact, other than the claw marks down his face and his wounded forearm, he seemed untouched. But he was injured. The fact that he wasn't moving told her that much. He continued to slowly damp a strip of his shirt on his face. The blood flow had almost ceased.

"We go back to the hall now?" Gina didn't realize she was shouting until she finished.

Cassius glanced at her and nodded mildly. Then he stood holding the katana and the Colt .45.

"Okay!" he said loudly enough to gain their attention. He pointed with the katana. "We go up this staircase! I'll take the lead, and Gina will guard the rear! We'll move safe and slow back to the Hall! Does everyone understand?"

They nodded enthusiastically.

To release a little anger—*at least he's human*, Gina thought—Cassius kicked what remained of the shattered door out of the way as he mounted the stairwell. Gina made impatient gestures and commands as the others followed.

She made certain that the children, Melanchthon and Jaqual beside them, were last so that she was close enough to protect them. She didn't know if they'd be attacked again before they reached the Hall. Anything was possible.

The huge broken section of stone wall was the last thing Gina saw as she entered the stairwell. Whatever had hit that section was far, far beyond Raphael's power.

Retreating from the corridor with the MP-5, she gazed once more over the carnage. Her head was clearing faster now, and she could once again feel her heart.

And the fear within it.

The return to the Hall was mercifully without incident, and none of them wasted any time in drinking and eating everything they hauled from the nearby kitchen where no less than six of the ten surviving monks stood guard with spears.

Poor Jaqual was almost frantic as he alone scurried back and forth with plates of heavy fruit and, finally, a roast, retrieving bottle after bottle of water and wine. Gina almost felt sorry for him and petitioned for him to sit and rest. But the monk was apparently working out whatever nervous energy remained and demurely resisted her protestations.

Finally Melanchthon made him sit and rest and eat. Gina wasn't sure if the old monk had done it for Jaqual or himself. She only knew that Jaqual's repetitive ministrations had begun to grate on her nerves.

Only Cassius, having laid his weapons to the side, was not approached for any embrace, for when they entered the hall, he displayed no emotion and inspired none. He simply walked, cold and stoic, to the table and removed his weapons and began rewrapping the bandage on his arm.

The others seemed to have dismissed his presence. And their demeanor said what words did not. Though it had not been revealed, they knew who he was. She could see it in the way they all but bowed before him when he passed to claim a bottle of wine. They had retreated or bent their faces or clasped hands in silence, though Cassius seemed not to notice. He had taken bread as well and walked back to the table, where he continued to work alone.

It was indeed a far cry from the rest who encouraged and supported one another as if there were now no threat.

Yeah, Gina thought, *it's one thing to be lost and alone in the catacombs of this place. It's another to be surrounded by friends, supported emotionally and physically, though the reason to fear remained the same.* But she also knew that numbers were false security. There was only one man in the Hall who offered any hope for survival, and he rested alone at the north corridor.

When she looked toward him again, Cassius had finished rewrapping the bandage. And as Gina watched him more closely, she saw that he had quickly recovered whatever strength he seemed to have spent in his encounter with Raphael.

Gina's cold, surgical ability to evaluate—inculcated so deeply within her—was not a hindrance anymore. She had seen this man drop sixty feet to shatter a wooden floor with the impact and then rise up almost instantly to engage a Nephilim in physical combat.

She had heard them speak so hatefully to each other, and someone can only hate what they know. Finally Gina rose and walked to him and sat casually on the table. She stretched out a bottle of water. "Want some?"

Cassius smiled and accepted the bottle and drank heavily. "Thanks." He handed it to her. "This heat can wear you out."

"Amazing, isn't it?" Gina muttered. "An ice age outside, hell inside."

He only laughed, and Gina waited. Then, "I don't think I ever thanked you for saving my life. So...thank you. And thank you for saving Josh's life."

Emotion caused Gina to suddenly tighten her face. She blinked and quickly wiped a hand over her cheek. Cassius, if he noticed, gave no indications.

"Is he all right?" he asked casually.

"He's fine—just scared." She smiled again. "About like me. How about you?"

He smiled faintly. "I'm fine."

"What about your arm?"

"Just muscle." He suddenly frowned. "Pain is just pain— you can live with it, fight with it."

Yeah, he's in bad pain. So cold...so indifferent to his own life or death...but he risked everything to save Josh....

She began quietly, "You don't have to talk if you don't want to, but I'll listen, if you do." When he said nothing, she said, "I saw you snap an iron bar like a twig, Cassius. I saw you drop sixty feet without breaking a bone. And so did they." She paused. "I'm sorry about the stairway. I called you...by your name again. I was...so scared for Josh. I only had one thing in my mind."

He shook his head. "It's okay, Gina—doesn't matter. It was coming a long way off." A sigh. "Nothing matters now, except getting all of you out of here."

"I understand you doing the tourist thing with us, Cassius. The best way to reach any destination—for you—is to go in a group. You attract less attention that way. So I don't resent that you came here with us. But, somehow, I don't think you ever expected this."

He barked a harsh laugh. "No...no, I didn't."

"What *did* you expect?"

His frustration was visible. "I just came here to make sure that something remained undisturbed—something I placed here long ago. No one would have known anything, then I would have left with you and probably shown you a good tour of Rome."

Eyes softening, Gina blinked once, sadly. "I would have liked that."

Strangely, he made no effort to hide his emotion. "Me too."

The question couldn't be withheld.

"You never—"

"Not anymore." He cut her off. "I've made enough mistakes." He became more pensive. "Once, I tried to live like a man. It was too good. I was a monarch.... I ruled a kingdom, at peace with God. But people grow old...they die. Even children grow, and they wonder why you seem not to have aged. And one day the dream is over. Now I only want to live long enough."

He stared at the ceiling.

"So you have no one?"

He shook his head.

"Did they know? Your wife? Children?"

"My wife knew. My children didn't know until the last. But I saw them when they were old and comforted them. I didn't want them to die uncertain of...some things."

He sighed, as if knowing Gina's mind.

"No, she had no regrets. She grew old gracefully, peacefully, and was glad of the years we'd had together. She knew from the first that I wouldn't grow old and die, but—" He surprised Gina with a soft laugh. "—she said it was *her* advantage, not mine."

Gina leaned back against a square column, gazing at a distant corridor that led into the Hall. She wasn't surprised that she did not fear to see the creatures.

"Sounds nice," she said.

Faintly, she noticed Cassius was gazing in her direction, but not quite. He was looking at her, but past her, and she knew he was thinking. But she regretted what she'd said because she felt she had imposed upon him, or made this more difficult for him.

"I need to get back to the kids."

He said nothing as she walked away.

The festive mood had faded, suspicions had been slowly cornered, and then the discussion went from the practical and understandable to the fantastic and incomprehensible.

Gina watched as Father Stephen and Melanchthon faced off, as if in an arena. Melanchthon's doom-like voice projected forthright anger and even condemnation.

"I warned you of this!" he said solidly, pointing at the father abbot. "I warned you that lives were in danger and still you refused to act! And now, every body laid at death's door will likewise lie heavily upon your shoulders!"

"Legends!" Stephen retorted, struggling to contain true rage. "No man can be expected to believe the impossible!"

From beside his place at the radio, Monsignor DeMarco rose angrily and stepped between them. "That's enough! Both of you will calm down or I will ensure that your next assignments are in the middle of the Sahara Desert! Right now we should not place blame but find some means of dealing with whatever has come!" He took a breath. "Now, do either of you have anything constructive to say?"

Only Barnabas remained outside the fray.

Gina looked toward him and saw that he had removed the armor of the centurion and was polishing the breastplate, oblivious to the tension and discussion. The cloak rested across an ornamental couch, and the sword had been unsheathed. The silver blade was as finely honed as a razor. Intent upon his work, Barnabas did not even lift his head at the harsh words that crossed before the altar.

The monsignor had taken control. "I no longer doubt that this creature is a Nephilim any more than I doubt that he has concealed himself within this abbey for centuries! But that is not my primary concern! My primary concern is to make this radio functional and summon assistance! There is plenty of time for accusations if we survive!"

"Melanchthon!" Professor Halder said forcefully. "Tell them what we discovered in Dominic's room!"

"We found what *may* be the Spear of Destiny," he said quietly. "The spearpoint of Gaius Cassius Longinus."

The implications, as far as Gina could determine, were incalculable. But she didn't know what they were. She could only see the genuine fear upon every face.

"Are you certain?" asked the monsignor.

"No."

"Let me see it. I will know."

Without an air of grave ceremony, Melanchthon removed an object wrapped in brown sackcloth from his habit. He laid it upon a table and untied the string. When he threw back the cloth, a large and obviously ancient spearpoint was visible.

Almost as long as Gina's forearm, the spearpoint was badly aged. It seemed frail as shale and was wrapped in tightly closed copper wire that also held three long iron nails. The nails were black and rusted and seemed equally as ancient, equally as frail.

None spoke, and Gina glanced at Cassius. He was paying no attention to the activity, which surprised her. Perhaps he was unaware. Then she laughed lightly at the thought. Cassius was never unaware—not of anything.

Finally Melanchthon spoke. "I do not know if it is, in truth, the Spear of Destiny. I only know that it is what I have read of—a spearpoint with nails taken from the crucifix attached to it with copper and gold and silver. It is supposedly the spear of the high priest, Caiaphas, which he gave to the captain of the temple guard. The spear that Cassius took from the captain's hand on Golgotha."

Gina was impressed that the monk did not look in Cassius' direction. But the others were not so controlled. Several of the monks passed more than one glance toward the lone figure.

It was enough.

The monsignor's words were forthright. Nor did the pro-foundly formal tone seem out of place. "It is time for truth!" He turned and stared fully upon Cassius and extended his arm. "I abjure you by Almighty God: Are you Gaius Cassius Longinus, the centurion who crucified the Son of God?"

Cassius did not move, nor did he give any indication of surprise or anger. Then his dangerous eyes rose, and he gazed with what seemed like judgment upon the monsignor.

That everyone did not run screaming through the room seemed a most remarkable thing to Gina. She felt her heart racing, felt sweat upon her palms and rubbed them on her legs. A glance at Rachel and Josh told her that they were the only ones not terrified. In fact, they seemed encouraged by

Cassius' demeanor, regardless of the implications. Both of them turned their gaze to the centurion.

With a stern effort Gina took a deep breath and held it, reducing the oxygen in her blood, erasing the tunnel vision that encircled all that she could see.

From everything Cassius had done since the battle began, the answer was obvious. Those who respected, or feared him, did not wish for Cassius to answer, and he knew it. Only those who wished to know for a purpose other than survival would have demanded that he speak, and Gina knew it was time.

Her words were certain with the kind of quiet someone uses when they acknowledge a betrayal of love. "The spear is why you opened this abbey in the first place, isn't it, Monsignor?"

The monsignor scowled. "What, Ms. Crockett?"

"You heard."

"Yes. I heard your question. Which is no question, as you well know. Yes, some seek the spear for they believe that the ancient relics contain power."

"Like you?"

"No," he said flatly. "No, I am wiser than that. And as we discussed earlier, I was a skeptic. I did not believe these walls contained anything but weapons, chariots, statues—a wealth of treasures, to be sure, but not the treasure they sought."

Gina stared. "Which is?"

"Which is nothing anyone needs to possess," Cassius said beside her, and Gina's heart leaped.

He had moved silently across the Hall, but she had not seen or sensed him. And neither, apparently, had the others, who reacted with even more alacrity. With the air of a commander, Cassius gave Gina the reloaded MP-5 and a belt of fresh clips.

Cassius turned to the monsignor, and the monsignor involuntarily stepped back, though Cassius made no sign of approaching.

In the moment that lasted, Cassius seemed revealed in an entirety that only Gina had witnessed. He was imperious and lordly—a king among them who held their lives or deaths in his grasp. No one spoke as Cassius cast a long gaze.

Melanchthon did not raise his face. Father Stephen cast his cowl over his head, and Jaqual fell to his knees, hands folded, face bent. Then Gina saw Josh and Rachel. They were glancing to the monks, to Cassius, back again. But even Josh sensed the power, the fear of the moment, and didn't speak.

Cassius' voice was the tone of stone intoning a deep resonance of strength, as though he had dipped his hand into an abyss of immortal might that he summoned at will.

"Don't be afraid.... For I am Gaius Cassius Longinus, the centurion who crucified the Son of the Living God. I was once a soldier of Rome. But I serve in another army now. And if by my life or death I can save you...I will."

It was easier to deal with the situation, Gina discovered, by simply watching and listening—at least until her mind no longer reacted against the thought that Cassius was the two-thousand-year-old centurion who crucified Jesus. And as she listened to the professor and Cassius discuss the situation, she found reason to make the impossible seem less impossible.

Cassius knew all there was to know of these creatures. Clearly, he had hunted and killed them for centuries. He knew their habits as any good hunter would know the habits of his prey. He knew their limitations, their instinctive reactions, preferred tactics, and could anticipate what they would do—to a point. But he was also honest enough to admit that they were ultimately unpredictable.

Although the initial discussion focused on the Nephilim, it was not long before it spiraled out to embrace other subjects, as if Cassius realized that further discussion of the creatures only fueled their already heated fears. And Gina noticed several of the others—Melanchthon, Jaqual, and Monsignor DeMarco—as they appeared on the edge of the group, listening attentively.

The casual, easy manner in which Cassius described historical events was genuinely fascinating. He described the fall of Rome, the rise of continents, lost civilizations, abandoned cities the world was not fortunate enough to remember. He discussed the founding of the New World and, he added, that Christopher Columbus was the only person who *hadn't* seen America when it was "discovered." He spoke with intimate knowledge of the Celts, the Druids, Julius Caesar, Genghis Khan, Hitler, and a dozen more characters who were only partially captured by historians.

Gina was intrigued that Cassius had never contributed anything to man's memory of history, not even anonymously, and wished to know why.

Cassius sighed. "I saw events unfold through my eyes just as others saw them through their eyes. We all had our prejudices, our philosophies. I don't know that my memories are better than the next man."

Staring into flames within the hearth, the professor laughed. "How true—no one man comes to history with a blank page. We come with what we have already decided is true."

"Yes," agreed Cassius, "but I've read your work, Professor. You have an ability for impartial analysis that escapes most so-called historians." He laughed. "I've seen history rewritten a hundred times, and each time the evil and the good have changed. But, as far as I could discern, you simply described events as accurately as historical documents and physical evidence allowed."

The professor was stunned by the quiet comment, but Cassius did not seem to notice as he continued. "But still you err in understanding the fall of Rome."

"Describe it to me," said Halder, rapt now.

"People look at Rome's decline in population, the disintegration of the army in the second century, the plague that wiped out half the city under Marcus Aurelius, and these were forces of the decline. But those events were as nothing. Rome would have survived—it had survived worse. Yes, Rome fell because its god fell—a god named Caesar.

"In the end, even legions turned on one another—those who worshiped the Christian God and those who remained loyal to Caesar." Cassius grew more still. "Rome could have survived anything but the Messiah. But Christianity was the one thing no army could overcome—a kingdom beyond this world that made all authority and suffering as nothing when compared to the glory of it.

"Rome simply did not know how to deal with a religion that denied the ultimate reality of this world. Killing was no answer because it did nothing to affect what Christians claimed to possess."

"When did you come to believe?" the professor asked.

"I began to wonder as I watched Him day after day. I don't know how anyone could watch Him...and not wonder. Then He was brought before Pilate." Cassius shook his head. "I had never seen Pilate tremble. But he trembled before this beggar—this homeless, wandering Jew. And he was not alone."

Cassius expelled a hard breath. "A crucifixion is the most painful death that any man could ever suffer. It was meant to deter others from attempting the same crime. I'll spare you the details. Your English word *excruciating* is taken from the Latin *crucifix*.

"I expected Him to die before we ever reached Golgotha. But His strength was so great He would not die until He decided. Everything that happened up the Via della Rosa was just a doomed attempt to make Him ask, just once, for mercy. But He never spoke, as I knew He wouldn't. Because by then I knew this man would overcome death on that hill as He had overcome everything else."

The crackling of flames was the only sound, and Gina's mind returned to something else. "You said you only wanted to live long enough.... Long enough for what?"

Cassius frowned. "That has nothing to do with this. I will kill this beast. He's escaped me too many times. And he's inflicted far too much harm on the world."

He held the katana close, the .45 at his side. Gina felt confident that he stood a good chance against the creature with the weapons. But in hand-to-hand combat, he stood no chance at all.

"How much longer before we know about the radio?"

"The monsignor says the components are made to adapt," Gina answered numbly. "He's hopeful, but I don't know...."

"It'll be night in five hours. If it's not fixed before night, we'll need to barricade the room as much as possible. Its power is greater at night."

"Why?"

"Night plays well with its preferred methods for stalking and attacking." He nodded at the tunnels. "It can see in the dark as well as we see in the day. And it will take risks in the dark that it won't take in the light. But out here we have the advantage of the light. We don't need to lose that."

Jaqual bent slowly over Josh and Rachel and motioned to the table, where he'd prepared a meal for them. Gina smiled thankfully at the young monk, and then the kids rose and walked, quite content, across the Hall. Cassius watched them leave before he spoke. "Do you ever wonder why children are instinctively afraid of the dark?"

"Yes...I have."

"Because memories live longer than the conscious mind," he said quietly. "And some memories are older than the mind itself."

When no one spoke, Cassius continued. "Just as the Jews have a strange, intimate understanding of God that other races seem to somehow lack—racial memory, they call it—there are things in everyone's mind that are older than years. Just as poets wrote of neuroses, obsessions, and their psychological effects hundreds of years before science followed, the heart knows things that science will never comprehend.

"We fear the darkness because the darkness once contained the source of our greatest fear—a fear that has been suppressed, but never completely vanquished, from the deepest part of our being. We fear the darkness because *it* was once out there in the darkness—stalking us, waiting for us, watching us.

"Nightbringer, they called it, and the fear of it was so great that generation after generation inherited that fear in a thousand ways and passed it on in a thousand ways to generation after generation. Now men say they're too rational to fear the darkness. What they don't know is that the part of them that fears the darkness is beneath their mind."

Gina sighed and lowered her face to her knee. "But most of the Nephilim are dead, Cassius."

"Most of them," he agreed. "But even if I killed the last, there is always the chance that another would be born."

"I don't understand that at all," Gina murmured. "These things are as old as you? Don't they ever die?"

"They die—eventually. But their years are beyond my knowledge. I've killed Nephilim born in the days of Jericho, and some no older than a century. The old ones are the most dangerous because they understand the secrets of sorcery."

Gina felt confident enough to say, "If God is God, then why didn't He simply prevent these creatures from ever existing? They're evil, right?" She raised her hand. "Wait—I know they're evil. The question is: Why did God allow them to inhabit the earth?"

It was obviously a question Cassius had heard and even asked before. "Why is there suffering?" he answered finally. "Why did God create Satan? What good purpose have these creatures served in a world that was not—is not—theirs?"

He paused a long time. "I believe Satan is as beyond the understanding of the most brilliant man or woman as God is *within* the understanding of the simplest child."

No one spoke, and finally Cassius placed a hand upon his sword and stood. He took a deep breath, staring into the tunnel and the entrance to the catacombs. "I'm going to make a quick circuit of the corridors." He looked at Gina as she raised her face. "I won't be long."

Gina didn't like it but knew it would do no good to dispute it with him. This was beyond her—all of it. Besides that, she didn't want to leave the children alone any more than necessary. She nodded.

"Keep the MP-5 and let Melanchthon have the other. If it gets past me—"

"It won't." Gina smiled tightly.

"You bet."

With that he turned into the tunnel with the .45 in hand and the sheath of the sword pushed through his belt.

Only at the very end, when he was within the very shadow of darkness, did he stop. He stared into the gaping black as if it were the jaws of a dragon and racked the slide of the .45. Then, without looking back at all, vanished into the corridor.

When he returned, his face glistened with sweat, his form possessed a great aura of fatigue, and Gina restrained herself from asking what horror he had beheld.

———

In the aftermath of what Gina could only classify as some-thing beyond, everyone worked with a far steadier calm, a far greater courage. Gina saw it in the way they spoke concisely and businesslike, securing the entrances, assisting the monsi-gnor, tending to the wounded.

And if they had never witnessed hero worship, they had the opportunity to see it personified in the eyes of Josh and Rachel as they shadowed Cassius' every move. Even now, Josh sat upon the table that had been so avoided earlier, asking Cassius question after question, which he continued to answer patiently, more often than not finding humor in the endless dialogue. Rachel, attempting to be more mature, asked Josh to "cease and desist," but the nine-year-old boy didn't seem to respect the authority of his sister anymore.

Worried that Cassius might eventually become annoyed, Gina continued to search his face, but his smile was easy and unforced. Nor did he seem imperious, as she knew he could be. He was almost like an uncle—someone who dropped in to tell fascinating stories and promised to return. She didn't know what Cassius was speaking of now, but she heard plenty of "oohs" and "ahhs" to judge the entertainment value.

Gina knew he was simply taking their minds from the situation, and she was more grateful than she could communicate. So she continued to check progress on the radio—less than three hours, the monsignor reported—and ensure that the monks were safe.

As she exited the kitchen, the Hall seemed to glow with an atmosphere not created by the lamps. She saw easy smiles and friendship and encouragement flowing like light. Where some had been crippled with despair, they worked strongly, confidently. Others, previously terrified beyond encouragement, were encouraging others.

Gina enjoyed her smile. It was amazing the difference a hero could make. But she was tired, deathly tired, and she knew it was because she could finally relax. She didn't want to sleep, but to rest her eyes, and lay down on a blanket spread across the dais. Laying down the MP-5, she closed her eyes for just...a little rest....

She took heavy, comforting breaths....

She saw the people, all wrapped in gray against a black sky and low black clouds. But she was not dressed as they were. No, she still wore the clothes she had worn in the abbey. Nor could she feel the sheets of ice that washed across the sky casting light only because of the torches raised from the hundreds and hundreds who wept and moaned as if they had lost a father.

Old men, holding torches aloft, were white with fear and did not move, as if they did not trust their legs not to collapse, and yet they could not turn their eyes from the low hill before them.

Gina looked to the hill and saw Roman soldiers working quickly over a man who lay upon a crucifix. The man seemed no different from any other—neither comely nor unsightly—but not an inch of His body was unstained by the blood ever deeper than the royal red robes of the Roman soldiers. She could not clearly see the man's face but noticed a black ring of thorns crowning His head.

Thunder emerged from the core of the earth, and sprawling spiderwebs of lightning flashed across the sky as if innumerable angels slashed in rage to tear through the clouds.

Never had Gina seen such an awesome display of fire so far beyond anything man could conjure. For if all the cities in the world had been set aflame at once, they would have paled against it. She looked back at the haunting, surreal scene on the mound.

The soldiers had finished, and one of them—a man who seemed stronger than the rest—made an angry gesture to the others. Though Gina could not discern the Latin words, she recognized harsh anger in his voice and knew he was terrified for some reason.

Without patience he struck the soldiers, ordering them to raise the crucifix quickly as lightning cascaded from heaven to earth and the air solidified with thunder. And the soldiers complied, immediately lifting the crucifix with ropes so that it stood between two more crucifixes where two men already hung in agony.

As it was lifted, hundreds fell to their knees in the mud, crying aloud, praying for death. Gina looked back toward the old man who had held the torch. He, too, was upon his knees, and then he sat back, the torch held so that no light shone.

Across the field itself a thousand more were spread headlong, blind to anything but the black water and the stench of this graveyard. Even children, who surely could not have known this man, were motionless, hands clasped tightly before them.

Gina looked back at the mound as the centurion whirled with a bolt of lightning that flashed from sky to earth so close that the sound struck with the light. And in the blazing, blinding instant Gina thought she herself had been struck and was dully amazed how she did not feel the wind that lifted shawl and cloak, the ice-rain that beat people to the ground, or the mud that enclosed her feet. Yet she felt their fear—a fear so complete she could not move.

Upon the hill that resembled the white of a skull, the centurion continued to pace, unable to remain still. Nor did he speak as the three Roman soldiers about him finally fled the hill in fear, leaving their spears behind. They brutally knocked aside those who stood at the base and in moments were lost in the throng.

Gina knew....

She looked directly into the face of the man who hung upon the center crucifix. His entire body was black now with blood, streaked with red only from fresh wounds, and the crown of thorns had not been dislodged. It was amazing that He was still alive, but He *was* alive because His eyes, so completely unreadable, stared over the crowd.

Gina tried hard to read a single thought in those eyes. But she didn't want Him to look upon her—no, certainly not her. And there was no reason why He should. She was only one among a thousand here, and she did not even belong.

And then He looked upon her.

It was strange—His gaze. His eyes were dark beneath, like a man weary with suffering. But there was no pain as Gina recognized pain. No, His gaze was pure, somehow, with a knowledge and compassion beyond understanding. Even now, she thought, it was as if He held the end of all things in His power, as if He knew everything and feared nothing, but felt the pain of those surrounding Him so deeply that no expression upon the earth was sufficient for His thoughts. And yet it was an expression so far different from those who felt nothing. No, it was the expression of one who so well knew the heart and mind and suffering of everyone before Him that His very substance was suffering.

Gina had wondered what it would be like to stare into the eyes of God...and now she knew. Just as she knew that if the man had wished, that crucifix would have instantly sprouted leafy green branches, and roots would have instantly stretched far into the earth. But what He was doing could not be done with life. So He was here to endure this as He endured every-thing else—for a purpose only He knew.

She almost stepped forward to scream at Him—to tell Him to change all this because He had the power! But His dark eyes only narrowed as the thought crossed her mind, and He smiled.

He would do as He would do.

Anger, rage, then despair were all Gina felt as the crowd continued to writhe upon the ground. But she did not care or notice them any longer. *This* was the Hour of Darkness, and if they could not at least stand on their feet for His last hour, they deserved what they received. But she would not fall. She would stay with Him until the hour had passed.

Imperial shouts parted the crowd as dozens of soldiers wearing purple and yellow shouldered their way to the cruci-fix. And Gina saw the man nod faintly—a nod not of approval, but satisfaction. Then Jesus raised His face to the sky and roared—a roar that struck the place where thunder began, and thunder returned from the cosmos in response, tearing apart the clouds to separate them as though God had blown a breath that could have laid the earth open to the marrow.

The centurion turned to gaze upon the gigantic display of strength that mocked the crucifix, the nails, the blood, and the power of the man at once. It was such a display that hundreds fell back, and even the centurion fell to a knee, staring up and uttering words that could not be heard. Then the thunder rolling through cloud and space faded quickly into the distance, and Gina was aware of nothing but a dead man hanging upon the crucifix and rain, falling gently, tears of the earth.

Never had she heard a silence as the silence of that moment. In all creation—as far as she could see—all eyes were upon the man, and no one spoke. Nor, as she faintly anticipated, did anyone move. It was as if they had been struck eternally immobile and would never, for the rest of their lives, leave this moment.

Movement...she looked as the huge soldiers mounted the base of the Hill of the Skull. Armed with spear and sword, they assumed control of the mound despite the centurion who stood alone at the base of the crucifix, staring angrily.

Gina heard the words clearly.

"We have come to break the legs of the one called Messiah!" the captain of the temple guard proclaimed. "Caiaphas insists that we ensure He is dead!"

The centurion gazed over them.

"You cannot pass," he said.

The captain stepped forward. "Think not to defy us, Cassius! If He is dead, then your duty here is done! And, according to law, you have no further authority!"

"Yes," the centurion answered and drew his sword, "that is the law. But we have broken the greatest law today, so no other laws matter."

"You are a Roman. You have no right to protect His body, Cassius."

"You had no right to crucify Him, and yet you did." Cassius' eyes were saddened, and he shook his head. "I say again—you cannot pass."

At that, the captain looked over the mound. "Have you noticed, Cassius, that you are alone? Your men were not so stout of heart!"

Cassius said nothing.

"No more talk!" The captain made a rushing gesture to the thirty soldiers behind him. "Take him!"

With a long leap and the flashing hum of his sword, Cassius split the breastplate of the captain who dropped his spear and plummeted into the men behind him. And, as if the temple guards had been confronted by a legion, they quickly backed in a wide semicircle, half ascended upon the mound, half ringing this side of the hill.

Cassius stood where he had stood, sword raised. His voice was filled with a rage Gina would have expected to have come from the man who hung upon the crucifix...had He been just a man.

"Touch Him and die!" he snarled, lowering the sword for another blow. He stared savagely over them, face twisted.

Gina was still unable to see his eyes, but she knew that his voice was pure and without doubt.

"The first and last man to touch His body will go with Him to wherever He has gone!"

The guards hesitated and looked to one another.

"You exceed your authority!" The captain was tightly holding a hand against his chest. "I say it *again*! It is *forbidden* for anyone to interfere with our rituals! For even a centurion!"

"From this hour I am no longer a centurion!" Cassius shouted in a voice that swelled and fell over surrounding hills. "From this hour I am a servant of the Son of God who hangs upon this crucifix!" He held their hostile gaze. "Will you die for Him?"

"Will *you*?" shouted the captain.

"Yes!"

Even from where she stood, Gina felt the rage like invisible fire spreading from the mound, sweeping out with the speed of lightning to wash over everyone who watched or heard.

"Take him!" the captain commanded.

Thirty men were instantly clawing and scrambling up the mound to battle the centurion, and the centurion descended to meet them. His slashing brand sent three of them reeling at once, sliding into the rain-soaked field, and Gina heard screams and howls of men grievously wounded. She knew that the centurion and the temple guards would die now because neither would retreat.

Then the centurion cast his sword aside and snatched up a spear—his or the captain's, Gina didn't know—and thrust it into the side of the man who hung upon the crucifix.

From a distance, it appeared that water and blood erupted from the wound, drenching the centurion. And at the impact the centurion cried out and staggered back. Then he fell heavily to a knee before struggling to gain his feet, roaring with shock and pain as he stood. He whirled instantly into the captain of the temple guard, spear held tightly in both hands.

"You said Caiaphas ordered you to break His legs to ensure He was dead!" Cassius shouted so that all could hear. "But I just proved He is *already dead*! You no longer have a reason to break His bones! Unless you wish only to break the words of your prophets!"

The captain of the temple guard glanced to the sudden chorus of angry voices that swelled from the hundreds surrounding the crucifix—voices that were immediately amplified by other voices and still others so that a riot began to rise.

Cassius stood, poised for battle.

The captain glanced nervously to the crowd.

With a quick gesture—as if he did not even want *word of this* to spread—the captain ordered his men to follow him through the crowd. Gina wondered if they would be attacked by the surrounding mob. But they roughly shouldered their way through the crowd as if they feared nothing, though she knew they feared because they wasted no time in their retreat.

Afterward, Cassius stood alone upon the hill at the base of the crucifix, still holding the spear. He did not raise his head again to Jesus but, with a strange expression, lifted his wounded hand, staring. Then he scowled before raising his face to gaze upon the crowd, as if he had not previously noticed them. Only when a group of older men slowly climbed the hill did the centurion lower his gaze, as if remembering where he stood.

"What do you desire?" he asked, and it seemed that he would collapse.

A big man with a flowing white beard and a tunic worn only by the very rich replied humbly, "I am Josephus. I have prepared a tomb for Messiah. I ask only for your permission to remove His body from this cursed place, for cursed is any man that hangs upon a tree past sunset, and bury Him, as our rites require. We shall gently care for Him, nor shall a bone be broken."

Cassius stared into the old man's eyes and nodded. "Take Him...and bury Him as your ritual requires."

Slowly the old men moved farther up the hill as the centurion, still holding the spear, walked down the mound. The crowd parted reverently, though many hesitantly reached out to touch his cloak. Many fell to their knees. Women moaned. Children stood frozen with fright. Old and strong men wept.

Holding the spear so that it did not touch the ground, Cassius passed Gina with steps made solemn with sadness, pure with purpose. Then he removed his helmet and cast it to the mud so that Gina recognized the ice-blue eyes, weary now with weariness like death—the familiar, sad bend of his head.

Cassius...

A hideous bellow from somewhere deep within the abbey brought them together to their feet. Then the bellow was followed by a scream that continued on and on and on until the children raised their hands to cover their heads and fell to the floor.

Gina was struggling to awaken—deep inside slumber—and snatched up the MP-5. It took her another moment to clear her head—*Yes!*

Livid, she spun to Melanchthon. "Who's not here!"

It took him only a moment. "Barnabas!" Melanchthon pounced on Jaqual. "Where's Barnabas!"

Jaqual dropped a bottle of wine, stammered, "H-He—"

"Speak, boy!" Melanchthon roared.

"He-He went for more food! Only a second—"

"Foolish old man!" Melanchthon bawled and snatched up a spear. He spun toward Cassius, just as Gina did, to see Josh and Rachel, alone and in shock, at the table.

Cassius was gone.

Frantic shouts erupted everywhere, and Gina learned that Cassius had moved with the first cry, snatching up the katana and his Colt .45 and within seconds was in the corridor that boomed with the sound.

"He said don't follow him!" Rachel and Josh screamed at once. "He said for nobody to follow him!"

Exactly what she expected, but Gina couldn't do it—not with the sound so close. Still, she had to ensure that the children remained safe. The professor was before her.

"Give me a weapon!" he said quickly. "I'll watch the children!"

"Here!" Gina threw the SIG to the professor and tore out the MP-5 as she grabbed a torch. She spun to Melanchthon. "I can't let him go alone! If Cassius dies, *we all die*!"

The monk snatched up a spear.

"We go!"

The howls continued as Gina, Melanchthon close behind her, descended far into the corridor, angling quickly around corners with less caution than she would have preferred. But from the distance of the cries she knew they weren't even close to the creature. Yet in another five minutes they were in the center of what happened, and she held out an arm to slow Melanchthon, who obeyed instantly.

A strange thought passed through Gina's mind—the kind of thought that happens even in life-and-death situations—that the monk would have made a good FBI agent. Then she saw a cave-like tunnel completely unlike the rest.

"The catacombs," Melanchthon rumbled. Sweat glistened silver on his face, framed by his white hair. "It's the only entrance. But there are twenty miles of tunnels."

The screams had ceased, and Gina felt a distinct temptation to retreat back into the Hall. But if they were even close to one of the creatures now, which was likely, maybe she could get a clear shot with the MP-5 and do more damage. The memory of how fast it moved in the stairway flashed across her vision.

No time to debate. She moved into the tunnel, sweeping left and right to the corridors that instantly sprawled into the vastness of the catacombs. Somehow she managed to ignore the bones resting in crude niches, the gaping mouths of skulls, the depthless black eyes.

By reflex she searched the floor for a sign of direction, but all she read were multitudinous tracks of hundreds who had walked through here across centuries. Only then did it occur to her that tracks in this place would never vanish because there was no wind, no rain.

She whirled, crouching.

A sound...

She'd seen this creature move. It was incredibly fast and struck but once to kill. So if she didn't catch it when it was at least a hundred feet away, then it would survive the onslaught of the MP-5 to kill her and Melanchthon together. Even a human being could travel twenty feet after they'd been mortally wounded—this thing could easily triple that.

A scrape...

Gina shouted as she spun.

In a well of torn gray clothing and a widening black pool, Barnabas lay unmoving.

"Barnabas!" Gina shouted as she pitched forward and was over the old man. She saw at once that he was wounded.

Melanchthon knelt beside him and, despite the obvious lightness of his wounds, felt along them. Even at the slight touch, Barnabas moaned, and Melanchthon bowed his head, quickly working to bind up the old monk's wounds.

"Barnabas!" Gina said loudly enough to get the old man's attention. At a faint stir, Gina leaned closer. "Was it the same Nephilim that Cassius fought on the ledge? Could you see?"

Nightbringer

Rubbing his neck, Barnabas groggily formed a reply. Gina waited without a breath. "It was...another."

Then the answer continued in a long breath, and whatever animation remained in the old man's eyes froze over like frost over glass. No one needed to say it, and no one did. Slowly she and Melanchthon stood, staring down, and Gina shook her head.

"Come on." She held the MP-5 closer as she turned. "Let's get out of—"

Dreaming, Gina wondered why light wavered across the ceiling, why she was floating.

She heard a howl and a roar and felt her face against dirt. Dust rose around her, and she wondered why she wasn't standing, and some reflex told her she'd been hit. She cried out, rolled, and saw shadows wrestling across the ceiling.

No...not the ceiling.

She didn't know what had happened, but whatever had happened was horrifying. She screamed in pain as she gained a knee, seeing the MP-5 on the ground.

She'd been *hit*....

Clumsily she grasped the weapon and saw a gigantic gargoyle shape holding Melanchthon aloft as it flung the monk into a wall. But Melanchthon was strong and rose almost in the same breath. He crouched barehanded—as Cassius had—though he stood no chance against the beast.

Both torches were lost, so they were fighting almost in total darkness. Gina couldn't see any details of the Nephilim's form, though she sensed somehow by the way darkness faded at the silhouette that it was far larger than Raphael.

Melanchthon laughed through mashed lips. "Now we face each other in our true forms!"

The Nephilim seemed to laugh and sank farther into shadow, farther and farther until Gina could barely see the scarlet reflection of its eyes. And then they, too, were gone.

From the opposite direction of where the eyes sank into the darkness, Gina heard movement. A sharp step caused her to shout and whirl, firing the MP-5 in the darkness. She glimpsed nothing in the muzzle flash. The brain wasn't fast enough to transmit images at the blasts, but she realized this section of the catacombs was an amphitheater.

She froze on the trigger and, remarkably, remembered to sweep the barrel slowly so as not to leave any man-sized holes in the pattern, and then the bolt locked. *Change clips!*

Sound.

Black rising...

Raphael—

A massive hand hit her throat, cutting off a scream, and Gina was smashed against the wall. Her head cracked painfully against the stone, and she must have lost consciousness for a second because she awoke with hot breath steaming across her face. Turning away as much as possible, Gina gasped painfully and drew a burning breath.

Her hand was empty. She'd lost the semiautomatic.

Eyes inhabited by a red world of lost souls gazed deep into hers, and it laughed.

Gina closed her eyes and tried to kick, to fight, but there was no fighting stone and iron. She had as much chance of moving it as she had of lifting a ton of granite.

The Nephilim threw back his head to laugh, and it was an unearthly howl of the blackest mirth, inhuman at its source, in its sound. Gina screamed, and in the next second her legs caved as she hit the ground.

Stunned and surprised—her mind not fast enough to catch up with what had happened as she scrambled back—she grabbed wildly for the MP-5, and then it was in her hands again.

By force of will she saw the beast—this one was Raphael—less than a stride away. But it was bowed back, and a human arm was locked around its neck, another arm hooking its bicep, holding back the blow that would have severed her head from her neck.

Cassius!

Enraged, the beast whirled, swiping, but it couldn't reach Cassius from such a position. It bellowed in mindless animal fury, spinning, raging, and rebounding from wall to wall. Fangs gaped and snapped again and again, but Cassius didn't release either neck or arm. And although they seemed equal in strength, Cassius began to lose his hold inch by inch. It was simply too powerful. Gina saw it in an instant as her head cleared.

As Gina stood she ejected the spent clip in the MP-5 and slammed in another, pulling open the bolt for a quick burst. But she couldn't fire with Cassius so close and moved to the side for the best angle if they separated.

With a thunderous bellow it finally tore free from Cassius' hold and spun with its claws rising, but Cassius took a quick jerk-step backward, and the katana flashed like lightning from ceiling to floor.

Raphael—she had no idea where the larger one had gone—howled, and Gina fired an entire clip. She knew she'd done massive damage when the Nephilim turned and staggered into another corridor. A clawed hand swept out to blast a torch from its pedestal, and it was swallowed by darkness.

Gasping, Cassius stood in the center of the corridor, but he didn't pursue as Gina expected any man caught in the heat of combat to pursue. Instead he turned to her and seemed to check her visually for wounds, then walked to Melanchthon. He rolled the old man onto his back. He had a severe cut on his forehead.

Cassius bent and lifted him from the floor with ease. Then he pitched the monk over his shoulder and gazed upon Gina.

"Can you walk?"

"I think so. But Barnabas is badly wounded."

Cassius hesitated for only one instant, but it was enough for Gina to know his sorrow. He nodded as he motioned for Gina to help him lift Barnabas. Clutching Melanchthon tightly, Cassius gently hoisted Barnabas onto his other shoulder, looking into the old monk's glassy eyes. Cassius' tone was somber but also tempered. He would not allow sorrow to dull his thoughts.

"We have to go to the sanctuary."

"The sanctuary? Why?"

"I have to know something."

"I figured."

Despite the ominous air that surrounded the sanctuary, Gina sensed nothing so special when they entered. Even after Cassius lit torches they had retrieved from the main tunnel system, she saw nothing that should inspire awe or even fear.

No larger than a typical small church, it seemed that it had once been a cavern but had also been carved from the granite by iron chisel. She saw endless narrow grooves along the walls and felt amazement at the hours and steady labor it must have required. It was a testament to the dedication men once held for their religion—to chisel a sacred place of worship out of solid granite for whatever magnificent purpose.

But there was nothing magnificent about this cube of empty space within solid stone. But for its size, it could have been a tomb. Then Gina saw Cassius standing in the center, strangely immobile, and walked forward, sensing rather than seeing that there was something terrible before him.

As she passed his wide shoulders, she saw that the back of the sanctuary had caved in. And the wall, she noticed, was far different from the others.

Where the others were scarred with iron, this one was perfectly smooth but for the gaping hole in the center behind what had been a stone altar table.

Cassius slowly lowered Melanchthon and Barnabas to the floor. Then he expelled a long breath as he stood, and Gina asked, "What is it?"

"It's gone into a cavern beneath the abbey," Cassius intoned solemnly. "I needed to know."

"Know what?"

"If it had discovered the entrance."

"It goes to the catacombs?"

"No." He shook his head. "To a cavern far beneath this place—greater than the catacombs...deeper. I walled up this entrance long ago so that no man would ever trespass there. There are two more entrances, but they can't be discovered. "

Gina *had* to know. "Why did you wall it up?"

His voice was so weary that Gina feared he was about to surrender to this ageless struggle.

"Because it contains what man cannot and must not possess," was all he said. "But we must wait for Melanchthon and Barnabas to awaken. We cannot leave them."

Gina studied Melanchthon's head. There were several discernable marks, but the most serious was the cut on his forehead. Barnabas seemed to be resting peacefully, the blood of his many wounds having been stanched thanks to Melanchthon's hasty first-aid job. "They might not wake up for awhile, Cassius." She didn't want to say the rest.

"It's a chance I'll take for as long as I can." Cassius stepped to the entrance of the sanctuary where old wood lay in a heap. He retrieved a handful of shattered boards and set them against a wall. "We'll stay warm until they wake."

There was no arguing with him. Gina knew that, in this, he was in total command. The thought of argument didn't even arise in her, for she recognized the futility of it.

Experiencing a vicious bodily alarm of endless aches, bruises, and those indescribable painful muscles that one knew they possessed only when they were in pain, Gina slowly sat. She coughed, realizing her lungs were beginning to gather fluid.

It was incredible what she was enduring. After this she could qualify for SWAT. And she wondered what type of superhuman endurance Cassius must possess. It wasn't natural—certainly not what a man could achieve in a normal life span. And, knowing more deeply that it was just an excuse, she said, "So... two thousand years. Mind if I ask how?"

Eyes closed, Cassius laughed gently. "I was wondering when you were going to get around to that."

His laugh, thankfully, made her relax. Until this second she wasn't certain whether he was going to shut her down or open up. She breathed easier knowing it was the latter.

"You laugh.... But I guess you know how something like this can shake a person up."

His smile was almost a grimace. "Believe me, I know." He seemed to grow more considerate, even pensive. "I've seen it time after time. Monsignor DeMarco's handlers didn't open this abbey for the good of mankind. They opened it to lure me back, hoping I would reveal to them the treasure they seek."

"The spear?"

His voice became distant. "Fools...they seek a holy weapon—a weapon that they think contains the power of God." His expression was bitter. "Holy wars, noble crusades, heroic quests for ancient relics that mean less than nothing now, but for what men make of them."

Gina shifted so she could more clearly see his face, but when he looked at her again, she could read nothing in his eyes. And she could only surmise that it was because he was no longer concealing what she had already known.

Still, it was as if she were looking into the eyes of a lion or tiger. What was there simply could not be understood.

Cassius asked, "How do you feel?"

"Fine," she replied, touching her forehead.

"You've got a bruise—maybe a concussion. But you should be all right by tomorrow."

She stared at his forearm. The bandage was soaked with fresh blood. "You're still bleeding."

"I know."

"The wound is deep."

"Not deep enough."

Which led into what Gina wanted to know. "How is it that you're so strong, Cassius? Is that part of the gift?"

"The only thing that reduces a man's strength is that he must eventually grow old. Only age reduces his strength, his endurance, whatever. And just as a man gets stronger even into his sixties, if old age did not begin, he would continue to get stronger with each decade." He shrugged. "I'm strong, but it's only because I've lived so long, immune to age or disease."

Surprisingly, that made sense. Gina realized she'd been searching for a more cosmic explanation, but, like most things, the most obvious answer was probably correct.

"I was expecting something more dramatic."

"Sorry to disappoint you."

In the ensuing silence, Gina allowed herself to wonder how this man could even relate to a normal human being when he had, doubtless, witnessed the fall of a hundred nations, the conquest of Rome, and had probably accompanied history's greatest figures in journeys, wars, and trials. She could only imagine all that he had seen and what he had done. Then she thought of Barnabas and the seemingly secret bond he shared with Cassius. She wanted to know.

Cassius nodded slowly. "At the beginning of World War II, I found Barnabas in the ruins of a village near Lausanne. His parents had been killed. I couldn't leave him, so I brought him here. When I haven't been hunting something that had to be destroyed, I've spent time just as you. I've worked at a trade, made good friends, enjoyed life."

"People always talk about how it would be a curse to be an immortal," Gina said absently. "They hypothesize that you get tired of seeing friends and family die. How you can't love anyone because they will grow old, and you won't."

He was strangely still. "True.... But I've never wanted to die. And I have loved more than once. Love—true love—is more than strong enough to survive age...and death. It's no different for me than anyone else. And sometimes I've loved despite myself. It happens." He sighed. "You live long enough, everything happens."

"I guess you're living proof of that." Gina muttered. "Do you know how it happened?"

He studied her.

"How you became an immortal."

"Oh...that...no, I don't know for certain. I saw Him raise the dead again and again."

"You mean, like Lazarus? You were there?"

"No." Cassius shook his head. "I wasn't there when He raised Lazarus. But believe me, I heard about it. But there were others. Jesus did a lot of things that aren't recorded in what you call your Bible." His tone was stunningly casual. "I watched Him for two years, and I never tired of it—not for one moment."

"What was He like?" Gina asked, and from the center of her, she wanted to know. In fact, she felt slightly amazed at how much she wanted to know.

Cassius laughed lightly. "He laughed a lot. That's what I remember about Him most." He leaned back against the wall. "I wonder, like that painting in the Hall, why everyone portrays Him as a man of such tedious sorrow."

"He wasn't?"

"Yes," Cassius said with a vague gesture. "Yes, He knew great sorrow—greater than anyone that ever lived. But He also laughed and...and *enjoyed* people—all kinds of people.

"I had seen many people—the very poor, or sick—and I had never seen them smile. But when He was with them, they laughed and sang as if they didn't have a worry in the world. And He wasn't constantly performing miracles. Sometimes He was just there, and people would stay at His side until they were starving and fainting, simply because they couldn't bear to leave."

"So the Bible is true?" Gina asked and didn't blink as he turned his eyes on her.

Cassius smiled. "If I tell you it's not true, you wouldn't believe me. What does it matter what I say?"

"Because you were there, Cassius."

"Yes, I was there. And so were many that didn't believe, despite what they saw Him do. You want to know the truth, don't you? Yes...so do I. But you know something? I can't. And neither can you. Neither of us will know fully until we shuffle off this flesh."

"But you saw Him."

"Yes, I saw Him. But I never spoke to Him." He paused thoughtfully. "I did have a friend, though—another centurion—whose servant that he loved like a son was healed simply because Jesus spoke. Scipio was never the same after that. He died years later, when Caligula ordered all centurions loyal to the Christian God executed by their brother centurions."

"What about you?" Gina asked.

"I had already left Jerusalem and Rome. I was no longer part of that world." He sighed. "I didn't know of the decimation until I returned to Israel forty years later, when Tiberius laid siege to Jerusalem. I went to fight with the Jews, but...there was no fighting. They were betrayed from within, and the city fell almost without a blow. I cut my way through surrounding legions and escaped into the desert." A pause. "I've fought many wars. I've come close to death many times, but that was one of the narrowest fights."

"So you can die," Gina announced, musing that being ageless didn't prevent him from being killed.

"If a man bleeds, he can die. Yes, I can die—like you or anyone else." It was as if he were watching thousands upon thousands of pages lifting, as if blown by the wind, before him. "I can't count the number of times I thought myself dead. But the will to live is great—greater than many know."

"I heard you call him 'Messiah.'"

As if a mask settled on his face—a mask of grief—Cassius stared long into the flames. "I believe He was the Messiah, born to save this world. And we crucified Him, and I...died that day...died in ways that you can never know.

"I was the one who presided over His torture, His death. And only at the last...did I understand. But it was too late. He was already dead, not that I could have prevented it. No one could have prevented it.

"Then, three days later, He rose from the dead...as I knew He would." He took a breath. "I was there in the area of the tomb and saw Him. He was standing on a low hill, and there was a single tree there—I can still see it—and He just stood there, staring over Jerusalem as if He had all the time in the world. I couldn't move...I had watched Him *die*. But then He turned His head and looked directly at me and...smiled." Cassius' face was purest wonder. "He smiled...."

"Did He say anything?"

"No." Cassius laughed. "He didn't have to."

"But...why not? I mean, how did you know that you were... immortal?"

He shrugged. "I continued to live, and it dawned on me little by little. There was no bright light, no announcement. It was something I came to understand as the years passed. But it was not the greatest change in my life. The greatest change came the hour He died, and my eyes and hand were healed."

"Your eyes?"

Cassius seemed wearier, and Gina began to worry.

"Until the hour of His crucifixion, I was nearly blind with cataracts." He stretched out his hand. "Men looked like trees walking around in the street. In fact, that's why I was stationed in Jerusalem. I was no longer considered fit to command a legion. But in that hour my eyes were healed. Nor, since then, have I known a single day of sickness."

"And your hand?"

"Ah..." He smiled and lifted his right hand before his face, staring into the palm. "I sliced it open on my spear after I pierced His side. And moments later...it was healed."

Gina was surprisingly comfortable but didn't know how and didn't try to know. She didn't care to overanalyze it.

"So, Raphael...old friend of yours?"

Cassius stared into the flames. "*Long* I've tracked him across this world—through battlefield after battlefield. Through cities left in ruins. Through countries devastated by disease. But he always managed to escape me—for nearly a thousand years—until now."

"Do you think he knew you'd come here?"

He shrugged. "This was the last place I thought he would hide."

There was something tragic about his tone that caused Gina to concentrate on the pensive brow. Her voice was quieter than she would have preferred. "Cassius..."

"Yes?"

"Do you *want* to live?"

"Long enough," he answered simply.

"Long enough for what?"

"To know."

He wasn't going to answer that one, she realized. As silence drew, Gina lifted her chin to the cave-like opening in the back wall. "So what's down there?"

"Something I'm going to bury once more."

"So why don't we just throw a few antipersonnel grenades down the stairway and be done with it?" That seemed to Gina, at least, like the most sensible idea she'd had yet.

"I would, but I have to make sure it's there first." He glanced at the monk. "Okay, Melanchthon and Barnabas aren't coming around. So this is what we're going to do. I'm taking all of you out. Then I'm going to get you and your kids on a helicopter and come back to finish this. If the Nephilim are down there, they're not going anywhere."

"No," Gina said in a dead tone.

"What?"

"No, Cassius." Cassius stared upon Gina as if she'd angered him, but Gina knew he was only confused.

"Why not?"

"Because I'm not letting you go down there alone," she answered, unblinking. When he didn't reply, Gina thought carefully. "I'm not going to let you face them alone."

With a frown Cassius stood and Gina was with him, facing off with him. He seemed to search for words, then, "You have your children. They're your first priority."

"I'm not forgetting my children," she replied steadily. "I'm not forgetting myself, either."

Cassius wasn't looking at her anymore. He was staring at spans of centuries he had lived by hard rules.

"You're not dead yet," Gina said. "Don't act as though you are."

"Do you realize—"

"I'm not scared, Cassius." Gina searched his eyes. "At least, not as scared as you."

After a time, Cassius' face revealed thoughts, feelings, fears, and doubts that Gina could have never imagined on the face of the ultimate warrior. Then, as if he had longed for something he had been too frightened to think, Cassius nodded. But it took a moment longer before his thoughts could find words.

"If we survive," he said quietly, and paused, "I would like... to know you."

Even now, he was so formal, and Gina couldn't prevent her smile. But she didn't regret it, and then he smiled too. "Yes," she replied as quietly, "I'd like that."

They turned as Melanchthon sat upright with a bearish groan, as though he had been dead and they had disturbed him. He rubbed his head a moment, growled, and winced as he searched his surroundings, looking first at the sleeping Barnabas next to him. Then he saw Cassius and Gina and nodded.

"Ah," he gasped, "I'm not dead yet."

Cassius laughed and looked at Gina.

"That makes two of us."

CHAPTER TEN

A fter leaving Gina, Melanchthon, and Barnabas in the Great Hall, Cassius elected to make a last quick circuit of their surroundings, insuring they would at least have an unimposed beginning into the storm. Holding a torch in one hand, the Colt .45 in the other, he walked openly through the catacombs, alone. There was no way to catch this creature unaware. He couldn't move silently enough, nor were shadows that inked the corridor more than shades of gray to its keen eyes. At least with the light of the torch, Cassius could see it when it closed—a small advantage because it was a small distance, but better than no reaction room at all.

Hyperalert to react—like a boxer inside his opponent's reach—Cassius prevented his mind from wandering. But after he had made the first circuit of the closest corridor—empty and secure—he began to surrender to the mistake every sentry makes when the night is cold and silent and dead but for wind and stars. He began to think—only fleeting shadows of thoughts, at first—of what had brought him to this hour of reckoning.

He stood upon Golgotha, always upon Golgotha, for he would never leave Golgotha...but he stood in another place— an unexpected place—as well. He stood in the Castille de Matisse with the woman who knew him and loved him, Julie de Lespinasse.

And...more...

He stood before the grim and implacable Cotton Mather arguing a defense that, at last, brought a hard ending to the hysterical persecution at Salem. And then there was Cedric the Great, who almost defeated him in that titanic duel that lasted an entire night on the steppes of Russia.

In all his years, Cassius had never known a man of such great strength. Sword after sword shattered in his hands, and as fast as he could measure his last wound, he received another while giving three in exchange so that it was all lost in the speed of giving damage faster than he received it. He used all he had ever learned of fighting—from the sword-shattering blows of Musashi to the finesse of La Boessiere—but the battle had been decided not by strength or endurance, in the end, but by the will to win.

As Cassius fell to his knees over Cedric's slashed, titanic form, he knew he should have died from his wounds, as well. But he had built strength upon strength, year upon year, and it had been enough for him to stagger numbly from the hill.

It took a full year for his injuries to heal. Nor, for a time, did he think they ever would. He thought that at last he had suffered more damage than even he could endure. But after a year he stood once more. And then he began the hunt once again.

A thousand faces of a thousand men who had trampled kingdoms and continents—men who had executed millions for nothing more than savage delight—had died because he decided they would terrify the earth no more. Nor was there anyone to tell him he was right.

He had fought his way through the darkness of war after war with no light to guide him but his own. And for centuries he had prayed that God would give him some fleece to confirm the choices he made again and again, but there was no fleece.

He had asked a thousand times. Then, after a battle he could barely remember—so fierce was the collision and the bloody end—he had risen up, wounded and exhausted in a field of dead men, horses, and chariots—the only survivor—and knew he would ask no more. He knew his purpose, and it had to be enough because answers would not come in this world. He only knew what he believed was his purpose.

He noticed the flames burned lower in the passageway before him. He wasn't concentrating.

Concentrate...

Cassius searched every space illuminated by the torch, but there were entire canyons of darkness. Not that the darkness was an advantage against him—not like the others. For his senses were acute to react to what others would not notice. Also, the strangeness of the corridors affected him.

He had overseen construction of this tunnel system almost 1,400 years ago, but it had been altered and rebuilt a hundred times. Not unusual because Cassius had hidden far more than bones in this refuge.

Also, the Knights Templar, which Cassius began, had kept a guard in these quarters until their numbers grew too few. And word of their habitation had spread so much that entire nations whispered of the hidden treasures buried at what became known as Saint Gregory's. Cassius could have issued orders that the abbey must never be abandoned, but that would have drawn suspicion even within the Knights.

The shadow rose tall against a wall.

Cassius swung the .45 to the left and fired—that simply.

No emotion, no anger, no fear. Then the shadow was attempting to move behind him, and Cassius swung the pistol smoothly—no flinching, no dramatic turning or spinning—and fired again. He fired from behind his left hip, bending slightly at the waist to get the best point-shoot aim as possible, and the explosion cracked in the corridor.

Hit.

The Nephilim snarled in anger.

Cassius didn't fire again, as most would have emptied the clip. He was turning into the pistol and took a moment to bend his face, letting peripheral vision read the edges of what was around him. It was the perfect tactic to draw his attention to one line of attack so that another line opened. And, like a great chess player—or a great fighter—Cassius never forgot to keep his alertness scattered. When he finished turning he was facing back the way he had come, but he didn't rush forward. He took a step backward, negotiating for room to slip, turn, be thrown, or brace—head still bent, still searching.

Which was good, because the death that came upon him from the corridor to his right made no sound and gave no warning.

If Cassius had not wisely taken a step backward, he would have been facing the first image and firing, both blinding and deafening himself to the threat much closer at hand. And when he dropped, passing the .45 under his outstretched right arm—his right hand settling over his left, his right hand grasping the hilt of the katana—Cassius fired five full rounds point-blank into...

Raphael!

No time!

Raphael smothered Cassius with the next rushing stride, and then they were on the ground again. And although Raphael had been hit, Cassius knew he hadn't hit low enough because Raphael had barely staggered at the shots.

At the first twist, Cassius instantly released both the katana and the .45, grasping Raphael's neck and chest, holding the fangs and claws at bay. It was still superior in pure brute force and speed, but Cassius hoped desperately that its earlier wounds had bled away some of its strength, especially the blow with his sword that glanced off its collar and ribs before rebounding from the floor.

"Melanchthon!"

Gina had not needed to scream. The old priest had spun and was gesturing largely for the others to gather on the dais of the Great Hall while holding aim at a half-dozen tunnels.

"Go!" he shouted.

Gina was already running, covering the Hall in seconds to reach the north corridor. She couldn't determine exactly where the shots originated but knew she would find it in seconds because there would be more—she prayed.

For the next few seconds she ran in the direction Cassius had selected and heard the suppressed snarls of a struggle. Then the beast howled again—they were 150 feet in front of her. Breathless already, Gina didn't flick off the safety on the machine gun yet. She didn't want to accidentally fire too soon and hit Cassius.

Duck!

It was like an immense white cloud that emerged from nowhere, something moving quickly, and Gina sensed rather than saw part of the cloud extended like a layer of cotton— beautiful in its own way. And she dove and rolled underneath the blow that would have killed her whether the claws struck or not. She gained her feet, extending the MP-5 back in the direction of the blow and fired.

She turned into the weapon, pulling the barrel down as she screamed and backed up, searching the corridor for a sign and felt nothing as she realized the corridor...

Was empty.

"We battle our last!" Raphael spat as Cassius placed a boot against the Nephilim's chest.

Cassius made certain his foot was secure and tightened his leg while retaining his hold to hurl the Nephilim back—much like a pilot will rev an engine before letting off the brake. Then he released his hold, and the Nephilim slammed into the wall behind it.

Plates of stone broke at the impact, light brown dirt cascading through the rivulets, and Cassius reached his feet, recovering even quicker than the Nephilim. Taking no time to wipe sweat from his eyes, Cassius picked up the katana and leaped forward.

He feinted a blow—something high that Raphael would take because it was easily blocked by his tree-trunk arms—then the katana dropped in a sharp arch, and Cassius' arm straightened as he twisted low and to the right, putting all his weight, all his strength into the edge of the blade.

Still, quick as Cassius was, Raphael was no student of war—he was a master. The Nephilim whipped his body back at the waist so that the katana barely cut flesh, and Cassius knew he was in a bad position. He was within Raphael's striking distance, and the katana was too far to the side. He tried to bring it back across for a return blow, but Raphael had already lashed out.

Sometimes there's nothing to do but...take a blow.

Unwounded, Cassius had supreme confidence in his ability to receive the most brutal blow to either the head or body. Now he wasn't so certain. Then he had no more time for hope as Raphael's hand—wide open, claws separated, fingers hooked like steel talons—was but a foot from his chest.

With a shout Cassius turned into the Nephilim, hoping to take the impact on his shoulder, and he did. But the blow was worse than he anticipated, both in brute force and the wicked effect of the claws. Raphael caught the side of his arm—the best Cassius could have hoped—but the impact sent a shock-wave through his bones.

Cassius made a doomed attempt to catch Raphael again with the katana as he was blown to the right, dragging the sword to at least make contact with the Nephilim. But if it did, it had no effect—Raphael didn't even grunt.

Cassius was staggering—the worst possible reaction.

If he had been retreating, the blow would have blasted him twenty feet to the side. Yet surrendering to the force would have also passed the force through him. But since he could not *surrender* to the force, he had to stop the force.

As Cassius staggered to the side, his entire body felt dead, only his head retaining any sensation. Retreating, his hand tightened on the katana, though he knew he didn't have the ability yet to strike. With a sharp curse, Cassius leaned back— the best he could do—to shift his weight, hoping his legs would follow.

He staggered back and fell awkwardly against the wall as Raphael closed far more slowly.

Familiar thoughts assailed him—each Nephilim was different, just as each man was different. Some preferred to attack from ambush, some liked a stand-up, forthright fight in full armor. Some had fangs surpassing a tiger, some appeared almost human, though all could alter their shape for periods of time and were the original inspiration for the American Indian's terrifying "shape-shifter."

"You surprise me, Centurion."

Cassius blinked, trying to focus, and realized that he wasn't recovering fast enough. Gasping and streaming blood, Cassius extended the katana, as if to threaten.

Laughing, Raphael paused. "So this is how the great Cassius ends—holding his sword like an old woman."

Unseen, Cassius' left hand withdrew a poniard—with its slender dagger blade—at the small of his back. The Nephilim approached once more. "No, there will be no peace, Centurion. You began this war, but *I* shall end it."

Raphael was gloating. "I actually feared you, Cassius—so many stories of how the great centurion had killed this brother or that. How you burned down the temple of Tel-Gedi, killing a hundred of my kind at once. How you were the supreme hunter. How none could escape you. How great was your strength, your skill. Did you know you have become a legend? Even among my kind?"

Cassius' extended right arm began to drop, and he groaned in pain. Raphael's mirth knew no bounds. It took another stride, its right hand drawing back once more. "But now it ends!"

Twisting hard, Cassius spun and struck with the dagger in his left hand, but Raphael wasn't caught off guard.

"Fool!" The Nephilim shouted as his right hand swept down to swipe the blade aside. "I saw it!"

"I know!"

Cassius let the poniard spin-wheel through the corridor as both hands found the hilt of the katana, and the blade flashed out and straight down—the samurai's most powerful blow. It struck Raphael's extended right arm cleanly, deeply, and Cassius straightened his right arm, his full strength locked into the perfect technique, and the katana sank deep into the muscle, striking the bone.

With the katana buried deep in his forearm, Raphael howled as he had not howled until now.

Yes, he had been struck before, but none of the blows had done this measure of damage. This blow severed muscle and nerve and the critical radial artery so crucial to arm strength.

This time it was the Nephilim that staggered back, reaching up with his left hand to rip the katana from his arm, and Cassius bent, finding the .45. Raphael saw and hurled the katana forward, and Cassius was forced to leap aside. Then the Nephilim raced into the darkness as the centurion once more found the .45, slammed in a fresh clip, and fired seven rounds at the shadow.

With the .45 still extended, smoking, Cassius stared over the black steel barrel, watching and listening. But he saw no distant shadow stagger or fall. Finally, he lowered aim.

"Cassius!"

He spun into Gina and saw instantly that she was alone. He knew the other Nephilim was in the corridor. It had been there all along. Raphael had done the work, yes, but the second one...it had planned the ambush, had used Raphael like a commander would use a platoon.

Gina spun, staring back the way she had come. "I don't know if this corridor is clear," she gasped.

As she drew hard breaths, Cassius' face revealed nothing. "Time to leave," he said simply. "Did you see the other Nephilim?"

"No."

Cassius saw no reason to tell her of the four long claw marks in her back—sliced so perfectly through the thinnest layer of skin that Gina had not even felt them.

The blood seeping down her back probably felt like sweat at the moment, but she would realize the stickiness soon enough. By then, he would have her back in the hall and bandaged.

"Follow me," he said simply. "And stay close."

CHAPTER ELEVEN

Remarkably, Melanchthon said nothing when they emerged into the Hall. But, then, not so remarkable, Gina realized. If the monk had spoken his mind, he would have alarmed both Cassius and herself, because she knew they were a ghastly sight.

Cassius, during the last few feet, had told her of the claw marks across her back, and Gina finally understood why the stiffening wetness did not feel the same as sweat. She knew how it happened. As she dove under the larger creature's blow, it had swiped backhanded before she gained her feet and turned into it.

The thought disturbed her, for the creature must be astonishingly fast, far faster than Raphael. It must have hit her a tenth of a second before she turned, but when she turned it was already gone. But if it was so powerful, why did it run?

The others tried to wipe her back with clean gauze, but Gina angrily shook them off. Her wounds were barely skin-deep, but Cassius' were puncture wounds that sank beneath the muscle. She didn't doubt that they dug to the bone.

For the first time, Gina was amazed at how stoically Cassius could endure pure, simple pain. She knew any single one of the wounds, for a normal person, would be agony. She had seen strong men suffer one-hundredth of this and go into shock.

She glanced at Cassius' face. His head was bent, eyes closed. He was breathing deeply, rhythmically, as if subduing the pain with spirit and mind. And no doubt he would—for awhile.

It took her more than an hour to completely stop the bleeding—an hour before she could concentrate on herself. But after dealing with Cassius' injuries, she almost laughed when told once again of her own. She wasn't surprised at how easily and quickly she had realigned her definition of an injury.

By some reflex, when they had first entered the room, Gina searched the dais to see who was present. Most of the monks were now milling about the room, retrieving water or weapons. They had obviously relaxed since chaos had died in the corridor and no unearthly sight had stalked into the Hall, but that wasn't the reason she had searched.

No, it was because there had been something else in her brief exchange with the creature, something she didn't under-stand. It was a fleeting glimpse of a vision she could not isolate or define, but it was there—an identity she *should* know but didn't.

Mostly for the sake of the children, Gina revealed no fear, but she had no illusions. Cassius had won time and again, but it wasn't because he was unkillable—he was just hard to kill.

Also, he had the advantage of high-tech weapons, an advantage that would end quickly enough when they ran out of ammo or the weapons were damaged. And, sooner or later, that's what the creatures would do. They would take away Cassius' fangs.

Yes, Cassius had somehow managed to match Raphael's might when he was uninjured. When half his blood hadn't been drained from his body by wounds. When he was at the peak of his strength, rested, and ready. But that was hours—it seemed like days—ago. Now, and Gina could see it in his eyes, dark and deeper in his face, he wasn't recovering so quickly. He could recover enough for another full-strength encounter, but his endurance wouldn't be there.

Usually no matter how badly the body was hurt—even if it was exhausted to the point of death—it could recover quickly enough once core temperature dropped and oxygen was restored to the muscles. But if the muscles were bleeding freshly oxygenated blood, the heart would be working twice as hard, even at rest, so neither would the core temperature drop or the muscles regain oxygen.

Gina could see it on Cassius' face. He drew hard, long breaths.

Though he did not seem to notice the full measure of his wounds—and perhaps he did not because he was concentrating on breathing—he was crisscrossed with claw marks. A thought flashed through Gina's mind—the image of two wrestlers grappling face-to-face—of what it would be like if humans left bloody furrows wherever they touched the other. And she knew the answer. They would be as Cassius' wounds—all but uncountable.

Even when she had completely stopped the flow of blood, Cassius had still not regained his strength. His face was sheathed in sweat, and his voice was hoarse.

"Water," he whispered, "and bread."

"Go!" Gina said to the monks and they were gone. She leaned close to the centurion. "Cassius?"

"I'm all right," he groaned, as if to allay her fears. He opened his eyes and gazed about the room. He focused at last on Monsignor DeMarco, sitting safely in the distance. Cassius' teeth gleamed in a silent snarl. "Come here, Priest."

The epitome of caution, DeMarco wiped palms on his frock. He arose and approached with hesitant steps, though his tone retained some of its original dignity. "Yes?"

"Why did you lure me here?"

The monsignor stared, then, "Because we knew you would come to protect...your secret."

Cassius closed his eyes and inhaled deeply. Then he shook his head—almost tragically. "Fool..."

"No," Monsignor DeMarco said quietly. "Not all men who disagree with you, Centurion, are fools. You took it upon yourself to hide what the world deserved to possess." He came closer to Cassius. "Alone, Cassius, you decided that men cannot possess the great treasure you have hidden somewhere inside these walls. But you are only a man. Who gave you the right to decide for the world? "

Cassius laughed sadly. "I was not the only one who saw Him rise from the grave, Priest. And many of them did not believe even then. Do you think a relic will convince anyone of the truth? Do you think it holds any power?"

"It may," the monsignor replied. "In any case, that is not yours to decide."

"I did decide," Cassius said simply.

"You have no right."

Cassius' eyes were the purest purpose, the purest image of death as he looked upon the priest. "No man has greater right."

"The Church disagrees with you." At Cassius' curiosity, the monsignor nodded. "Of course we know of you, Cassius. We have known for centuries. Just as we have known of others like you—as we have known of the Nephilim. But the treasure is not yours to claim."

Cassius laughed, genuinely amused. "You truly *are* a fool, Priest." He enjoyed his mirth a moment. "A *treasure*...I've never heard it put like that."

"It represents life."

"It represents death, Priest—it *is* death." Cassius recovered from his amusement and stared with disappointment. "You forsook the truth long ago, Monsignor. Do you have any idea what He would say if He were beside you?"

The monsignor stepped forward, whether from unthinking anger or true boldness, no one could say. "You have no right, Centurion! The end draws near! The time for secrets has passed!"

After a sip of water, Cassius wiped his mouth with his forearm. "Did you know that Martin Luther was my friend?" he asked casually.

The monsignor's control was impressive. "I am not surprised, Centurion."

"Yes...the peasant was my friend. And he will always be a peasant in my eyes as well as his own. Luther was proud of being a peasant, Priest. A man of humble position and humble ambition. But no one, before or since, has stood more forthrightly against Satan. And yet he asked for no weapons. He did not even believe in resisting evil, except by professing faith in God and scorn for the devil."

A violent cough choked Cassius, and he leaned forward until it passed. With a deep breath, he reclined once more. "I don't suppose you would be amazed to know that Luther, too, thought the end was near. And my hairy little friend, Paul, thought the same. *All of them* thought the end was near, Monsignor—and they were all wrong."

Monsignor DeMarco did not reply but glanced at Gina as Melanchthon patiently bandaged her back. "Men did not understand then what we have the benefit of understanding now, Centurion. We have the advantage of teleology, science, numerology—a thousand disciplines of the mind that—"

"That men had then," Cassius muttered. "There is nothing more to say, Monsignor DeMarco. Foolishness never ends.... Always men seek the Holy Grail—so be it. Find it, if you can. Destroy your enemies. Conquer empires—make your empire great in the world. Rule from a throne of gold above all others."

Gina gasped at the pain on Cassius' face as he lifted himself up on an arm. "I serve from the foot of a skull, Monsignor. I know nothing of glory."

Although impressed, the monsignor still replied, "You have fought too long, Cassius. And killed too much." He stared sadly. "You have lived too long, my friend."

"Perhaps...perhaps I have lived too long, and seen too much, and killed...far too many men. But my heart cannot be taken from that hill, and what rose beyond it when He conquered death. Say what you will of me—here I stand. Nor will I give you...what you seek."

"Cassius," Gina said gently, placing an arm upon his chest. And, slowly, Cassius sat back. His head was bowed, eyes closed. She whispered, "You don't have the strength for this."

An opportunity—the monsignor saw it.

"At my word, Centurion, the world would converge on this place. They would know your secret. Nothing that is hidden would remain. You call me a fool. Perhaps, yes. But perhaps you are a fool for believing that your secret will remain so." Though resolute, even the monsignor seemed to hesitate. "Don't you understand, Cassius? All things must end! Even you! You and your life! Men must know! They will know! Even I cannot stop that now!"

Cassius laughed blindly at the ceiling. "And, so...the children of God—children I have defended through age after age—would destroy me, in the end." Sadly, tragically, Cassius opened his eyes to stare upon the monsignor. "Look at the work of your hands, my friend. These children will die now because of your righteousness—your plans. How many more, if I gave you what you want?"

Slowly, Cassius tested his hands, clenching and unclenching. The bandages had stanched the flow of blood. He was recovering strength, though slowly.

"Then you doom to death God's kingdom on earth," the monsignor replied, equally as tragic.

"Perhaps." Cassius nodded. "And perhaps...God is wiser—more powerful—than you think." He paused, breathing. "I am only a soldier, Monsignor DeMarco. I know nothing of glorious things. But I know that with my last breath of life, with my last full measure of strength, I will serve the Lord. I cannot answer your questions. I cannot give you what you want. And why? Because men think strength is equal to glory...don't they?"

No one spoke, for they knew the answer.

"It's not," Cassius said at last. "I will pray for you, Monsignor. I will pray God gives...a reformation...of your heart."

The monsignor bowed his head, then walked across the Hall, where he pulled a chair from the table and sat. No one approached him as he folded his hands and closed his eyes.

Staring down at his hand, making a fist once more, Cassius nodded, then looked up at Gina. "I promise you...both you and your children will live. I promise it with my soul...my life."

Gina shook her head.

"How can you promise that, Cassius?"

Cassius raised his eyes to the great domed ceiling.

"I can promise," he said.

———

Jaqual—little more than a child, himself—was playing a game with Rachel and Josh. He was as without restraint as they were, and Gina realized that the monk was carefree with them because he was somehow frightened and intimidated by adults. It was the first time she had seen him genuinely smile, and she was glad the children had him.

She was in no mood for serious conversation as she sat beside her children, though Jaqual cast her an anxious glance. Gina smiled sweetly at him—*it's all right, go ahead*—and he continued to play some game with colored stones that he'd retrieved from the front office. She was thankful that, at least for awhile, the children seemed to have forgotten the worst of their situation, nor was she going to remind them.

It was movement by Barnabas—who had only just awoken—that drew her attention, and she watched as he lifted the breastplate and robe and sword of the centurion and carried it carefully upon a couch in a far corner of the room. Even from a distance the armor burned like silver fire—the sword so highly polished it seemed born of the sun.

Cassius was smiling faintly and spoke loudly enough for Gina to hear. "Come here, Barnabas."

Head bowed, Barnabas did not move, and Cassius waited. Then the old man turned and walked cautiously, slowly, across the room. He did not lift his gaze when he stood before the centurion.

The voice of Cassius was the voice of one brother meeting another after a war, when both thought the other had died. Gina only heard, "Sit, and speak with me."

Something about Cassius in that moment seemed old beyond imagination. Though Barnabas had aged and the centurion was the same as he had been seventy years ago— the same as he had been two thousand years ago—an aura of gigantic age had settled about him. There was no way Barnabas would have felt his superior in years. As Barnabas sat, Cassius settled an arm over Barnabas's shoulders. Then he smiled and began speaking so quietly, and before long Barnabas was also smiling, and nodding, and seemed to glow with strength. They were still sitting and speaking when Gina felt her eyes, so tired now, closing and laid down beside her kids.

She didn't know what the night would bring, nor did she care as she had cared before. What she was beginning to believe gave her a peace that she knew would survive even death.

It took Gina a moment to realize where she was, what had happened, when she awoke. She knew by instinct where the children were—eating breakfast with Jaqual—and the next thing she saw was a gray weight against the tall picture-glass windows.

Her heart sank.

The snowstorm, after two days, had not lessened at all. It continued to pile crust upon crust of snow, literally burying the entire massive abbey in a white grave. She knew it wasn't natural. Knew that whatever the larger creature was had brought it...as he brought the night, and death, and everything evil that had passed.

She lifted a hand to her face, brushing away the sleep, not surprised that she didn't feel refreshed. Then she remembered the dreams—dreams of a warrior in slashed and burning armor fighting upon an island of dead men, broken lances, and shattered armor in a sea of blackening blood. Refusing to surrender, refusing to die, the soldier struck down each barbaric shape that rose against him. None seemed to realize that to challenge him was death, for he was the ultimate warrior, the strongest fighter, the purest survivor. His armor bore the marks of a thousand parried cuts so there was no separating the silver from scarlet. Each time he dropped a man upon the mound, he did not cast him another glance, as if he had dropped tens and tens of thousands. As if strength was his birthright and nothing within war—not the savagery nor the butchery nor the field of dead men that stretched in every direction with abandoned banners waving drearily in a battle-heated wind—could enter his mind, for he fought for more than banners.

In her dreams, Gina had seen the sight again and again, the man fighting unknown wars in unknown lands. There, he wore black armor and struck and roared like a hurricane against the backdrop of a sprawling white castle surrounded by a raging battle of hundreds of thousands. There, he wore the uniform of a Templar Knight, standing defiant and alone, sword in hand, in a hazy desert thundering with scimitar-wielding, black-cloaked riders. There, he was a sea captain on a splinter-blasted ship outnumbered fifty-six to one, but he gave them blast for blast. There, he stood over a wounded priest, beating back those who howled for blood in some city of the damned. And there, again, he stood, gravely wounded, over the monstrous body of some manlike thing in an ancient city overgrown with vines and forgotten by time. And there, he was a monarch, a Puritan, an assassin, a priest, now in black, now in white, yet always the man was the same. Shaking her head, Gina tried to no longer remember the dream, for she knew that any dream that lasted so long should not be remembered.

When she saw Cassius, she sighed in relief.

He was different from when she last saw him. He was dressed utterly in black, having raided the abbey for what he required. He stood before a table spread with the MP-5, reloaded clips, the katana, the two Colt .45s, his poniard, and a row of grenades. He raised his face as she stared, and winked.

Gina rose and walked to him. She began speaking before she stopped moving. "I guess we got lucky last night?"

He frowned. "No...not luck. You hurt it bad with the MP-5. I cut it pretty bad with the sword. It was crippled, bleeding. I thought it might not attack last night because it needed time to heal."

"Think it's healed?"

"As healed as it's going get."

"So you're going to do it again?"

"I wanted to try the storm but...Do I have any choice?"

"Guess not." She leaned back against a table. "Cassius, it's time for us to talk. Seriously."

"Go ahead."

"There's something bothering you—something you're not sharing with me. What is it?"

It didn't seem as if he would reply, then, "Things don't fit, Gina."

"Like what?"

He glanced at the tiered cathedral ceiling. "The sorcery needed to maintain this snowstorm is complex. Besides that, this entire ambush was perfectly played. This Nephilim even took advantage of Rome's desires to trap me here. And even though Raphael is strong, they do come smarter."

"Cassius...there's been so many people killed—Molke, the monks. But I never actually saw Molke killed. It could be any of them. All I know is that it's not anyone in this hall because they were all here when you fought it in the catacombs. And as far as Rome goes, any fool could have taken advantage of that."

Cassius shook his head. "No...whatever did this is wise." He seemed afraid for a moment. "It's someone unknown, Gina. Someone we don't suspect. It's Melanchthon, or—"

"No, Cassius, not him. I saw him when you were wounded and—" Gina grabbed his shoulders. "Cassius! It's nobody in this hall, remember? You've fought it too many times now for it to be someone that's been *with* us."

By instinct, Gina reached up to feel his head—fever.

"Cassius, listen to me. You're not thinking well. You are... too...*hurt*."

With a faint smile, Cassius looked at her. "You think I'm dying?"

Gina sighed. "I think you're feverish and not thinking well."

He laughed. Then, with a surge of strength that defied logic, he sat, lowering his forehead into his palm. "Fever...yeah...had it before. It makes me mad." He frowned, then gathered what was left of him. "No, I know these things, Gina. If the first Nephilim is Dominic—or Basil—the second is not who we think—not even close. In the end, it'll be the last person you suspect."

"The second one?"

"Yes..."

"Wait...the first is now *either* Basil or Dominic." She shook her head, then frowned pensively. "Samuel said the Nephilim that came to the Hall was wearing Dominic's robe. But that could have been a simple ruse to throw us off."

Cassius nodded.

Gina continued. "But the second is neither of them, even though both have been missing since all of this started?"

"Right."

"Cassius, you're gonna give me a heart attack!"

He laughed.

"So what's the plan?"

Slowly, Cassius raised his face. "We can't depend on the radio. I don't trust it now." He took heavier breaths. "And now, I'm too hurt to take you through six miles of snow, so our options are—"

"Limited. Yes. I know."

"...so we have to kill 'em."

"And how do we do that?"

It took a moment, but the centurion took it all in—Gina could see it—before he stared once again at the crowd.

"We take 'em all with us."

Gina had known it, had *known* it from the first, and shook her head angrily. She bent and began to shed the first tear, then felt Cassius' hand on her face, lifting it. She raised her head, took a heavy breath, and stared into his eyes.

Cassius' gaze was grim.

"I *will* kill them, Gina—both of them. My strength—His strength—is sufficient." He stared into her eyes and smiled. "There's no reason for you to ask further...if you trust me."

Gina stared into eyes of pain—into eyes that had fought countless battles against foes that the world remembered with fear.

"I trust you," she said, so simple.

Cassius' head bent, and his frown deepened. He reached out and grasped the katana, closing his fist upon it. He looked over the Hall and feared nothing that he saw.

He stood.

Gina was on her feet as well, hands close to him.

"Cassius?" she whispered.

He did not turn.

"Get them ready," he said with a force she could not comprehend.

"It's time to finish this."

CHAPTER TWELVE

Gina spoke quietly to Josh and Rachel, assuring them that what she was about to say to the others was only to make them cooperate. They nodded, trusting.

With no semblance of mercy, Gina told the others that if they wanted to live, they'd better come with her. There was no debate. Only the monsignor did not move, gazing quietly at Cassius.

"A dangerous gambit, Centurion."

"Yes..."

The monsignor stared. "And so, why?"

Cassius' voice held the tone of last words. "You seek the spear to defend an institution." Almost tragically, he laughed. "Foolish man...God needs no defender."

"And so what are you, Cassius? How many men have you killed to defend an institution?"

"None," Cassius answered and slowly stood.

Watching from the side, Gina gasped as Cassius rose upon the pedestal. Even now—incredibly—he was recovering. It was impossible, she knew, but his strength now was not the strength of those who wished to survive. He was calling upon a strength that lay within everyone, but once it was spent...life was spent as well.

Yes, it would be his last battle.

"I fought to preserve life, Priest...because I believed that no man—tyrant, emperor, or monarch—owned the life of another. Men condemned another to death for their faith...as *He* was condemned...and so I spent my life to help those who were the same...but I was a twig in a river destined to overflow."

"It is not an institution that wages war, Cassius."

"Fear is the beginning of hate, priest. And hate is the beginning of war. And nothing more needs to be said of that."

With little sign of emotion Cassius lifted the katana. He nodded to Gina, and she smiled.

"Let's go," he said.

In an elliptical shape they moved slowly down the corridor that led toward the catacombs. Cassius moved slowly at the front with a host of spear-carrying monks in the rear. Josh and Rachel were on the inside of the pack, well surrounded on all sides. The monsignor had removed his soutane and carried a long Roman spear in his hands. Beside him, Father Stephen and Jaqual were similarly armed, their eyes shifting at every shadow, every sound. Rounding out the small platoon was Melanchthon, the professor, Rebecca, Miguel, and the other surviving monks.

Cassius stopped when he reached the tunnel where, according to his description of the battle, he'd last seen the Nephilim. He looked slowly over them.

"Remember," he said quietly, "if it attacks, form a solid line. Hold your spear hard in front of you and stand your ground. Do not retreat. If you run, you'll die."

If that was for inspiration, it worked. Gina saw everyone's hands tighten on the wooden hafts of the spears. Every face, glistening with sweat, was a vivid picture of fear—eyes wide and darting, lips partly open, perspiration dripping from brow and chin.

Standing close to Cassius, Gina's sweating hands tightened on a Beretta and an Uzi. She had given the second semiauto to Rebecca, who held it in a low hand. It had only taken her a moment to train Rebecca how to use the weapon, and although Rebecca had said she hated guns, she certainly loved them at the moment.

Cassius suddenly knelt, studying tracks. His eyes roamed far ahead and he nodded. "It's been busy. But it was too badly hurt to lay as many tracks as it did in the other section of tunnels. It came this way once. I'm betting it's still in here."

Gina bent, then, quietly, "No tracks leading out."

Cassius moved cautiously forward. He spoke to Father Stephen without taking his eyes off the corridor. "Did Basil request this abbey?"

Father Stephen gazed curiously at the centurion. "Yes—he requested it. For his own reasons."

"And everyone else was already here?"

"Yes."

"Raphael is...*Basil*," Gina whispered.

Cassius muttered as he lifted his torch before an opening. "How long has Basil been here?"

"Perhaps a year. But how could he have known that the abbey would be reopened?"

"He didn't. He came here for another reason."

"Like what?" Gina pitched in. "The spear?"

Cassius shook his head. "The spear won't help it." His frustration was visible. "Basil didn't pick this abbey for no reason. But this would be the last place it wants to hide unless..."

Gina was rapt. "Unless what?"

Cassius stared into the corridor. "So...they are in Rome...."

"What, Cassius?"

"Rome," he said simply. "All of this comes from Rome." He lowered his weapons. His head was bowed.

"I did not intend to trap you, Centurion."

It was the monsignor.

"You didn't," Cassius smiled faintly. "You're a pawn, Monsignor, because it trapped you as well. You were ordered to obtain the spear. But your orders came from a higher authority."

"It cannot control the Vatican itself!" retorted the monsignor. He appeared shocked. "This plan was approved...there is no way—"

Cassius' face blazed with anger. "This creature has lived for six thousand years, Priest! It's created and destroyed nations! Nothing is beyond its reach."

Monsignor DeMarco stared bitterly.

Shaking his head, Cassius searched the corridor again. "Now it has infiltrated the last, great throne of the Earth."

His expression disturbed Gina. It was almost like fear.

"They've never done that...."

"And so...the game is up."

The voice had emerged from the darkness before them, and only Cassius did not flinch. He turned to stare evenly into the darkness. "A cunning move, Raphael: But it is not yours."

Raphael laughed from somewhere within darkness. "You are a great warrior, Centurion. But it is time to end this fool's dance around the world."

Cassius nodded. "After you."

"Ah," Raphael cooed. "I think not, old friend. I have much work yet to do on this meaningless rock cast through space and time, as these creatures understand it. But we know a far different dimension, don't we, Centurion? Yes...we know of a dimension teeming with all manner of creatures as far beyond their understanding as the sun beyond the earth."

It laughed, and Gina glimpsed Cassius' finger as he flicked off the safety of the Colt.

"No more games, Raphael."

To Gina's shock, Cassius began walking forward.

"You wanted me, you got me. Forget the rest of these people."

A sound like a huge rug rustling rose in the darkness.

Cassius tilted his head slightly to the side, poised to catch the faintest sound. But Gina heard nothing more, and, apparently, neither did he. The voice finally came again from a site higher and to the left. It was at least thirty feet above the floor.

"Have you told them everything yet, Centurion?"

Cassius' mouth was drawn in a bitter line, and Gina felt an unexpected tendril of fear. In this, there was no room for mistakes because there would be no chance to recover. The last thing she wanted was another surprise.

"Tell us what?" she asked.

"Nothing," Cassius replied, lifting the barrel of the MP-5. "Don't listen to it."

Raphael's laugh was joyous. "Yes, woman, I'm lying to you. I'm not *honest*...like the centurion." He laughed long and loud. "Did he tell you what *else* he buried here so long ago?"

"What's he talking about, Cassius?"

"Don't listen to him, Gina."

"Cassius! Is he lying?"

Cassius' teeth gleamed in anger. "No, he's not lying. But whatever else is buried here has nothing to do with this! He's trying to confuse you!"

Fear said what she did not want to say. She began backing away. "Cassius, I have to know. What else did you—"

Cassius turned into her. "Gina! Don't listen to him!"

An avalanche of black and red swept down from the darkness, arms reaching toward Cassius with claws outstretched and fangs open in a silent roar. Gina reacted fast, but it was nothing compared to the speed of the beast. The violent collision carried them into a tunnel where they were instantly rolling and striking at each other.

Gina saw Cassius submerged by the creature, and a quick rush carried her into the corridor, where she saw a revolving, hulking bulk, an arm rising to strike with a long knife, and then an arm rising to strike with rending claws.

They were too close for a shot, but Gina leveled as Cassius placed a foot against Raphael's chest and threw him a short distance away. Instantly the centurion was firing, a .45 in each hand, and he emptied both clips within two seconds. Raphael bent and howled at each wound, and then he lashed out to strike Cassius hard across the face. But at the last split second, the centurion seemed to know the blow would take his head off at the neck and ducked so that claws and hand were turned on his shoulder, saving his life.

He didn't even try to reload the .45s. In an instant his hand reached the katana, and steel flashed like lightning, impaling Raphael on the blade.

It was a move so smoothly executed that it seemed no move at all. Cassius' hand had reached the hilt, and then the sword was parallel to his right side, his right hand tight against the guard. He launched himself forward, plummeting the sword through the creature's body as if it were paper.

Raphael's rage was prehistoric, and Gina realized with complete clarity why these creatures were so greatly feared.

The blazing red eyes beneath the heavy brow were the purest animal fury with a bloodlust far beyond any thought of survival.

With a single hand it lifted the centurion from the ground and flung him down the tunnel toward Gina.

Gina dropped for a shot, but she couldn't risk it as Cassius almost instantly reached his feet, spinning back toward the creature as it pulled the sword from its chest and, holding it as a man would hold it, smashed it against the granite wall. At the impact, the ancient steel shattered into a thousand shining shards that ricocheted up the tunnel like shrapnel.

Everyone instinctively ducked, and Gina raised the Uzi, searching, finger tightening on the trigger to open up with a full clip even if Cassius stood in the line of fire.

Dust swirled in the corridor like an angry demon, and it took Gina a moment to realize...

Empty...

The corridor was empty.

Cassius and the creature were gone.

———

Cassius couldn't let it escape—not this time.

He dropped from a ledge, falling the same sixty feet Raphael had dropped. As he hit the ground he rolled smoothly and came up running.

He knew he was wounded yet again. The wet flow on his neck and arm confirmed it, but he wasn't losing strength as he'd feared, nor did his agility or speed seem affected. But then, he also knew why. His body was drawing upon all that remained within him.

Even now he could feel his heart laboring with a fatigue he had never experienced. And everything, no matter how fast, seemed to be happening slowly. Even the blows of the beast, sweeping in blinding combinations, were read as if they were in slow motion so that Cassius twisted, angled, or neutralized them with the faintest touch.

As Cassius had discovered, Raphael almost always launched an attack with his right hand, and this last exchange had been no different. But as the beast surged in, right hand withdrawn, Cassius had reached out with his left hand to lightly strike Raphael's right bicep. Just a touch, something Raphael did not even notice, but it took all the momentum from the arm. And as Raphael turned, all his weight in his left hand, Cassius leaped inside the blow, striking the beast's left bicep with his right shoulder, again defeating the blow.

Cassius had not managed to escape unscathed, but they were little more than scratches. One advantage of having repeatedly fought Raphael was that he had the creature's timing now. Also, like a man, Raphael had certain moves that he repeated over and over. But, unlike the best fighters, he didn't seem to adapt. If Raphael threw a blow that didn't work, he simply threw the blow again and again, relying upon his superior strength to overcome. And that was a mistake because it burned deep strength—the kind of strength that did not recover as quickly.

Cassius, by using finesse—like a boxer allowing his opponent to pummel him round after round—was conserving his strength for one last, decisive confrontation.

He still had more than enough to take Raphael to the ground, but he wouldn't do it until he was certain that Raphael's exhaustion was complete. For once it happened, there would be no second chance. Cassius had seen it, and known it, too many times. A blow thrown late in a fight that would finish an opponent would have no effect at all thrown early in the fight. It was only a question of choosing the opportune moment to unleash.

Cassius ignored the wetness warming his back. Shallow wounds. They look bad enough, but a small amount of blood loss isn't enough to affect fighting ability. He'd bled his entire life and was familiar with it. Even encouraged by it, because in every other battle where he had fought and bled, he had won. Blood bought victory.

Already they'd descended more than a mile into the catacombs, and Cassius didn't question how much farther this would go. If Raphael led him to the center of the earth, he would follow because he wasn't letting it escape this time.

No, not this time.

He had chased it across the world a dozen times, and always, through some act of diabolical cunning, it had eluded him at the end. More than once it had simply injured an innocent child. Not killing, but severely wounding, forcing Cassius to make a hard decision—save the life of a child or allow the child to die and finish the fight. Cassius had never been able to finish the fight.

But here, in these catacombs, there was no one it could use. It had come down to the two of them.

Cassius didn't hesitate as he reached a thirty-foot gap, leaping across the ravine in a rush of air that rose beneath him like an invisible wing, the height of his jump lasting long enough to clear the distance before he began to descend. He was running as his foot touched the far ledge, nor did he hesitate, searching for an ambush. In fact, he preferred a hand-to-hand situation now. At least if he had his hands on the infernal beast, he knew where it was and could kill it.

Cassius didn't need to crouch to read tracks. Raphael was moving quickly, not turning around to see if he was followed, because he knew he was followed. Yes, Raphael was searching for a place to launch another ambush, a place that would be high and dark, and Cassius mentally counted his remaining weapons.

He'd snatched up and reloaded a single Colt .45 before he fled after Raphael, so he had nine big rounds. He retained the poniard, steeped deep in the beast's blood and...that was it.

A surge of fear rushed from the center of Cassius into his fingertips. He shook his head violently to scatter sweat from his face as he came down in a low crouch where eight tunnels connected to a huge chamber with a climbing ceiling.

Huge boulders and rocks littered the floor where they had fallen for probably a thousand years and would fall for a thousand more until the ceiling reached the surface and the cavern became a gigantic sinkhole. It was inherently unstable—not a wise place to fire a handgun.

Cassius heard a growl emanating from every tunnel at the same moment. He stopped moving. It was impossible to isolate the origin, for deep sound carried farther than high-pitched sound.

Raphael was close, yes, but how close...

Sweat dropped from Cassius' brow. He blinked and shook his head once more. His neck and chest and arm were warm with blood as if he lay in hot water—utterly comfortable. He didn't even feel the pain yet. But he had learned long ago to judge an injury by sight. He understood delayed reactions, nerve points, and the minute complexities of blood pressure and blood loss and what pain could and couldn't indicate.

Centuries and centuries ago he had come to regard his body much like a machine. He pushed it like a machine. He depended upon it like a machine.

The growl shuddered across the cavern floor once more.

Cassius stood poised, the handgun hanging at his side. He did not draw the poniard, hoping that he would have a chance to put more than one clip into Raphael before the battle again disintegrated into hand-to-hand combat. And he sensed that he stood a good chance against the Nephilim—*this* Nephilim, at least.

It was flesh. It could bleed; it could starve; it could die. Fire or water or swords or guns could destroy it. Its strength was not unlimited. Its ability to heal was much the same as his, nor was it immune to fear.

Cassius listened in stillness until the low growl faded to such silence that even the stones seemed to whisper from the trickles of an underground stream. Then he heard confused shouts somewhere in the distance.

Gina...

Cassius couldn't allow the distraction, but it had come at the worst possible moment. He had sensed that the end was near, but now there would be other factors—Gina and whoever else came into this section of tunnels. He had to force a confrontation—fast.

"It's over, Raphael."

Cassius walked toward a tunnel. If it was the wrong tunnel, it would only compel Raphael to attack him from the back. But not even Raphael could move across these brittle crumbs of slate without making a sound. It was all the warning Cassius would need.

"Raphael!" he shouted and began walking before all the tunnels, gun at his side, tempting the Nephilim. Then he decided on something more. "Since we have this moment, just you and me, tell me how it feels to be alone."

A snarl rumbled from the far side of the chamber. "You should know better."

At a soft scrape, Cassius lifted his head.

Closing...descending...

Cassius moved to the middle of the chamber. "Gladimus is gone, Raphael. And Barbatos—Vassago of Jerusalem, Berith of Rome, Marbus...even Bael."

"Yes," Raphael whispered—close, now. "I heard of your battle with Bael. They say it lasted an entire night and that Bael died...badly."

To the left...forty feet.

"It was his choice." Cassius didn't look in Raphael's direction. "Bael showed no mercy. I returned the same."

"But now you are trapped, Cassius, and even your great strength is not unlimited." A rough laugh. "Yes, you are right. We care nothing for the spear. As you say, it would do us no good. But to see you die will be worth the years of planning, the sacrifices."

Lower...twenty feet.

Clearly knowing the end, Cassius, strangely, was surprised with an impulse of regret. "I did not wish a war with your kind, Raphael. If you had only remained in your place..."

"I will never return to that place!" Raphael snarled. "I choose this world!"

The Nephilim was as close as twenty feet now—*too close.* Cassius had to make the creature move *now.*

"Enough," he said and turned his back to the beast, walking away. "You choose to hide here. You can die here. I'll bring down the tunnel and bury you."

The fast, muffled sound of steps racing toward him was all Cassius needed. He waited a full second and then spun and dropped.

The clawed hand that tore through smoking black air made no sound until it struck the limestone wall, slicing off a chunk as large as a shield. Cassius dropped the .45 to his left hand as Raphael spun into him and blocked a backhand blow with his right arm, firing past his own ribs to hit the Nephilim with three big rounds.

The consecutive impacts seemed to affect Raphael far more than the earlier rounds that he'd absorbed with little more than a curse. And Cassius knew the Nephilim was approaching the end of its strength. He spun to face Raphael head-on and fired the final six rounds straight into its chest.

Raphael, as any creature, was forced back by the thunderous impacts of the .45. But when the slide finally stopped, the Nephilim bent for a split second and then launched itself forward. Cassius had no time to consider anything but evading. He caught its arms and twisted, using its momentum and bulk to carry it over his shoulder.

It was a good move—strong and balanced—and cast the Nephilim a dozen feet. But it was no more than a brief respite, for Raphael reached his feet almost instantly and charged again, roaring this time because there was no more cause for silence. The chamber and tunnels rolled with the tremendous bellow, and Cassius also charged, ripping his poniard from its sheath.

They collided in the center of the tunnel, arms intertwining and locking in a dozen holds, releasing and locking again until they froze in position, swaying back and forth.

A snarl burst from Cassius' lips as he resisted Raphael's supernatural strength. He could feel his grip slip inch by inch and knew he would lose control faster than the Nephilim. He tried to shift, to bring its head down and avoid the fangs, more dangerous than knifes. But Raphael was prepared for that and jerked his head back as Cassius reached for its neck.

Then in a blast of frantic motion the Nephilim reached up to tear out Cassius' throat. Cassius saw the hand only when it touched his neck and turned explosively aside, hurling the creature again. It was like hurling a boulder, and yet again, Raphael rose.

Cassius knew a thousand ground-fighting techniques, but ground fighting was primarily a matter of brute strength. There was no finesse, just a savage encounter of muscle against muscle until an opponent gained a superior hold on the other's neck, and even then the ending did not come quickly.

Falling into a crouch, Cassius held the poniard low in his right hand and waited. He would strike once and hope that he pierced the cartilage between ribs and struck the heart. Then there was only time to react as Raphael closed the final step and his gigantic arms opened widely for an embrace.

Bringing the dagger up, Cassius leaped inside the arms and stabbed savagely toward Raphael's chest. The tip of the blade plowed through ribs, and Cassius shoved, throwing his full weight behind it, pushing, driving the dagger to the hilt.

Instantly he released and the arms closed around him and Cassius resisted, twisting, spitefully pushing the beast back, but he quickly discovered that Raphael was nowhere near death, as he would have been if Cassius had hit the heart.

Still, a bellow erupted from the beast as Cassius broke its hold and staggered back. Wildly flinging out an arm to sweep the centurion away, Raphael grasped the hilt of the dagger to rip it out of his chest. Instantly he staggered, pressing a huge hand against the wound. His eyes, when he looked at Cassius, mirrored true fear.

Breathless, Cassius nodded. "Yes..."

As Raphael began to respond, Cassius heard steps and whirled. He flung out an arm. "No!"

It was too late.

Gina and the others rushed into the tunnel, and Raphael moved, leaping past Cassius with agility unaffected by the wound. As it landed, Gina had time for a single burst from the Uzi. Then Raphael struck her and bounded into the heart of the monks, sweeping aside a half-dozen spears lifted desperately at the last moment. Raphael struck but once before a monk fell back, blood erupting from his neck.

Then the monsignor leaped forward, driving the long leaf-shaped spear-point into Raphael's back. Arching and howling, Raphael turned into the attack like a bear. He lashed out and struck the monsignor. Cassius recognized the sound of the impact—the sound of a meat cleaver cutting through bone—and knew the monsignor was dead.

The priest staggered back in shock, and Cassius knew the monsignor did not even know the blood was erupting from his throat with each heartbeat. Then Cassius had no more time as Raphael turned on Rachel and Josh, clearly intending to wound them as he had always wounded an innocent bystander or child, forcing Cassius to abandon the fight.

Cascading with blood like a bull pierced with swords and spears, breathing bloody froth, Raphael reached the children one step ahead of Cassius, snatching up Rachel.

"No!" Gina screamed.

Cassius collided with Raphael as the Nephilim attempted to leap outside the melee with the child, and his hand locked hard on Rachel's arm. It was a move that might have torn her shoulder out of socket, but Cassius had no choice, and then Rachel crashed to the ground.

Cassius rose instantly, knowing from Rachel's screams that she was still alive, but Raphael was only a split second slower and spun into the centurion. His rush was the rush of a wild bull—arms raised and head lowered to reveal heaping mounds of muscle that could pulverize wood and stone alike.

Cassius caught a glimpse of a solid wall behind him and in the same breath knew the impact would kill him—crushed between Raphael's irresistible rush and the immovable stone.

But as they struck the wall, they blasted stones into dust, and then they were rolling, Raphael passing over Cassius' head. Cassius tumbled wildly, falling, descending down a long, hidden staircase, swallowed by a white sea of skulls that rose about him, and Cassius knew that here were the graves of the evil and the good together, and that he had returned to the beginning.

As he knew he would....

CHAPTER THIRTEEN

G ina reached the door in time to catch a glimpse of Cassius and Raphael as they disappeared beyond the light. She spun and grabbed Father Stephen.

"Where does this go?"

The father abbot was astounded and confused. He could not even form a sentence. Gina shoved him back and snatched the Uzi as Melanchthon rushed forward. He stood in the entrance and stared down only a moment before he unceremoniously grabbed two torches from Jaqual. Melanchthon gave one to Gina, and then he picked up what she recognized as a traditional Roman fighting sword—a gladius. He turned to the professor, reaching out for the small medic's bag the old man had in his left hand. The professor gave it to the monk and nodded. Melanchthon grimaced, then turned and instantly began down the staircase, neither asking Gina's permission nor appearing to care.

She had to take control of the situation, but the monk was fiercely committed now and would do what he would do. She grabbed Rachel and fell to her knees. "Are you okay?"

Fast nods, but Gina knew she and Josh were in shock.

Gina's eyes blazed as she focused on Rebecca and the others. "Get them to the Hall and wait! If I'm not back in an

243

hour, bundle them up and get out of here!" She looked into their eyes and hugged them hard. "I love you! Now go!"

They shouted, but Gina had no choice. She had to finish this or these creatures would be with them forever.

Grimacing in pain, she stood and entered the newly revealed stairway, careful not to miss a step because the blocks were set so steeply that one slip would likely be unrecoverable. Dead or alive, she would plummet to the base, just as Cassius had done. But she knew Cassius was alive because roars—human and inhuman—thundered from what she feared was hell itself.

———

Cassius was beneath Raphael when they crashed together at the base and instantly placed a foot in the Nephilim's chest. Cassius hurled it back, where it crashed upon an ancient altar, shattering stones.

Remarkably, the torch had survived the descent, and Cassius took a single second to hurl it to a mound that ignited instantly, casting the cave in a sphere of light that grew brighter in seconds.

The mound, in the growling light, comprised hundreds and hundreds of chariots and wagons—all wooden relics of some tremendous military campaign of a nation that no longer existed. The fire grew quickly, feeding itself on the ancient wood that had not rotted because it had been protected from wind and rain and heat and cold, and was not petrified because the cavern was utterly parched.

At last, Raphael stood. His arms, glistening and black, hung stiff at his sides. His jaws were distended, but not in threat. He was dragging deep breaths across bloody fangs and lips. Then, slowly, he slouched toward Cassius as the mythical Beast might slouch toward Jerusalem during the final scarlet night of the world.

Grimacing, Cassius shook his head.

So it comes to this....

They embraced against a wall of liquid flame that consumed chariots and wagons and shields. Cassius brought the gladius up hard, stabbing Raphael through the torso. The blade sunk deep, and Cassius turned it inside the Nephilim, drawing it out to do even more damage. But if Raphael felt any pain he did not reveal it. With a snarl shuddering in its chest, the Nephilim grasped Cassius' neck and lifted the centurion fully from the floor.

Gasping, Cassius brought a knee up into Raphael's chest and then placed a boot against his clavicle. With a shove he broke the grip and fell awkwardly to the ground, and instantly Raphael crouched over him, lifting him again toward gaping fangs.

But Cassius twisted and took them both across the floor, the sword rising and falling—rising and falling with flat sheets of blood flowing off the blade as it rose, red rain following as it fell to stab the beast again and again.

It was not surprising that neither of them moved with breathtaking speed now. Rather, they were like two arm-weary fighters standing in the center of the ring in the final round of a fight that had lasted far, far too long, neither willing to lose as they hurled exhausted punch after exhausted punch to finish on their feet. They fought without air, without feeling, without sensation, only muscle memory hurling a blow, and then another, and another as the mind faded into itself, safe and soft within its own veil, void of pain.

Cassius stumbled back as he stood, falling over a small boulder. But he righted himself quickly, focusing on Raphael as he slouched forward yet again. The flow of blood from the Nephilim's mouth and nose was foamy, as if his lungs were bleeding into his breath. No, the Nephilim did not have much time, now. But it did not need much.

In two strides Cassius met the Nephilim, and they locked arms once more. Instantly Cassius was bent back, but it was not the strength of stone that Cassius had resisted before. And the difference, little as it was, was critical.

It was like the difference between bronze and steel. Even the lightest touch intimated that one could be broken, the other could not. The Nephilim also seemed lighter, as if whatever titanic force of will that had given it gravity was gone.

Cassius knew that Gina and Melanchthon had descended into the cavern. He peripherally saw the torches and glimpsed their silhouettes against the sloping stone wall. But he knew they would not enter this contest. Whether by conscious reason or some sensation they did not understand, they would let man and monster finish what they must finish alone.

With amazing clarity of sight, Cassius slipped the fangs again and again by a margin so slight that anyone watching would have thought that they'd touched flesh. But with each attack Cassius saw something, sensed something that revealed the direction, and threw up a forearm, a shoulder, ducked or leaned or parried, and finally they staggered back from each other, gasping heavily.

Cassius shook his head, sweat and blood glistening on his face like a crimson mask, as if he had painted himself in blood for this battle, but the blood was his own.

Each of them stood, bloody and bent, face-to-face with hands low because each could read the other so easily now. It mattered not how a blow originated—the feint or combination—because the movement was known before it began, as if each could read the other's mind. And if the blow landed at all, it landed simply because the other was too weary to parry or block.

Then, abandoning any façade of subtlety, Raphael simply walked into Cassius and lifted him from the ground. Only then did Cassius realize his intentions, and with a hateful curse the Nephilim hurled him into the burning heap of chariots.

As Cassius landed in the flames, he reacted with strength he did not know remained in his battered body. The flames sliced skin from his arms and legs and he rose, roaring and charging and violently blasting wood from his path to exit the blaze. He took three steps before he fell to the floor and rolled, smothering small flames that clung to his clothes. Even before he reached his knees, bent and breathless, he knew Raphael had fled farther into the cavern.

Gina was beside him speaking quickly, but Cassius couldn't catch his breath. He bent until his forehead rested on the heated floor and tried not to think of his wounds. If he were not mortally wounded, then he would survive. And if he were mortally wounded, then confirming it would do no good. There was little more than that, now.

Gina was talking fast as she lifted him from the floor and placed her shoulder beneath his arm. He didn't try to understand her words as he raised his eyes to gaze deeper into the cavern. He sighed, then nodded and spoke, as if to himself.

"So be it...."

Still nodding, Cassius reached and took the gladius from Melanchthon, who gave it up willingly. The blood that melded his hand to the hilt was blood as far back as he knew—to a place where his destiny was decided. He gazed into the darkness, and his face expressed pain that has no true expression, so that the face was void and empty of emotion, pain, or will.

Hand tightening on the hilt, Cassius shook Gina away and stood alone. She regarded him in shock and moved carefully to the side. Melanchthon said nothing and did not move.

With steps that left a wake of blood, Cassius walked slowly, as if drawn by a force beyond them all, toward what seemed a tremendous underground chamber much larger than the subterranean layer in which they stood.

With Gina and Melanchthon trailing, Cassius stopped in the huge, black mouth of the entrance. Then Cassius drew back his arm and flung the torch so that it arched long across the cavern to land in yet another mound of chariots, siege engines, shields and armor and weapons of war.

It took only a moment for flames to feed on the crisp wood, and then a tremendous, towering shape began to take form in the center of the cavern, casting its shadow upon a distant wall. Then mounds and hills and dunes of skeletons also rose from the darkness, heaped in hundreds of thousands across a haunting underworld of bones uncountable that lay like rags upon ravines and knolls with skeletal hands even now clutching broken swords and shattered spears.

And upon a low hill that dominated the gargantuan graveyard like a haggard skull stood a towering black crucifix that rose between jagged fangs of stone.

Empty eyes of a million skulls danced in torchlight, as if in warning. And the crucifix cast a lordly shadow over them all, as if in hope. As if beyond here were the gates of hell, and here all the dead of the earth must come, and pass, to enter.

<hr />

Staring up at the crucifix, Cassius did not move.

Gina cast a single glance toward him as she walked forward, afraid, for some reason to move in front of him. Mouth open in shock, she gazed over endless mounds of skeletons.

Then she sensed Melanchthon. He had walked forward and was also staring up at the crucifix. But his face did not reveal alarm or even surprise. He stared upon it as if, from the very beginning, he knew that it would be here.

Cassius' ravaged face was a kaleidoscope of astonishment, grief, pain, and regret that was freed degree by degree—some together, some alone. The gladius hung limply in his hand.

"*You...*" whispered Gina, "you brought it here!"

Cassius' voice was stone. "Yes."

"But...*why*? To protect it?"

"So men would not war over it," answered Melanchthon grimly. "As they would have."

Gina gazed again across the mountains of bones. What had happened here had been the purest war. And despite the uncountable death, it did not seem that they had died together.

"Cassius...who were these people?"

Cassius gazed across the skeletons, the broken swords, lances, and shields. "Those who sought to use it as a weapon," he said at last. "Warriors, adventurers, legionnaires, centurions, conquerors, tyrants...and those that served them."

His eyes softened. "I did all that I could to keep it in secret, but it was no secret, and they came for it...kings...mercenaries... armies...all with dreams of power, of immortality—dreams to change the destiny of nations." He nodded slowly. "For two hundred years I guarded it. Until all those who knew of it were dead. Until it faded into legend." He paused. "Until *I* faded into legend."

It was amazement beyond amazement, and Gina could only stand numbly in what was certainly shock. She would have realized it, but her mind was overloaded with so many images, she couldn't clarify thought.

Cassius walked slowly forward, gazing up at the crucifix, and his gaze seemed to pass over every crevice, every line and circle of age in the tree. He stopped when he reached the base of the hill and looked over the sea of skeletons that lay, arms outstretched toward the crest, as if they had each been killed trying to reach the base.

"If you could have seen Him," Cassius whispered, fearful or awed. He was silent a long time. "It's strange...what men say about Him now—what they say He would say or do. Because I watched Him for two years—I studied Him—and I never knew what He would say, or do. Just as I knew that no army could stand against Him."

His laugh was poignant. "I was terrified that day.... When we raised Him on that tree, I knew that He could destroy the world with a single thought—that He could destroy *us*." He paused. "You think that centuries are long? No, centuries are not long. *Long* is standing upon Golgotha for six hours, watching Him die, knowing that between His word and His death rested the fate of the universe. You have never known fear unless you have known that fear. You wonder why I do not fear Raphael and his kind? Because I have known true fear—I stared into the eyes of God, knowing that, with just a word, He could destroy the entire earth. But He did not. And, at the end, when I was begging Him to die—to finally claim His victory—" He laughed, but it was a laugh of tragedy and pain. "—which I knew He would, in the end, He just gazed upon me with such...such mercy...and love."

Gina had closed the distance as Cassius talked until she stood silently beside Melanchthon. She saw the big monk softly wipe a tear from his face.

Cassius' voice was a whisper. "Even when He said nothing... He commanded death."

A scrape caused Gina to spin, staring hard. But the far corner of the cavern was hidden behind the curving slope of a wall. Holding the MP-5 tightly, she looked to Cassius.

Yes, he had heard. But he did not immediately react, as if he dreaded his next act. Then he turned, gladius in bloody hand, and walked toward the origin of the sound. He did not reach for any of Gina's weapons, nor did she expect him to. Where he was in his spirit would not allow guns. It was something he had to do with a sword.

Closing close behind him, Gina and Melanchthon rounded the curve to see a broken wheelchair in the dirt. The steel was bent as if whatever was contained within it had exploded.

"Dominic?" Gina whispered. "It wasn't Basil?"

"No, not Basil," rumbled Melanchthon. "Dominic, who wore the darkest mask of all."

Cassius continued into the curve and saw Dominic lying naked upon a mound of broken skulls. His neck was torn and ravaged, and blood on his chest masked the depths of his wounds. His mouth was open in silent petition, as if he might speak. But he did not speak as Cassius approached. Did not speak as the centurion stood over him and shook his head.

"No," Cassius said quietly. "I truly didn't know it was you."

Dominic struggled to rise, to speak, almost pleading.

Cassius scowled. "Even now, Raphael, you would deceive me! Even when the game is over, and you have nothing to gain by lies, you would lie. You are truly...tragic." Cassius' hand tightened on the gladius, and he stepped forward.

Somehow, Gina felt that this place belonged to another world that she had no right to enter or remember. And what had to be done, had to be done. Yet, still, there was a great sadness in it. She turned her face away as Cassius closed the final stride.

Dominic's mouth twisted mutely.

Cassius shook his head, somehow reluctant now to finish this—as if he were finishing a part of himself.

"We belong to another world, Nightbringer." Cassius' aspect was tragic. "But that world has passed, and so must we."

With frantic strength Dominic reached out to Cassius with a mutilated right hand, pointing to the nearby darkness, then rolled his head from side to side and breathed his last. And the centurion saw it at once—the ravaged reflection of a lurking Raphael in the eyes of the silent monk. Cassius dove forward.

Yes, Raphael—*Basil*—had played his last gambit—an attempt to lure Cassius into position for a final, finishing blow. As Cassius rolled past the body of Dominic, he spun just as Gina's distant scream boomed across the cavern and Raphael surged into him.

Combat reflexes and instinct saved Cassius' life, and he was instantly in a fighting mode—a change made in a tenth of a second that cast aside tragedy and compassion and any thought that didn't search out the life in his enemy so he could destroy it.

Baleful, Cassius rose. His eyes were red. His voice was ravaged and bitter. "The long night has ended, Raphael.... Time for you to return to your kind."

Cassius was stunned when the MP-5 erupted, but with the blackest animal fury, Raphael spun into Gina's attack.

It covered the distance on its huge bowed legs with horrifying speed. It, too, was holding nothing back now, though Cassius knew that the beast was as good as dead. It just didn't know it yet. Still, he did not know how long Raphael could continue before his body finally burned out oxygen and acids and adrenaline.

Cassius surged forward, hurtling a boulder with hesitation, knowing that he had to intercept Raphael before he reached Gina. Cassius blasted a heap of skulls into dust and staggered, unable to recover quickly enough as he crashed into a skeleton fixed in a chariot still arrayed in iron armor, and in a nightmare flash Cassius *remembered* the moment he had driven the man's own javelin back through his heart. He crashed through the skeletal spectacle, scattering bones and splinters and iron fragments like ashes, and one step later he collided with Raphael and Gina together.

A lightning-fast blow by Raphael tore the MP-5 from Gina's hands. As the clawed hand closed on the steel it exploded, a round in the chamber discharging at the force. In the next moment they were locked in a chaotic tangle of arms and legs with Cassius taking blow after blow intended for Gina. But it couldn't last and it didn't last because Cassius spun to lay a hand on her arm and spun again, hurling her clear of the battle. He spun back into Raphael, reading his opponent's moves fast.

Claws swept in low from the left and Cassius had no move but to jerk his body back, head and feet remaining in place as the claws missed his guts. But the move left him off balance, and there was no way to avoid the left hand that rushed toward his neck, and Cassius knew that it was the end.

Go to the ground!

Cassius grabbed the arm and spun, and the momentum carried them sprawling to the ground.

There was no finesse to this last grapple to the death. It was war—pure, savage, truthful, and without regret. Again and again the gladius rose and fell, and then Raphael surged with hysterical strength and broke free, reaching his feet to flee yet again. But Cassius was equally as quick and spun to hurl the beast through bones that exploded like dust. Raphael was dazed and disoriented as he rose, searching instantly, and saw Cassius as an arching leap carried him into the fangs of the beast.

Raphael had time for an abrupt half-twist to avoid the gladius Cassius held aloft with both hands tight on the hilt, but it was too late. The blade descended to hit Raphael solidly in the forehead in a blast of flesh and blood and bone.

Cassius' weight bore the Nephilim to the ground, and Cassius remained on top, tearing the gladius free to stab again through its chest. Enraged, Cassius reached up to grasp Raphael by the throat and ripped the blade through and... stared into lifeless eyes.

Unable to catch his breath, Cassius gazed with something like amazement into the black wells that had commanded such bestial strength, such power, knowledge, and the wisdom of ages, as well as the evil. The blood that joined them was older than this world, more powerful than this world. It was the rubric of gods and fallen gods.

It seemed like forever that Cassius held the mammoth neck in his hand, his forehead bent to Raphael's chest. It seemed like forever that the great wedged head, fangs open in a frozen roar, was silent. Like forever...that the gladius dripped darkly to the dust.

Dusk had darkened the edge of all Cassius could see. He sensed someone speaking to him but could not answer—his mind separated from his body in what he knew was the beginning of death. He did not know he had fallen forward, did not know that he lay upon the breast of the beast as if they had died together.

Gina rolled Cassius off the carcass of the beast and didn't even glance at the violent, frozen gaze that even now searched the darkness, as if to beg for an answer.

"The professor's bag!"

No question. Melanchthon knelt and opened the bag, and Gina was checking one vial after another before she cried, "Epinephrine!"

She drew half a syringe and plunged the needle into Cassius' heart, emptying it. She ripped it free as Cassius convulsed, his right arm reaching high and violently, as if to appeal to a higher power.

"No!" he cried—pleaded.

His eyes blazed in asking, then closed.

And he fell as dead.

Strange, thought Cassius as he walked through the cavern he had not visited in so many long centuries...yes, so strange, and so familiar. Things were as they had been, but gray and transparent and benign now, and beautiful in a misty, fog-edged way.

Cassius gazed upon the mountains of bones and saw the chariot of the warrior who had called himself Sulieman. He had come to claim the crucifix for Mecca, as convinced in his own mind that he must claim the treasure for his faith as Cassius was that *no one* must claim it.

Still resting inside the iron chariot that bore him to the castle walls, Sulieman's skeleton was suddenly fleshly white. And Cassius remembered the titanic power of that mighty arm. Remembered how Sulieman hurled that battle-ax with such force that wood and stone were reduced to dust.

No, the Moor had not listened to reason even when Cassius at last struck him down and stood above him, offering life if he would leave in peace. But there would be no peace, and Cassius finished him, as he had finished the rest.

Battle after battle rose again and again inside Cassius, and he saw himself again and again—he was cut, broken, dying, only to rise up once more to kill. Sometimes they had come alone—sometimes together. It had made no difference in the end. They had all died.

Some part of Cassius' mind wondered why he did not behold a river of blood, but the only blood he beheld was his own. And, then, there he was, standing in a field of dead, painted with blood, head bowed, alone and guilty and...

Condemned.

And then Sulieman raised his head, as Cassius knew he would. But the magnificent Moor did not smile, did not frown. Nor did he reach down to grasp the huge battle-ax even now at his side, as Cassius had left him. Rather, it was as if whatever he and Cassius had fought for, however just, meant nothing now. Then, slowly, Sulieman lifted his arm toward Cassius and waited patiently, a single hand outstretched.

Cassius' eyes narrowed in amazement.

This is where I belong...not with the living....

A world of war in countless faces and names flooded before Cassius, and he was amazed that he remembered them all—the children, the men, women, the ancient, and the innocent. He saw evil in human form, and he again felt the cold wind and a deeper cold as he moved silently through the night to find it and destroy it. He again saw guards walking terraced gardens where he would descend to the terror of man. And the scenes continued and continued for centuries—more faces, more cities, more balconies and gardens and guards. But always the blood was the same, and always his hands were the same in the blood.

An overwhelming fatigue rushed up, and Cassius lay on a soft cloud in which he could rest and which would bear him through the ages to come. And he almost closed his eyes, surrendering to the mercy of it when he saw more faces emerging from the hills.

They were here—all of them—the children, the old and the young, all standing, all waiting. The children smiled, and the old men nodded as if to assure him that the end was not war, or death, or the grave. Nor did their gazes reflect anything but peace. And then Cassius did shut his eyes—not to surrender to the cloud that lifted him but to pray...to thank them—to thank Him—and remember.

A heartbeat, slow and subdued, thumped in surrounding corridors, and Cassius bent his face, listening. He smiled, laughed once, and cast a last gaze at those who held out their hands.

There was nothing to say that a hand raised in peace did not say, and Cassius nodded, but then he lifted his head and heard Gina speaking to him and in a transparent, white, rising rush felt her touch his face. And she continued to speak, as if to hold on to whatever part of him remained in the world of the living by words alone.

Cassius stretched out his hand to the shapes that stood so close, their faces void of anger or hate or condemnation. Whatever they possessed now—what could not be taken from them—was far, far greater than what they were doomed to lose from the beginning.

Great Cedric bowed his head and smiled with the smile of a friend. "You have fought well, Centurion—you have honored our God. And now, my brother, is it your will to rest?"

Bent, Cassius wished for peace. He raised his face to the sky and looked once more into the eyes of God, but there was no more pain in His eyes now. No, the Lord of All the Earth recognized no more pain. Then Cassius thought of those behind him—those yet in the cavern, those who had not reached this place where pain and fear faded because the Lord was here. He grimaced, reaching toward the Lord. And then he thought again and again and again of those who would be left behind to the mercy of the beast, and Cassius bowed his head.

"No," he groaned.

The Lord stretched out His hand and smiled.
The sound rose like rivers around him.
"So be it, my child...."

Cassius' eyes blazed with life.

Gina was staring over him and cried out, "Cassius!"

Cassius stared into her, knowing life. Then he grasped her hand and closed his eyes, grimacing in pain before he saw again the spectral images that remained so patiently waiting—that would always be patiently waiting.

A single hand outstretched.

CHAPTER FOURTEEN

R est, Cassius."

Cassius heard Gina's words and rose slowly. He felt remarkably stronger and knew what she had done. He glanced at the professor's bag.

"What'd you do?" he asked, mostly because he was too tired to tell her, himself.

"I gave you the works," Gina said, checking his eyes.

"You did well."

"How do you feel?"

Cassius coughed and then—slowly, painfully—stood. He knew the best way to defuse her fear was to put the same question to her. "Did you get hurt?"

"Not really. You sure you're all right?"

"I'm all right."

They turned as Melanchthon spoke and shook his head. "Don't move too quickly. My legs are not what they used to be."

The journey through the duplicitous tunnels lasted longer than Cassius remembered, but in time they entered the last, final corridor that would take them to the chambers surrounding the Great Hall.

They had spoken little, but as they neared the Hall, Gina looked at Cassius. Her eyes held sadness, as if she did not desire this ending. But she did not say it with more than her eyes, nor did Cassius encourage her.

They had spoken of love, and afterward she had spoken of it no more. But Cassius wondered if he could love again—if he could endure love again. And with the question he knew that he could. Yes, he could endure it again. To not endure it would be worse than love itself.

But in the same thought, he knew he could not inflict his love on another, or accept love. Because he would not age, and she would grow old, and she would die. But long before that, she would feel guilt that he would not leave her in peace, then less and less worthy until she longed for death because of love. Cassius had endured it before, and some things did not change.

She spoke as they saw the distant entrance to the Great Hall. "So...what now?"

Cassius looked at her, eyes sullen. "I have to track the other one."

Gina fought back tears, wondering how much more Cassius—*even Cassius*—could take. She whispered, "Can you..."

He shrugged. "He escaped this time, but he can't escape forever. When this is finally over, maybe I'll take you on a tour of Rome." At her laugh, he smiled. "I think I can give you a better trip than most tour guides."

"I'll bet you can. And this place?"

"I'll handle the authorities."

She was amused. "How?"

"Believe me, I didn't live this long without being prepared for contingencies. I'll make a phone call. That's all you'll ever hear of it."

Nightbringer

They walked a moment in silence. Casually, Melanchthon trailed them by a half-dozen steps. Gina's voice suddenly became pensive. "And your friend Dominic?"

"Was a victim. Like the rest." He became more studious. "Raphael—Basil—wanted to distract me—get me chasing shadows. And it worked for awhile. But I knew something was wrong. I just couldn't figure out what it was. If I had more time, it might have been different. But I was as confused as you were."

"Yeah," Gina agreed and swept back her hair with both hands. "I don't know what to say. I think of returning to the world, and I don't even know what the world is anymore. Going through something like this changes everything. It's as though everything outside this place doesn't matter."

Cassius was quiet, then, "It does matter, Gina." He matched her gaze. "The good things—the small things you didn't think were so important—become more important than anything. And the things you thought were such a big deal—catching criminals—take a backseat to spending time with your kids. That's the way it should be, and it's something that most people don't discover until they've faced death."

Gina nodded slowly. "Nothing like a good dose of death to let people know what's truly important. A shame it has to be that way."

"It doesn't." Cassius laughed. "But when it does, you don't forget it too fast."

"Believe me. I will never forget this."

Cassius had stopped without warning. And when Gina looked back, she saw him staring high toward the roof of the Great Hall. They could only see a portion of a single window, but the storm raged even worse than before.

"Cassius...what is it?"

His eyes didn't leave the window. "He's still here."

"The *children*!"

Cassius caught her before she moved and slammed her hard against a wall. "No! It's *me* he wants!"

"But the children!"

"He hasn't harmed the children!" Cassius' confidence was complete. "He needed bait to make sure we'd come back!"

Gina's control was gone. "We don't have any more weapons!"

It was a long moment, both of them breathing hard and fast. Then, as if an idea dreaded and anticipated rose within Cassius, he lifted his gaze at the great domed roof of the cathedral-like Great Hall. His voice was a whisper.

"There are always weapons."

He turned into her fiercely, close enough for a kiss. "When it begins, grab the children! Get outside the abbey! The storm won't last much longer! I promise!"

"Cassius!" Gina was on the edge of frantic. "What are you going do!"

"Finish it," he said bitterly and stepped solidly away from her.

Gina's gaze flicked from the entrance to his face, as if trying to discern what invisible fate existed between them. She stopped when she saw he was staring gently at her.

He smiled faintly. "Remember what I said?"

"About what?"

"About my dying?"

She stared. "Only when you've lived long enough to know?"

He nodded.

"But...know what?"

He stepped into her fast and lifted her by the shoulders and kissed her strongly and embraced her and held her as if nothing in the world could take her from his arms. When he released her, Gina's hand slipped off his back as he angled fast around a corner and was instantly lost in shadows.

She stood alone, staring after him. She looked at the Hall again, and it seemed too...peaceful. The lamps glowed, the torches burned, as if nothing evil rested within it. But she knew that what was within it was beyond evil.

A hand braced against the wall, Gina leaned her face into her other hand, and what was within her rose to words.

"Jesus, *please*...help us."

CHAPTER FIFTEEN

J osh and Rachel sat motionless upon the divan as the lone Nephilim that rested before them enjoyed a pomegranate, relishing every drop of the green flavor, squeezing it so that the juice trickled, drop by drop—life after life of a corrupted world—into its mouth.

Beyond them, the Great Hall was magnificently and brightly illuminated with hundreds of candles. There was no trace of shadow. The arena was prepared so that color and action could be fully seen and fully remembered. For the first time Cassius was aware that the Nephilim would treasure this battle. Which was, perhaps, good because it also meant it considered Cassius a serious challenge.

The Nephilim lifted the last piece of pomegranate when it obviously sensed Cassius' slow, calm approach from the far end of the Hall. Then it stared directly at the centurion who walked from the darkness of a corridor.

Wearing the silver armor of the marble centurion, the bloodred robe descending almost to the floor, Cassius walked directly toward the altar and the beast.

The breastplate emblazoned with the gold lion enclosed Cassius' chest, and he wore the leather-steel gauntlets. Upon his feet he wore the knee-high sandals. His sword, the gladius, was sheathed low at his left side, and a long poniard was sheathed on his right. He held one of the polished spears from the wall. Cassius stopped a great distance from the altar. His face and his gaze were stoic, patient, unaffected. When he spoke, he revealed nothing.

"Good evening, noble Jaqual."

Jaqual laughed gustily in a deep voice so unlike the voice that had risen from his spindly form until now. "*Tanat potentia Centurius est.*" He laughed. "Been a while."

Cassius angled slowly toward the altar. An experienced eye could easily detect his tactical use of surroundings. For at every step there was a column, a display, a couch, or table between himself and the Nephilim. If Jaqual launched a sudden attack, he would be forced to hurtle or demolish two or three obstructions, giving Cassius seconds—all the time in the world—to execute a counterattack. But Jaqual clearly had no intentions of rushing his satisfaction.

No one else was in the Hall.

"The others?" Cassius asked.

"Ah," Jaqual gestured, "unfortunately, I was forced to lock them in the wine cellar for the moment. You know how it is—so many to kill, so little time."

His hands, quite human in appearance, hung relaxed at his sides. "Did you know you almost caught me once?"

Cassius carefully closed. "Really."

"Really." The Nephilim laughed. "You don't remember? 1892? That castle in London? Yes...you were trying to kill me, but like a bad marksman, you killed my *brother*, instead."

Cassius nodded. "To finish what David began."

Jaqual smiled, and jagged white fangs *not there* a split second ago were visible. The change had been instantaneous—something in the blink of an eye. Then the Nephilim's voice assumed a fatalistic tone. "Raphael is...?"

"As you will be...in a few moments."

Jaqual grimaced. "I see."

Josh made a faint motion to rise and move toward the side of the divan and Cassius instantly raised his hand. Gently, Rachel reached out and pulled her brother back. Cassius knew Jaqual was not threatened, but he wanted to keep him distracted. "Why now?" he asked, stepping even closer. "I didn't know it was you."

Jaqual picked his fangs with a splinter of bone. "Ah, well, I didn't know what my poor, pathetic Raphael might have told you. He never was very smart. In fact, none of this would have happened if he hadn't panicked when you arrived. But he feared that you might recognize him, and then the hunt would begin all over again. Oh, I tried to tell him he was making things too complicated—dragging that fool cripple all over this *holy* place. But nooooo...he wouldn't listen to me." His stare was ironic. "That's the problem with being a thousand-year-old teenager like Raphael. You think you know everything."

Still moving, Cassius was within twenty feet of the children. "Why didn't you help him? The two of you could have probably finished me in short time."

"Well, I did assist in my own humble means."

"More than once. Even let Raphael wound you at the start to play out your charade."

Jaqual smiled, as if to say, "It was nothing."

"But then Raphael panicked."

The Nephilim shrugged. "To tell the truth, I knew he would. You see, I easily recruited the wayward Raphael, who had always survived by my foresight, anyway. But there are others—others like myself—" A smile implied the unspoken threat. "—who were yet to gather under this roof.... But now, alas, I suppose I will be forced to find more hospitable lodgings."

"To create your own nation again?"

"Oh no, nothing so ambitious." Jaqual's gaze shifted from white to red—again, instantaneous. "To be completely honest, Centurion, there's another reason."

Positioning himself so Jaqual could not see the corridor Gina had just exited on the distant side of the Hall, Cassius took a risk and stopped moving. He knew that when he stopped moving, Jaqual would be twice as focused, afraid his opponent had found some unanticipated line of attack. And Gina would need the distraction if she had any hope of even getting close to the children without the Nephilim's inhuman senses detecting her presence.

Cassius was right. Jaqual's face became more sharply angled, as if he had prompted the first stage of his monstrous transformation.

"What reason would that be?" Cassius asked.

The Nephilim shook his head, as if in pity. "I have grown tired of you, Cassius—both you and your war. Endlessly preying on my kind to reconcile your guilt. Even before you arrived, I had devised the means of your demise. All that was required was for the remaining brethren to join me, and then we would have helped you rest in peace. But then they opened the abbey too soon." He laughed. "Yes, I knew you'd come, Cassius, when you learned the abbey was open once more. I simply wanted to eliminate the trouble of a 'fight,' so to speak." He smiled. "I much prefer a slaughter."

Cassius couldn't see Gina. She had disappeared amid the pillars.

Then, without removing his eyes from the centurion, Jaqual spoke to the children. "Please tell your mother she can come out. She sounds like a charging rhinoceros."

No one moved and then Gina stepped from behind a pillar a hundred feet from the altar. She had slipped out of her shoes so she could move without sound.

"Thank you," Jaqual said, and then his eyes narrowed. His mouth turned down. And where there had been patience, there arose an old and bitter anger.

"We could have ruled the world together, Cassius. But you had to serve the Hebrew dog to the bitter end. Do you really think He'll forgive you for what you did?" He shook his head, as if in disbelief. "Fool...you saw Him feed thousands. You saw Him *raise the dead*! Then you nailed Him to that tree for your *emperor*."

"I serve another King, now."

"Too late!" Jaqual snarled, eyes blazing red. "You have always been the fiercest fighter! The *perfect warrior*! The sea of men you killed lined both sides of the road from Jerusalem to Rome! Yes, Cassius, entire cities! Entire nations lay in ashes! As if you had the right to decide! An entire world, Centurion, has wept at the blood you have shed!" Jaqual continued with malicious calm. "And then there's always *Golgotha*...the most precious blood of all."

Cassius did not move, and in a blink...

Water and blood appear so much the same in the darkness, Cassius noticed with such clarity as the dull thuds continued. And yet the man did not move, but for deep gasps that lifted his chest on the wooden beam already soaked in His blood. Cassius looked out to gaze across the hundreds and hundreds of cloaked shapes, a remarkable sea of pale faces in the dusk—painful faces, faces that could be no more painful than the face of this man—this man who had caused all this.

Cassius' teeth came together hard as he turned back to the man, and he moved a soldier aside so that he might look into the man's eyes, so that he could look into His eyes once again to confirm what he had seen before—a hundred times before. But that was the fascination of the man's eyes. No matter how many times Cassius had seen Him—and most of the time he had not seen the man's face directly—he had watched Him gazing on some old woman, some child, some tax collector or harlot—Cassius had been...*confused*. Wondering what knowledge, what great secret the man *had* but never revealed.

Before cataracts had whitened Cassius' vision, he had prided himself on the clearness of his eyes. He had purposefully stared blue and clear upon those he confronted. The power of a man is in his eyes, he had been told, but not with this man.

No, this man never revealed himself with His dark eyes circled with dark rings as if He had not slept in ages, as if the grief He knew had permanently cast bruises beneath His eyes. But even when He did not look upon someone, there was a force beyond this world, even in the gaze He did not cast. A *power*—it was the only way Cassius could reckon whatever it was—that held history, even time itself, in its grasp, as if all *this* were always within His power.

And gazing upon the man as He lay upon the ground, Cassius prayed more desperately than he had ever prayed that the man would die, but the man would not die....

No, He would not die.

Until He chose.

Opening his eyes from a single blink, Cassius stared upon Jaqual once more. The centurion's smile was despising. "You feared Him, Jaqual. Even then, you feared Him."

Jaqual snarled. "So did *you*! But I had cause to fear Him! I even had cause to kill Him! You had no cause but for

Nightbringer

expendable Tiberius!" He laughed, equally despising. "What an *idiot*! You sacrificed eternity for a laurel wreath that fades like grass!"

As another vision arose before Cassius, he shook his head, aware suddenly that there was more at work within his mind than guilt. His teeth were tight as he bent his head toward the Nephilim, concentrating to remain within the moment. But the power was strong—vision after vision of depthless black storm clouds and thunder that rumbled across the sky, as if it began above where he stood.

His soldiers were laboring over the nails they hammered into the huge square timber. They had driven iron spikes through the man's arms easily enough but had hit a knot or some unseen density at His ankles that refused to allow the spike to enter.

Cassius cast a glance at the storm, moving impossibly fast now over Golgotha, as the Hebrews called it.

"Finish it!" he roared to his soldiers, who jerked their heads upward at the enraged voice. Cassius ripped his gladius free as he stalked around them, cursing. He didn't seek to understand the cause of his horror, for he did not want to.

"Idiots!" he shouted as he struck a soldier aside and pointed threateningly at another. "You have ten seconds to finish this or you'll be dead by morning!"

Cassius could threaten them with death. He could threaten them with anything, and it was a power he exercised without mercy in that hour. He did not worry about the consequence of what he said. He only cared that every fiber of his being, every nerve, felt naked and exposed to the lightning that struck from sky to earth to him.

271

Raising the hammer far above his head, the soldier struck six rapid blows, and the nail protruded downward from the beam. Whatever the spike had struck within the wooden crucifix had bent the iron like wax. Cassius had never seen such a thing. It was too much.

"Raise Him!" he bellowed, and as ten men struggled to lift the crucifix, lightning turned the night to day for a moment that cost Cassius his mind. He shut his eyes and raised forearms across his face to the brilliance of a world that threatened to invade this one....

"Cassius!"

Cassius jerked his head to the side. It was Gina.

"Don't listen to him!"

Again, Cassius found Jaqual. He was stunned and amazed at the power of the creature, which he acknowledged was far more than the power of flesh. He only had to barely consider that the Nephilim had brought this storm that had not broken in three days and nights. That he had lived twice as long as Cassius and knew twice as many dark secrets. That he had effortlessly blinded so many within this abbey for so long. Yes, its power was great.

Breathing heavily, Cassius waited for his head—his vision—to clear. He only hoped Jaqual did not know the true effectiveness of this power that reduced his mind to vision upon vision.

"No," Jaqual muttered, contemptuous. "Don't listen to me—to one who was there!" He pointed upon Cassius like a judge pronouncing doom. "You knew as well as I what He was, Cassius! We both condemned Him! We both killed Him! But then...then after you nailed Him to the tree, you began to hunt us! His brothers!"

"You were never His brother!"

"What do you know of celestial might?"

"I know this world was given to man!" Cassius shook his head to reinforce. "You have no place here...."

Jaqual erupted from the altar, fangs savagely separating in a thunderous snarl. The hair on his head rose like the hackles of a wolf. "And *you* do?" he barked. "What made you immortal, Centurion? Was it not an *accident*! His blood touched yours, and you were fated to live until you were killed by force! But if the Nazarene wanted you to live forever, would He not have lifted you *above death*? As He lifted Elijah?" Jaqual's aspect would have condemned even Moses. "Even your immortality is damned! Can't you see that? Can't you see? You are a casualty of war! An *abortion* of God's plan for man!"

Jaqual's eyes glowed—the truest monarch of hell. Then his fingers spread, palm uplifted, and curled like talons, crushing man's mind, man's world.

"Yes!" Jaqual hissed. *"Remember your guilt!"*

Thunder was the world, and the rain was hot and then ice and Cassius fell to his knees. Whatever he had known, whatever he had decided, whatever he had hoped or dreamed or believed was insignificant now.

Cassius shouted in fear, unable to contain his fear to silence, and his soldiers turned in confusion, but he did not care. He was not the greatest authority upon this hill—this hill that never seemed more like a skull than it did in this moment. Quickly, though the quickness did not reduce his horror, Cassius strode across the mud-slick mound, knowing he was shouting something that his men did not understand—something he did not understand.

Cassius gazed over the minions collapsing in hundreds upon hills that merged with ice that slashed in sheets until the hundreds and the hills disappeared into storm.

Mouth open in shock, eyes hot with tears, Cassius raised his face to the crucifix....

―――――

"Cassius!"

Gina was staggering forward, and Cassius shouted as he whirled. He'd dropped into a crouch, the spear lifted. Then he remembered and spun toward the altar to see that Jaqual had stepped from the dais—an electrifying threat.

Catlike and poised, the Nephilim began circling. "You believe you are strong, Centurion. But I will show you strength. I slaughtered a thousand of your kind a day at Jerusalem—at Carthage, at Askelon. Until even I tired of the blood."

Gasping, Cassius blinked. He shook his head to clear his thoughts and gritted his teeth. "There is an end to all strength," he said after a moment. "Even yours."

"You know nothing of strength, Cassius. You have known and fought Nephilim that were only distant descendants of we who began to spread our father's seed on this doomed planet— faint reflections, thin images, pathetic champions."

In the short space, Cassius had recovered. "Yes, I remember the great Raphia. Yes, great Raphia, who was brought down by Yahweh with a small stone hurled by a shepherd boy who became a king!"

Jaqual bent his face and growled. His voice was ice—a titanic wedge of ice that rose within him and fell like a monument to the end of the world. "I also remember Goliath...my *son*."

Cassius' lips opened partly in shock, but he had been here before—hearing secrets that shifted everything the world seemed to be, secrets not even he could have guessed. Then he exerted discipline gained across centuries and blew drops of sweat from his lips. "Man is lord of the earth, beast—not your kind. It was never your kind."

Jaqual's bark was sharp with spite. "Yes! That explains why I have killed a hundred thousand of your kind! Because your Yahweh is so great!"

Cassius frowned. "You haven't killed *me*."

Scowling, Jaqual ceased to circle. His scowl deepened as he glanced at the tapestry of the Nephilim fighting the Roman soldiers. Yes, the creature appeared to be victorious, but its true end was unknown. The Nephilim's mouth was a hard line as he stared once more upon Cassius. His words required reluctant resolution.

"Let me pass," Jaqual said bitterly. He waited for Cassius to answer, but Cassius kept silent. Growling, Jaqual stepped forward, and his cloak swelled to the limit of what it could contain, threatening with monstrous strength in the same way a man threatened with an unsheathed sword.

"I know you will not break your oath," Jaqual added coldly. "So grant me safe passage, and I will let the woman and her children live. Even more! I swear that none of my kind will ever harm them!" He searched Cassius' gaze. "Consider my words, Cassius! This does not have to end in death! We have always existed! We can continue to exist!"

Fangs bared, Jaqual took a single step. "Do you truly believe you can eradicate evil from the world, Centurion? Evil has always existed and always shall! It is foolish to rage against a balance that will only be decided with the Nazarene's return!"

From the divan, Rachel spoke in horror, trembling. "There's *more* of them?"

"Cassius knows I am not the last," Jaqual whispered.

Revealing nothing, Cassius looked to Gina. Her face was a kaleidoscope of emotion. Then he looked to the divan as Josh plainly shook his head, silently mouthing, "No!'

A thin smile creased Cassius' face, then faded as he looked to the Nephilim once more. "And how many more of their kind must die so you can live?"

Jaqual blinked, as if the question were insane. "What does it matter?"

Cassius nodded sadly. "It matters."

For a long moment Jaqual stood in silence. Obviously, he was half-hoping for compromise. Then he seemed to reconcile himself to the bitter alternative and began to circle.

"Then you must die," he growled.

Cassius remembered the vision in the cavern and knew without doubt that it had been more than a vision. "The dead are better off than I am today," he said quietly.

"Because they are with *Him*?" Jaqual crushed the comment with contempt. "If that is true, Centurion, then why have you cheated death for so long? Tricked it! *Defeated it* in war after war! You could have ended it any time you wished!"

"I'm a soldier," Cassius said wearily.

"You're a murderer!" Jaqual's force of will erupted like the wrath of a god. "Look! There is blood on your hands!" He flung out an arm toward the storm. "Listen! The blood of Jesus cries to you from the earth! I can hear it!" He pointed. "You are guilty!"

"The Judge of All the Earth can choose between us."

The answer hurled ice into Jaqual's burning visage. "My last words, Cassius. Join me. Or *die*."

"Everybody dies," Cassius said. "Once."

Both ceased to move.

"Yes," Jaqual growled. *"Even you!"*

In a split second Jaqual's clothes exploded into shreds, and he towered a foot above Cassius. His bear-like body was the purest white—white fangs, white claws, fur, and face. Only his eyes were bloodred. His tremendous tusks clicked in a shuddering snarl. He casually flexed long, knobbed fingers, and his white claws cracked in a gunshot staccato.

Cassius had fallen into a crouch, spear lifted.

Sinews within Jaqual's gargantuan chest and arms rose beneath the white skin like steel cables straining to withstand unbearable stress. The legs were thick, springlike hooks between enormous thighs and long, tapering shins that ended with humanoid feet.

"*Idiot* centurion!" Jaqual snarled. "I am *the first*! How will your God save you from me!"

In a blur of flashing white, Jaqual struck—so beyond human speed or ability to react that Cassius was caught flat-footed. He made a confused effort to evade, but he was too late. He was blasted across a display case and onto the floor, where he rolled, stunned and searching before realizing he had lost the spear. He ripped out the gladius as Jaqual grasped the broken display and sent it spinning into the Hall. The huge white beast strode through the ruin like it was the ruin of a nation.

Cassius fell back, gladius in his right hand and his left hand also lifted to double his chances of parrying a blow.

With a single blow Jaqual had put him totally on the defensive. Cassius knew he had to attack quickly or die because a defensive position was ultimately doomed. The only hope in this fight—in any fight—was to attack. Then he was defensive again as Jaqual roared with a rage that engulfed the stars and surged in to strike.

Cassius saw it this time. The Nephilim's arm withdrew deeply to its left and locked in a hook to sweep in with long white claws, intending to tear off Cassius' head or rip open his chest. The best counter, Cassius knew by reflex, was to leap inside the blow and hook the elbow with his left arm, imprisoning it.

He leaped as Jaqual leaned into the blow. Instantly the arm swept in, and Cassius hooked it and stabbed upward with the gladius, trying for the neck. But Jaqual was twice as fast or faster and caught Cassius' right wrist, crushing it with the force of a vise.

Cassius bellowed in pain, aware of the wide gaping fangs that hovered before his face. He saw the hellish joy in the red eyes and strained savagely to tear his wrist from Jaqual's right hand. But he couldn't break the grip, so he spun volcanically to his left, taking Jaqual to the floor.

They hit hard, but Jaqual's body absorbed the force of the impact, and the grip lessened for only a fraction. It was enough. Cassius jerked his forearm down, twisting against Jaqual's thumb, the weakest part of his grip, and the claws scraped furrows across Cassius' bones. Ignoring the agony, he rolled to gain distance and slashed as he rose, but Jaqual wasn't there.

Rising slowly, laughing, the mightiest Nephilim regarded the centurion as if he were mere sport. "I overestimated you, Cassius." He smiled as he shook his head. "No, you are not so strong.... Or perhaps Raphael's life sacrifice was not in vain."

As Jaqual walked slowly forward, seemingly willing to make the battle last all night, Cassius circled quickly to his right, trying to stay between Jaqual and the others. It was strange that even in the midst of his greatest battle, he would be worried for others, but Cassius didn't question anything now.

He saw that Gina and the children were still beside the altar, but they were shifting ground to avoid the greatest chaos of the battle. And Cassius knew the one place in the room where Jaqual would have to meet him—a place that would give Gina and her kids a safe path to the door.

With five strides Cassius leaped to land upon the dais supporting the two gigantic pillars that held the domed ceiling. He cast the gladius aside as he spun back toward Jaqual, instantly placing a palm against each pillar.

Jaqual frowned. If he was frightened, he did not reveal it. He stalked toward the dais, fingers clenching, unclenching.

With a roar Cassius pushed, surging, his entire being in his arms, but it was like pressing a house off his chest. Neither column budged, but then Cassius thought he glimpsed the chalklike dust cascade past his face. He groaned, leaning into the—

"It's been done, Centurion!"

Jaqual's hurtling leap propelled him the final thirty feet through midair, and he collided like a mountain against Cassius, who was blasted completely from the dais. Even before they landed they were spinning in a frantic intertwining of arms, wresting to a crippling grip, each trying to gain any advantage and then they crashed onto the floor.

Jaqual gained his feet and twisted angrily to send Cassius crashing into a marble statue that shattered like ancient pottery. Amid raining shards of white, Cassius covered his head and then rose, gasping.

Motionless, Jaqual relished the moment.

"Ah, it seems your renowned strength is greatly overrated, Centurion." He laughed and began to advance. "And yet I've heard such great accolades. Yes, of how you broke the neck of mighty Nimbus with your bare hands. How you pushed down the twin pillars of Koth to bring down the temple itself, killing a hundred of my kind at once."

Old anger boiled to the surface. "Yes," the Nephilim muttered, darker, "that was my last—my *best*—stronghold! It took me three hundred years to build! Yet you destroyed it in a single day." He shook his head with a snarl. "But that was not to be the end of all things, Centurion. Balance must be restored."

It was clear that the Nephilim would drag this out as long as he felt he was in control. Yes, he had waited centuries for this moment—had even feared it—and was probably both relieved and surprised that Cassius seemed nowhere near the adversary he'd anticipated. But he should also be somewhat confused, and Cassius could use that.

He made a faint show of appearing weaker than he was— nothing so obvious that it would have indicated a conscious decision—and the razor-sharp glint in the Nephilim's eyes narrowed.

Cassius knew the Nephilim's thoughts. He was wondering whether Cassius was perfectly luring him in for a deathblow, or whether Cassius was genuinely weakening so unexpectedly fast. But it was neither. Cassius was merely attempting to make the Nephilim pause. It bought him seconds to think and recover.

Jaqual's weight had been forward, but his torso straightened and his arms rose reflexively, as if to ward off a blow. His gaze froze like the gaze of a man stumbling upon a rattlesnake.

It was enough.

In the space of a heartbeat, Cassius considered: Gina and the children could still not reach the exit, and Jaqual was not so badly wounded that he couldn't run them down in the storm or hunt them down in the abbey. There was no hope for reinforcements. There was no weapon within the abbey powerful enough to destroy it with the safety of distance. This Nephilim was pressing the fight and was far more powerful than anything Cassius had ever faced in battle. He wasn't certain he could defeat it; no reason to believe that he could. And finally—there was no truce that Cassius could accept even if it bought the lives of Gina and the children, for he knew that if he retreated, hundreds more would die over the next century. Nor was there hope that he might once more find the Nephilim. Jaqual had evaded him for two thousand years. He could evade him another two thousand. If Jaqual escaped tonight, he might escape forever. Nor did Cassius consider his own life—nor the lives of Gina and the children—more precious or important than the life of anyone else.

Each consideration passed clearly through Cassius' mind as his heart began the beat, and he knew the grim conclusion before the beat finished.

No...no choice at all.

Cassius spun and punched his fist through a glass cover, and his hand instantly closed on the hilt of a second gladius. Then he whirled back, balanced on the balls of his feet, swords low in each hand for an upward cut—to hit the Nephilim across the stomach.

A blow across the abdomen wouldn't cause instant death, but the pain would be excruciating—skin split widely, white globules spilling in a pain that roared up and down legs and arms so totally that its origin was lost, each nerve firing chaotically across another.

Cassius knew from experience that shock struck in three seconds and instantly crippled. It was like being hit in the hollow located only inches above the knee. Upon impact, the knee held as if it had not been struck at all. Then one second later, the leg collapsed completely and pain rushed up from the abdomen to take away breath. Nor was it possible to recover quickly. Nerves would do what they would do, and force of will had little effect.

Cassius had learned the results of virtually every blow, every wound, so that if he were struck, he knew what the next seconds would bring, giving him one last chance to react. If his knee was struck, he knew he had one full second to kill his enemy before he was temporarily crippled. Yes, knew he had one full second to use that leg as if it were not injured at all. But then he was going down.

Everything Cassius knew—two millennia of fighting—every technique, every nuance of fighting and killing and pain—revolved like an index card file in his mind, spinning at blinding speed as he selected or rejected technique after technique.

But he knew that techniques could not win this battle. No, this fight would be won by an accumulation of wounds, fatigue, and will. Won by some narrow margin of superiority of body and mind impossible to know unless a man faced death, and yet within it lay a man's power to defeat death.

Jaqual knew he'd been tricked, and Cassius well knew that it was the last time the Nephilim would be deceived. Now Jaqual would attack straight and direct and strong—no more caution, no more words, no more sport.

And he did.

Cassius ducked the same blow that he had trapped earlier and the white palm cracked a railroad tie timber in half. The entire Hall thundered with the animal roar as Jaqual spun, his right hand duplicating the sweeping movement, and Cassius again angled outside the blow, slashing horizontally as he leaped past the outstretched arm.

A vicious curse—something like surprise—burst from Jaqual's fangs as he grabbed the gash across his ribs. Cassius backed up, knowing already that he would have to hit when Jaqual closed or between the Nephilim's blows. It was impossible for Cassius to close the gap, hit, and evade. Jaqual was simply too fast.

Cassius continued to back away, placing a small column between them. Yes, he would have to use the pillars, even if they provided no meaningful protection, because it was a battle of inches, of degrees—of the faintest flashing margin gained here or there.

Foam specking his snow-white fangs, Jaqual released his ribs. And Cassius saw that the two-foot blade of the gladius had barely reached beneath the skin, though Cassius had felt it slide across bone hard as steel. The Nephilim's jaws distended in a widening smile.

"Surely," he said with a laugh, "that is not the *best* that Cassius—the greatest of all centurions—can do!" He shambled forward, reaching out to push the pillar aside as if it were weightless.

Cassius frantically leaped back as flat plates of lapis lazuli cascaded from the ceiling, but Jaqual ignored them as they bounced without harm from his apelike shoulders and neck.

Quickly Cassius realized that the Nephilim was remarkably skilled at cutting him off from the rest of the Hall, like a boxer cornering another in the ring. Each time Cassius thought of angling to a side, the Nephilim's acute senses simply moved him a step in that direction, rapidly and radically reducing Cassius' space.

Jaqual cast a single glance toward Gina and the children. He still remained between them and the door.

In fury—awakened by the gaze—Gina raised a Beretta and fired a full clip of fifteen rounds into Jaqual's torso. But Jaqual simply expanded the enormous girth of his chest, allowing Gina a greater target. The bullets struck with a remarkable lack of effect. As Jaqual breathed deeply, seemingly unaffected, Gina hurled the semiautomatic so that it skidded far across the Hall. Frowning, she pushed Josh and Rachel behind her, backing away.

Jaqual was still watching them when he spoke to Cassius. "Know this, Centurion. When I finish with you, I will deal with the woman and her children." His bark contained malignant intent. "Perhaps I will allow the woman to live for years. Some punishments are far, *far* more terrible than death."

Cassius shook his head, scattering blood and sweat. The heat was suffocating, causing him to squint and grimace as he fought to keep his vision clear. And degree by degree, the armor and the wounds and heat and blood began to swallow him.

Cassius was aware of what was happening, yet he was too fatigued to resist it. He *chose* not to resist. He released himself into it so that he knew nothing but what he'd sensed in the most grim and terrible of the bitterest battles, finding his purest purpose *here in the blood*—sword in hand, crouching and breathless—laughing, snarling. Just as he knew that what was happening came from a far greater place—a place he'd sensed only in his dreams and heart. A place that he'd never fully known but stood closer to now than ever before.

Smiling at Jaqual, Cassius laughed.

Jaqual's snarl was an eruption of hate. His head tilted like a dog's, but whatever confusion passed through the Nephilim's mind was hatefully cast out. He charged with arms outstretched, filling the Hall with a guttural roar.

Cassius shouted and leaped forward, and they collided between the two pillars that supported the gigantic dome. Cassius knew that the Nephilim struck well—felt the fresh lance of a wound—but didn't care and returned the same, driving the gladius out hard to blast aside the apelike arm. He speared Jaqual deep in the chest and felt the blade shatter bone that had seemed hard as steel, plowing viciously through muscle but it didn't satisfy and Cassius grabbed the Nephilim by the throat, violently shoving the head back so the fangs were no danger. He ripped out the gladius and stabbed to penetrate the stomach muscles so he could shove down on the hilt and gut it.

Cassius was so far beneath fear that he was beneath even the thought of fear. And he cared nothing for all of Jaqual's titanic might. All his purpose, strength, skill, and speed were in the move as he shifted his wrist on the gladius. Then another smashing left hand from Jaqual—who obviously read his move—hit with the force of a locomotive.

The centurion was in the air, visualizing everything behind him by memory. Instantly he twisted in the air, bunching and somersaulting to miss a display. Then he opened up and straightened an arm, pushing himself from a pillar, landing like a cat.

With a smile Cassius whirled. His expression was keen with killer instinct and confidence at his own fantastic skill. But it was nothing borne of pride. It was meant to communicate a fearless contempt for the Nephilim's power.

Holding his stomach, Jaqual's eyes widened before he concealed his shock. Then the fangs parted in a roar, and he came forward, blasting the display aside.

"*HA!*" Cassius laughed and angled fast to the side as if to place another pillar between them. *"Too slow, beast!"*

Bellowing in rage, Jaqual withdrew his left hand to shatter the pillar as he shattered the first. It was exactly what Cassius hoped he would do. He leaped forward before the blow began, catching the Nephilim by surprise. He stabbed in the blade with the weight of his body thrust deep, and Jaqual bellowed fiercely at the wound. But Cassius could not avoid the forearm that descended like a sledgehammer.

The impact was like being struck by a beam that had fallen from the ceiling. It hit Cassius' shoulder with the force of a building, and it was only because he twisted so violently *in the direction of the blow* that Cassius' arm was not torn from his body. Dazed, Cassius found himself lying on the floor as two wide, clawed hands reached downward.

Even in the purest battle mind-set, a warrior does not forget tactics, and in a space of time infinitely beneath any human measurement, he remembers where that tactic was gained. It happens with the speed of a flash of lightning not even seen, but glimpsed by the light that exists after it has struck. And in the same speed Cassius saw the old Japanese who had trained him six hundred years ago to know that a man on his back had every advantage as a man on his feet. Either man was forced to reach up or down, and it was the man who reached first that gained the advantage.

Twisting with volcanic power that lifted his entire body from the floor, Cassius shouted and stabbed up between the monstrous arms, and the gladius struck deep. A hostile grunt exploded from Jaqual's gaping fangs at the surprise blow. Then Cassius ripped the gladius free and snatched the Nephilim by the fur at his throat.

As Jaqual staggered back, shocked, he inadvertently lifted Cassius from the floor, but Cassius also pushed off his feet, sending the Nephilim crashing like an avalanche in white to his back.

The frenzied fighting went on, and the blows that fell like rain inside hideous howls and cries thundering from each could not be counted or understood by any that watched. But at such close range a hand that seemed not to have moved at all struck twice before it withdrew, drawing a rainbow of blood.

Then it happened—that quick.

Jaqual's hand came in low, and Cassius did not even see it when it hit, but he felt himself lifted from the floor and held high above the Nephilim's head. Jaqual flung him hard through the air, and Cassius could do nothing to alter his direction this time.

What Cassius struck blasted the breath and almost the consciousness from his body and mind, and he knew he'd been hurled against one of the two great pillars that supported the roof of the Great Hall. Shocked and numb but *internally* aware of broken ribs grating sharply beneath the skin of his sides, Cassius pushed himself up.

Propelled from the floor by sheer will alone, Cassius roared in anger and freezing sheets of pain. And as he reached his feet, his face was the face of an animal. His teeth were bared like fangs, and his eyes were opaque with killing instinct. There was no fear.

Cassius didn't remember releasing the gladius when he hit the pillar but knew that he had. Just as he knew that the collision against the granite had knocked him unconscious. It was the painful impact against the floor that had awakened him.

The white fur of Jaqual's chest was drenched in crimson, and his ribs lifted slowly and painfully. Nor did he seem eager to press this fight. For a moment, he gazed at the door, as if considering escape. But pride caused his lips to curl and the fangs to shudder. His blazing red eyes gazed upon Cassius once more.

Cassius knew he appeared much the same. Breathing hard, he recognized dimly that his armor was rent with the evenly separated claw marks and breathed a sigh of gratefulness for the steel.

With a slight stumble, Jaqual came forward again. He held a hand over his stomach, and Cassius saw the glint of white beneath the blood—ribs and internal organs gleaming. "Yes," he whispered and circled slowly to the side.

He didn't look for Gina and the kids but knew where they stood by replaying every movement made inside the Great Hall since the battle began. They had moved across the room as the battle had moved, evading its fury. Now they stood a long space from the altar, which towered behind Cassius.

No time to think...draw him so Gina and the kids can run...don't worry about the rest....

Without glancing at what was behind him—he knew already—Cassius began to slowly retreat, Jaqual following step by step. The last wound hadn't injured Jaqual as much as surprised him, and he was watching Cassius carefully. When Gina and the kids had a safe path to the door, Cassius stopped and raised the gladius. Feet wide, bent forward, Cassius faced Jaqual squarely—an insult.

"You tire, beast," he whispered through mashed, bloody lips. "Perhaps you *didn't* underestimate me...."

Jaqual's fangs separated.

He charged.

CHAPTER SIXTEEN

T*his is the end....*

It was the last thought Cassius had before Jaqual's hurtling rush carried them together through display after display that exploded into splinters and spinning shards before they crashed and rolled across the floor once more.

Cassius had half risen when he glimpsed a blur of white whirling. What hit him—Cassius didn't know—sent him sprawling half-conscious. But at the same time—executing the one action Cassius did not anticipate—Jaqual spun and snatched up an oil-fed candelabrum and hurled it like a spear across the Hall.

Gina and the children were racing for the door as the fiery missile exploded in their path like napalm, mushrooming over a wide expanse of the Great Hall, consuming all that would burn in its path. They staggered, screaming at the flames that only narrowly missed engulfing them, as well. All hope of escape was closed.

"No," Jaqual growled angrily. "There's no escape!"

Cassius cared nothing for death. He had accepted death so long ago that death was like a cloak he had borne through ages. But he feared for Gina and the children. And as he stood, he did what he had never consciously done before in battle—he prayed.

Never, *never* in battles that rose into scores of hundreds of thousands beyond reckoning had Cassius ever consciously prayed...because in battle he had always been like unto a force of nature, pure and at home with war, with fighting, and killing until the battle was won. Until armies were destroyed, nations were freed, and those who had terrorized the earth lay in dust.

But now Cassius prayed clearly, distinctly. He prayed *simply* because all that remained within him now was simple— a simple hope to finish off this satanic beast. A simple hope to be at peace with God because he knew this was his last battle. A simple hope to see Gina and the children alive and safe as he drew his last breath.

He had spent every moment of every century searching for the peace that passes all understanding, as his friend Paul had said, and he'd never known such peace. It had been a fable and a curse...until now. Because as he finished the simplest of all prayers, Cassius felt what was the *source* of his spirit—the man he had trembled before, as he nailed Him to the crucifix, watching...and deciding. And it was greater even than what Cassius had hoped. He did not know why he had never felt it before, but it was perhaps because he had never faced a foe that he knew he could not defeat with his own great strength. Yes, because he had never possessed cause for such faith...until now.

Blood hid the depth of his gaping wounds as Cassius stood. His breath was hoarse and ragged, and what strength remained, remained beneath what he could know.

Slashed and beaten, Jaqual slowly turned like a gladiator awaiting some signal to finish the fight. But the thick, hinged right knee that had propelled his huge bulk across the Great Hall with such astonishing speed was crippled now. Still, the injury had no effect on Jaqual's bestial countenance. Beneath the pain, which he accepted as stoically as Cassius, the inhuman rage was undiminished. Nor did the scarlet eyes reveal any doubt of ultimate victory.

Reading every line, every blink in the Nephilim's face—measuring the smallest fiber of strength yet remaining in the colossal form—Cassius made his decision, a decision he knew he would make from the very beginning.

In three strides he reached the altar.

With a shout Cassius sent the altar table pin-wheeling to the side. Then he snarled as he bent and locked an iron grip on the iron crucifix, and in the next second he placed a boot against the wall and surged back. For a moment the bolts anchored deep into stone held, then they tore free in an explosion of white dust.

Impatiently Cassius hurled the crucifix aside as if it were meaningless chaff before he reached deeply into a crevice chiseled into the stone and withdrew a long thin object wrapped in layers of oiled white silk and cloth. Casting the rags aside, Cassius turned toward the Nephilim with *his* spear, the spear of Gaius Cassius Longinus—the spear that had pierced the side of Jesus of Nazareth.

Almost six feet long, the steel haft bore a broad leaf-shaped spearpoint that cast a strange, unnatural scarlet glow. It was chipped by battle and should have been brittle with age. But as Cassius slowly lowered the haft, the gray blade shone thick and deep and heavy with strength.

Cassius bent his face toward the Nephilim, staring without mercy or remorse. And Jaqual understood. He barked some harsh, guttural curse before glancing at the closest tunnel.

Only a quick glance, but Cassius understood.

As Jaqual rushed to escape, Cassius leaped and caught a lamp heavy with oil to hurl it toward the exit. Jaqual's crippled leg slowed him, and the lamp struck the tunnel, exploding in a nova of mushrooming flame. Instantly it was an inferno—certain death for the Nephilim in his injured condition.

Jaqual reared at the flames that engulfed him for a split second before vacuuming back from the tunnel. And when the Nephilim spun, Cassius clearly saw fear—the fear of a trapped animal determined to escape though he is killed in the attempt.

Instantly he raced for another corridor, and Cassius leaped like a tiger to snatch up another lamp and hurl it with all his strength as well. Leaving a trail of fire that stretched twenty feet across the Great Hall, the lamp exploded even more ferociously than the first, devouring the curtains and wood at the exit.

And again and still again the scene was repeated, Jaqual raging and racing against the flames as Cassius hurled lamp after lamp to imprison him in a final, flaming arena. Cassius' last throw cast the largest lamp completely across the great expanse of the Hall, where it detonated to close Jaqual's last chance of escape, save for the great entry doors that Cassius stood before.

"No," Cassius whispered. "There's no escape...."

Raging, Jaqual lifted hands aloft with forearms tight before his face as he twisted to escape the flames, but there was no escape. His voice shrieked with molecular fear.

"NOOOOOO!!!"

Still howling, the Nephilim whirled as Cassius came through the flames, his bloodred cloak trailing a wide fan of fire. Jaqual had time for a single cry before Cassius roared and leaped and powerfully drove the spear through the Nephilim's chest and out his back.

Instantly Jaqual knew what had happened—what the spear contained. He staggered back, oblivious to the flames now in the shadow of a death far more terrible that burned and devoured him from within. With jaws open and drawn—eyes wide and frantic and pleading—the Nephilim struggled with all his great strength to pull the spear from his chest but the spear held.

Jaqual staggered through the burning wreckage of the Hall, bellowing and surging with superhuman, bestial strength to tear out the spear, but the spear would not release. Then by some vivid death instinct, the Nephilim whirled to see...

Cassius stood once more between the two huge columns that supported the gigantic, sloping dome. At the point of the dome rested a thousand tons of granite and stone.

"No!" Jaqual gasped.

Bent between the pillars, Cassius glimpsed Gina and the children racing toward the massive entrance doors. Yes, they would be safe now. But halfway across the expanse Gina hesitated, searched desperately, and captured Cassius' eyes with her gaze.

Cassius' weariness was like death. There was not an inch of his body not covered in blood. But he held her gaze for a moment that lasted...and nodded sadly.

Gina shut her eyes and lifted her face in a scream that could not be contained—a scream that began in her life force and defiantly seared the abbey and the battle, the flames and whatever else could come because *she owned this now*!

For love lost, she would own it forever....

Her teeth were clenched tight as she lowered and shook her head. She whirled to Rachel and Josh. "Come on!" she screamed and instantly pushed open the huge portal.

Rachel reached plaintively toward Cassius, who smiled gently as Gina threw open the door and, covering her children, staggered into the howling blackness of the snow-slashed day. When Cassius turned his head again to Jaqual, he saw that the Nephilim had also seen them flee.

His defeat was complete at last.

Gazing upon the beast, Cassius shook his head—sadly, tragically, painfully. Then, with a frown, he slowly shut his eyes. His chest and shoulders and arms expanded, gathering the last, truest measure of his strength. It was enough to draw the Nephilim's mind back to where he stood. Aghast, Jaqual staggered forward.

"If you do this, you'll die too!"

Wearily, Cassius opened his eyes, and he stared upon the beast. "As I planned from the beginning," he whispered and nodded. "Let this mountain bury us both."

A shocked gasp burst from Jaqual as Cassius instantly pushed against the stone. Eyes shut fiercely, blind to where Jaqual stood, Cassius surged from the depth—*from the core*—of his strength as he had never done, because only death remained once this last, deepest strength was spent. Cassius' arms shook, and he felt veins straining to burst from his shoulders and arms as blood strained to burst from his forehead. A snarl burst from his lips but *the pillars held*!

Cassius heard Jaqual staggering, surging to pull the spear from his chest, and risked a glance.

The Nephilim twisted against the spear to snap the haft, but the spear would not break or even bend. Then his screams became hideous as he thrust a hand inside his own chest, claws rending to savage his flesh from the steel that had touched the blood of Jesus.

Bellowing, Jaqual instantly tore his hand free. It was smoking—scalded and blistered. Insane with pain, the Nephilim bent back, shrieking to a force unseen in a language unknown.

His words flowed like millions of rivers thundering into darkness without depth—like millions of beings from millions of dimensions dying.

Cassius threw his back against the first pillar and slammed both hands against the second with enough force to shatter bones that had never shattered. Roaring to endure the abysmal agony, Cassius pushed, and sinews within his chest drew taut as piano wire and began to snap, fiber tearing from fiber and *still* Cassius pushed until the pain in his shattered wrists and hands spiraled to where his body trembled, threatening to disobey even his undefeated will.

And then, at the crest of the dome, Cassius heard a brittle crack like molten glass plunged into ice.

Jaqual raised his head.

"No!"

Cassius pushed farther, and the pillars began to separate.

He had no thoughts. He had no dreams of victory. Neither did he long for love because he knew he was loved. What surged forth from him was beyond death. He walked forward, pushing the pillar, and stone plates the size of boulders cascaded into the Hall.

Jaqual staggered forward.

"Cassius! We can be free!"

Cassius laughed and shook his head.

"Only God is free...."

Jaqual threw back his head and howled against the words with a corruption that rose from bowels black, flinging angry curses at what might be beyond.

Cassius surged against the pillar, and it fell across the Great Hall like the death of a giant, of an age—huge stones crushing stone into dust—and Jaqual raised clawed hands for one final celestial cry of denial before he was gone.

Cassius lifted his face to the now-open clear, blue sky that blazed with sunlight—stones falling, destroying every semblance of a shadow that had once marred his life. Dying, he raised a hand into the plummeting stones with a single cry.

"Forgive me!"

Was gone.

CHAPTER SEVENTEEN

Long it was before the roar inside the abbey stilled. Until dust ceased to pour from the open double doors, flooding over Gina and Josh and Rachel like the breath of an angry dragon, until the sound of the all-consuming flames died to nothing.

It was even longer before Gina noticed that the bitter wind had stilled, that the snow no longer slashed and cut and sheathed the earth in ice. Very slowly, she raised her face, blinking at the mountain of stone inside the Great Hall—a skull of stone shone with sunlight, surrounded by fire, the ice slowly sliding down the crest of the skull, silencing.

It was warm, Gina noticed, as she staggered to her feet, but not from the Hall. It was from the blinding blaze of a white face that had struck and split the sun as if by a blast of breath from God. She barely noticed Josh and Rachel rising beside her and only slowly noticed that they were as motionless. Neither seemed eager to reenter the Hall, though it was obvious that nothing could have lived through that holocaust.

Finally, Gina placed a hand on their chests.

"Stay here," she said and swallowed. She took a deep breath, blinked, and took the first hesitant step up the stairs. She found herself biting her lip, knew her legs were trembling. But she could not—would not—turn back now.

Standing in the entrance of the Hall, Gina saw a colossal heap of stone surrounded by dying flames and dying ice. Then she was aware that Josh and Rachel were standing beside her, but she was not afraid. What had happened here was no longer a danger to them—not to any of them.

"Mom?" Josh whispered, "is Cassius...?"

Staring over the devastating expanse, Gina could say nothing. She inhaled once, remembering the look in Cassius' eyes—remembering his words. Words spoken before he entered his greatest battle against his greatest foe—a battle he knew would cost him his life.

Gently, she placed an arm around Josh.

"He lived long enough, baby." She reached out to Rachel and turned them away.

"He lived long enough...."

EPILOGUE

B roken across a cornerstone of the abbey, Jaqual lay in his true form, white and massive and bestial. But he was still now and bloody. Nor did those imperious eyes contain the hellish glow that had inhabited them in life. Rather, they stared emptily toward the broken dome above them, where the avalanche had shattered the floor and carried them into the cavern below to the forest of skeletons.

The spear of Gaius Cassius Longinus even yet protruded from his chest, somehow unbroken from the long descent into the grave of the crucifix. And in the shadow of the torches that haloed the cross, the spear cast the dark blade of shadow toward the stairway, which had survived.

Silence, darkness.

Stillness...

Then a hand—a bloody, wounded hand—stretched forth from the darkness. And the spear that had resisted the titanic might of the beast as he struggled to tear it from his chest surrendered effortlessly, and the bloody hand pulled it free.

A warrior stood on the edge of shadow and light, holding the spear and staring down upon his enemy, dead at last. On the far side of the cavern the torches began to slowly die, casting the cavern, slow step by slow step, into darkness until the shadows reached the resting place of the monster.

The warrior did not move. His head was bent, somber even in victory. But then the shadows reached the place where he stood, as if to tell him it was finished.

He turned, and vanished into the shadows as well.

ABOUT THE AUTHOR

A veteran novelist and best-selling author, James Byron Huggins' life story reads more like fiction than fact. His career as a writer began normally enough. He received a bachelor's degree in journalism and English from Troy State University, and then worked as a reporter for the *Hartselle Enquirer* in Hartselle, Alabama. Huggins won seven awards while with the newspaper before leaving journalism in 1985.

With a desire to help persecuted Christians in eastern Europe, Huggins moved to Texas to work in conjunction with members of the Christian underground in that region. From the Texas base, Huggins helped set up a system used to smuggle information in and out of Iron Curtain countries.

In 1987, Huggins was finally able to leave the United States to offer hands-on assistance in Romania. As a jack of all trades, Huggins photographed a secret police installation, took photos of people active in the Christian underground, and also continued his work as an orchestrator of smuggling routes. Huggins was instrumental in smuggling out film and documentation that showed the plight of Christians in Romania. He even found time to create a code that allowed communication with the United States. As in Texas, Huggins' life had few creature comforts. To survive, he would often remain hidden in the woods or in secure basements for days at a time.

After his time in Romania, Huggins returned to the United States and took up journalism once more. He again worked for a small newspaper and won several awards as a reporter. Later on, he worked at a nonprofit Christian magazine before becoming a patrolman with the Huntsville Police Department in Huntsville, Alabama. After distinguished service as a decorated field officer, Huggins left the force to pursue writing novels.

His first three novels—*A Wolf Story, The Reckoning,* and *Leviathan*—achieved best-seller status in the Christian marketplace. From there, Huggins broke into mainstream science fiction with *Cain* and *Hunter,* both of which brought him more than $1 million for optioning the film rights. Huggins then released *Rora,* a historical novel depicting the harrowing life of a European martyr.

Huggins currently lives in Kentucky.

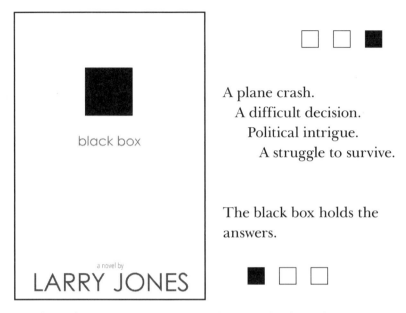

black box

a novel by
LARRY JONES

A plane crash.
   A difficult decision.
      Political intrigue.
         A struggle to survive.

The black box holds the answers.

Flight 027 out of Hong Kong has crashed in the mountains of central Asia. Four men and three women who, moments before, had been on a routine airplane trip suddenly find themselves stranded in a snow-covered wasteland, fighting for their lives. As the group struggles to endure, intrigue and mystery arise as some of the survivors seem bent on carrying out a hidden agenda—an agenda that centers on finding the plane's black box. Caught up in a web of deceit, the survivors must look within to find the deliverance they so desperately desire.

Black Box
a novel by
Larry Jones

ISBN: 0-88368-872-7 • Hardcover • 304 pages

www.whitakerhouse.com

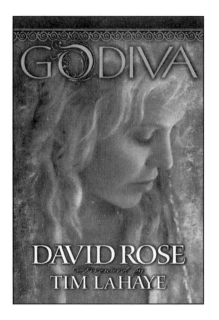

Bent on conquest, King Canute and his Viking legions have invaded England, cutting a bloody path across the peaceful countryside. In a flaunting demonstration of his power, Canute, the feared dragon king, destroys the fair town of Coventry, and a young girl watches as her once idyllic life turns into a nightmare.

Ten years later, Godiva has managed to rebuild her life and even find love in the midst of Canute's quiet empire. But the apparently sleeping dragon king awakens and threatens to devour her beloved Coventry once more. Godiva finds herself caught in the middle of the coming storm as she discovers that she alone can save Coventry.

But how much will she sacrifice? And can she save her people without betraying her faith and losing her very soul?

Godiva
a novel by
David Rose

ISBN: 0-88368-028-9 • Hardcover • 360 pages

www.whitakerhouse.com